Copyright © by Jo Calman 2020
www.jo-calman.com

ISBN 979-8-6709-6738-9

A Price for Mercy

by Jo Calman

With this there grows
In my most ill-composed affection such
A staunchless avarice that, were I king,
I should cut off the nobles for their lands,
Desire his jewels and this other's house:
And my more-having would be as a sauce
To make me hunger more; that I should forge
Quarrels unjust against the good and loyal,
Destroying them for wealth.
Shakespeare - Macbeth

Chapter 1 – London, Autumn 2002

Mercy was a great girl. Everybody said that. She was a hard worker, very bright, and a wonderful mum to little Etienne. Mercy was just twenty-one years old. She worked in the planning department of the council, just admin work, but she was going to night-school and she knew she would one day get a degree and a better job. For now she had the one-bed flat in a tower block for her and Etienne, who was three, and she kept it as nice as she could. Her sister Chantelle stayed over when she was at night-school or just wanted some company. Chantelle was just nineteen and adored her big sister. She had a room in a shared house not too far away, but she also had a key to Mercy's place. They were close.

Mercy had a good childhood. Mum and Dad were strict but loving. Then in her teens things had gone a bit wrong for her. She fell in with a bad crowd. She stayed away from school, did drugs and was in a gang with all that it entailed for a young girl in the city. By the time she was seventeen she was pregnant. She wasn't sure but she thought she knew who the baby-father was, and she had confronted him. He was full of bravado in front of the boys, but when they were alone he was different. He said he would take care of Mercy, look after her and the baby. Then he got on a plane back to the Island and she hadn't seen or heard from him since.

As Mercy's baby grew inside her she managed to withdraw from the gang. Her bulging stomach didn't appeal to the boys, and they also couldn't stand her morning sickness and crazy hormones. She went home to Mum, Dad having passed away two years back. She wasn't sympathetic and Mercy found herself effectively homeless. She went to the council and was eventually given the flat just before the baby arrived. Two days after her eighteenth birthday little Etienne announced his presence with a loud wail. Chantelle held Mercy's hand and she was the second person on this earth to hold little Etienne.

Mercy vowed to do good for her son, and to turn her young life around to do it. With Chantelle's help she arranged childcare and got an office job at the council. She looked after Etienne wonderfully; her social worker was full of praise for this young single mum who was clearly doing her best and doing well. Life, if not good, was at least OK.

Mercy's mum had never been wholly able to forgive her for having a child out of wedlock and without an identifiable father, so Chantelle was tactfully building bridges between the grandma and the grandson. She would take little Etienne to see their mother every week or two, and little by little the grandma warmed to the small boy with a sunny disposition, a good nature and a kind warm heart. The girls, Chantelle and Mercy, were quietly saving up to take their mother and little Etienne to the Island before he started big school in two years. There was a large extended family to meet, and although the girls had been born in London they felt that the Island was really their home.

The only remnant of the past for Mercy was the occasional Friday night relax every few weeks. Chantelle would come and stay over. They would get a bottle of wine and either Mercy would cook chicken or they would get takeaway sent in. As soon as little Etienne was settled for the night the sisters would open the wine, find some Island music on the radio and talk about how good it was going to be when they were there, in the Caribbean sunshine in their houses near the beach, right next door to each other. Each with a handsome and kind husband, with lots of brothers and sisters and cousins for little Etienne. And sometimes the sisters would do a few lines, not too many, just enough to get a buzz going, to lift the load of the week just gone. Mercy knew a small-time dealer who delivered, and she got her tiny hits from him. Not a problem user, not addicted or anything. Not hurting anyone.

This week had been quite tough. It was council budget time and there were lots of urgent requests for information and figures on this and that in Mercy's department, as well as compiling performance statistics. Plus night-school was ramping up for exams. Mercy needed to finish her A levels to have a chance of coping with the OU or Birkbeck or some other distance learning place so she could start on her degree and keep working at the same time. She wanted to do social science, to be a social worker. Chantelle, who worked on the beauty counter of a department store, had stepped up and looked after little Etienne a lot during the week and Mercy was planning to cook some really delicious chicken as a thank you. She couldn't manage without her Shan, her kid sister.

So on Friday evening Chantelle was already at Mercy's spotless tiny flat when she got home. It was nice to come home to the smell of coffee and the sound of the TV on. Little Etienne was burbling and bobbling about the place, delighted to see his Mum and pleased to be with Auntie Shan too. Mercy put the shopping bags down in the kitchen and kicked her shoes off. She chased the squealing Etienne round the flat before picking him up and swinging him around. He howled with delight. Mercy gave her sister a big hug and prepared a bath for little Etienne. He was still quite small for a three-year old, but he was doing OK. He was strong.

She tucked him up in his cot, which was alongside her own bed in the only bedroom. She read a story and sang an Island song to him, watching the child drift off into a happy sleep. All was good.

"How you doing, Shan?" Mercy asked her sister.

"Pretty damn good, sis! It's pay day and there's a nice bonus this week. We shifted lots of new make-up, a new line with big commission. Now, where's the wine?"

Chantelle and Mercy prepared the meal together over a few glasses. Chantelle had brought some too. They sat and ate together, swaying to the Island music coming from the radio. Afterwards they sat on the sofa chatting and dreaming. Mercy fetched a small bag of cocaine from its hiding place in the bathroom.

"No need, sis, I got some. Martina at work was given it – she does make up for videos and films and stuff every now and then. She went to an after-filming party and the main man was giving out coke to everyone. Martina doesn't use it but took some anyway. She gave it to me. And here it is!" Chantelle took a plastic bag from her bag. There was a good amount of coke in it, more than Mercy could ever afford from her dealer.

"Brilliant, Shan! Give it over."

Mercy carefully prepared four lines on a hand mirror and rolled up a banknote. She offered Chantelle first hit. Chantelle sniffed up her two lines and blinked rapidly as her eyes began to water. Mercy took her turn. Her two lines vanished too. Then she felt strange. This stuff didn't feel like it usually did. Instead of the usual tingle and numbness followed by the euphoria she felt herself getting hot, blood pounding in her ears. Her nose and head felt like they were on fire. Mercy looked at Chantelle.

"Shan? You OK, Shan?"

Chantelle was struggling to speak, gasping for breath. Her hands went to her throat and neck, blood trickled from her nostrils.

Mercy tried to get up. She felt a huge pain in her chest; she wanted to vomit. As she tried to stand there was a roaring noise inside her head, bile shot up her throat and exploded over the table in front of her. Chantelle was on the floor now, twitching and flailing, her back arching. Mercy collapsed on the floor, bringing the table crashing down on top of her. She tried to reach her sister's outstretched hand. As their fingers touched Mercy felt her heart being crushed; a pain exploded in her head, followed by a white flash – and then darkness and silence.

The sisters lay dead beside each other on the floor of Mercy's small flat in a suburban London tower block. Little Etienne had been woken by the noise and he was standing in his cot. He had wet himself. He called for his Mama, and for Shan. They didn't answer him or respond. They always came when he called. Little Etienne was scared. He started to cry. Apart from his cries the only sound in the flat was the Island music from the portable radio. Little Etienne's crying became wailing. He kept calling for his Mama, for Shan, but they didn't come.

The heating went off. Little Etienne was getting cold. His wailing was now just sobbing. His nappy was getting cold and heavy. Then there was a click as the electric meter ran out of credit and the lights went out. Alone in the dark little Etienne cried louder, but still no one came. After several hours there was a pounding on the door, an angry neighbour shouting turn that bloody noise off. Etienne howled but the neighbour had already stomped away.

As dawn broke little Etienne was standing still in his cot. He smelt of cold urine and faeces. He had run out of tears and no longer had the energy to cry. He was cold and hungry. He muttered Mama. He whispered Shan. Still they didn't come.

It was late on Saturday afternoon when someone called the police. They said they could hear music from Mercy's flat and there was a child crying. Someone had looked through the letter box and had seen a leg on the floor. Something was wrong.

A police patrol car arrived. The officers confirmed that a leg was visible through the letter box and called it in. They were given permission to put the door in, which they did. Little Etienne started to wail all over again.

Inside the officers saw Mercy and Chantelle on the floor. Both were clearly dead and cold. Their usually lustrous skin was dull and grey. Mercy was covered in vomit, while Chantelle had traces of blood around her nose and had clearly had convulsions. It didn't take the officers long to realise they were looking at a double overdose. The child made it more complicated. They called that in too. They asked for the Duty Officer and the weekend duty CID since it was a double unexplained death. They also called for a social worker for the little boy, the little boy who held his arms up to the strangers in their dark uniforms who had come into the flat. One of them picked little Etienne up and cuddled him, he had a child the same age himself. He rocked little Etienne and whispered "You poor little man. What just happened to your world?"

Chapter 2

Monday morning, 8am. Commander Julia Kelso was in her office at New Scotland Yard reviewing the weekend reports. Part of her job in the Specialist Crime Directorate was to oversee the Service Intelligence Bureau, the unit that sifted through all information and reporting that flowed through the veins of the Metropolitan Police. They looked for trends, they looked for timebombs, they looked for signs. They also looked for opportunities to get ahead of the crime and the gangs and the antisocial yobs who tormented Londoners. It was relentless; it was hard endless work.

The SIB weekend team prepared a summary for Julia each Monday about what had been happening in Greater London since she went home on Friday night. This Monday's list of tragedies was long. A double stabbing; a minor riot at a fast food restaurant in Croydon; a fatal car crash involving a stolen car; a drunken prisoner had choked on his own vomit in an outer London police station cell; and there had been a rash of unexplained deaths all over North East London, all seemingly accidental overdoses. The report highlighted the case of the two sisters, Mercy and Chantelle McMorrow, one a local government worker, the other a trainee beautician, who had been found dead in Mercy's one-bed flat with traces of cocaine around the place. A toddler had been in situ and was now in care until a relative or someone could be found to look after him. The report noted that the sisters weren't your usual accidental overdosers, who tended to be habitual heavy users. They were casual users at most, with no recent criminal history - Mercy had been in a bit of minor trouble some years before as a juvenile but seemed to have straightened herself out. There was a suspicion that some dodgy gear was in circulation.

Julia was concerned. Having worked the streets of Glasgow she knew all too well what 'dodgy gear' could mean. Not only could it lead to deaths and serious injuries, it could also signal the start of a bloody turf war between rival dealing gangs. She wanted to know more, and made a note for her assistant Raj to arrange a meeting in her office between the SIB, the Central Drugs Unit intelligence people, the Community Policing Coordinator for the Borough where Mercy and Chantelle had been found, and if possible the officers who had found the sisters.

When Raj got to the office he looked at the list of things he had to do.

"Boss," he said, "you do know Central Drugs don't like talking to Community Policing, and SIB don't like talking to anybody at all, don't you?"

"Well," she said, "maybe it's time for them all to start getting along and find out what each other knows. See if you can get them all here tomorrow morning."

She called SIB herself and asked for details of numbers and locations of presumed accidental overdoses in London for the last month. They grumbled, but not out loud, not to their Commander.

By lunchtime the Detective Inspector running SIB that day called her. He had the information she wanted. She asked him to come to her office.

Brian Kearney was a long-term old-school Inspector nearing retirement. He had been injured many years ago, in the line of duty, and he walked with a stick. Despite his old cardigan and his ponderous manner he had a sharp mind. He had a slim folder in his hand.

"Afternoon ma'am," he started, "here's the information you asked for. In a nutshell, there have been twenty-three apparent accidental overdose deaths in the last month. That's more than usual – the monthly average is eight to ten, and these are normally pretty randomly spread across all the Borough commands. In the current month there seem to be concentrations, but still only twos and threes, across a few Boroughs. These are Hammersmith and Fulham (three) Camden (two pairs), Southwark (one three and one two), Wandsworth (a total of seven) and four in Haringey. Within each Borough affected the deaths seem to be in close geographic proximity. So it could be that there's some dodgy gear in circulation, but it doesn't seem to be tied to any one distributor or distribution network. All the cases seem to be cocaine related. Historically most accidental overdoses involve heroin or synthetics."

"Thanks Brian," Julia said. "Do you know if the City police or the neighbouring forces are seeing a similar profile?"

"I don't ma'am, but I'll get on to it." Brian Kearney left her office, leaving the folder with her.

A couple of hours later Kearney sent her an email. The City of London Police saw nothing unusual, nor did Kent or Surrey. No figures yet from Essex but his contact didn't think there was a problem. Thames Valley said they had seen spikes in and around Milton Keynes and possibly Oxford but they would need to check.

Julia put in a call to her friend Mel. Mel, Demelza, Dunn was a senior intelligence analyst at the National Criminal Intelligence Service. They had been friends for only a few months, but they had come to know each other well and they trusted one other. They had been together, side by side, throughout the strange matter of the late DCI Alan Ferdinand and the web of extreme corruption he had exposed and disrupted, and that had rocked the UK's law enforcement community.

"Mel, it's Jake," she said when Mel answered her phone. Kelso's close friends knew her as Jake.

"Hello stranger. I was starting to think you must have eloped or something. I haven't heard from you for weeks now," said Mel.

"It's only been ten days at most, and you know I've been the senior officer on-call this last week. I can't let you lead me astray when I'm the person in charge of this great police service now, can I?"

"What do you want, Kelso? I'm busy." Mel asked, smiling.

"Accidental overdoses. Cocaine related. What are you seeing nationally?"

"I'll need to have a dig around. Fancy discussing it over a drink? Tomorrow evening maybe? Six o'clock at St Ermin's?"

"Sure, sounds good. I'll see you then. Take care."

Raj had succeeded in persuading and cajoling the disparate departments to come together in her office at 10 the next morning. Two bleary-eyed patrol officers, the ones who had been first on the scene of the McMorrow girls' overdose and just off night duty, looked perplexed. They weren't used to being summoned to the Yard, or 'the Big House' as it was known, especially by a Commander.

Julia was all charm and smiles as she settled everyone down around her large meeting table. Her gentle Scottish accent was a valuable weapon in fractious meetings, not that she thought this one was going to be fractious. She thanked everybody for making the time to come along and asked the patrol officers to start with an account of their discovery of Mercy and Chantelle McMorrow, and to give any update on the case since Saturday.

One of them took out a pocketbook and started to read. Julia stopped him with a smile. "Just tell us in your own words, Kevin, (she read his name badge and Kevin was clearly surprised to be addressed by his first name) I'm interested in your thoughts and observations. Was there anything striking or unusual about this scene?"

Kevin relaxed. "Well, it *is* an odd one. I mean, we've all been to ODs and there's a sort of look and feel to them. These two girls were different. They aren't, weren't, frequent or even regular drug users; the estate that Mercy lived on isn't one of the bad ones, very little crime and not much in the way of drugs. The odd mugging and car breaking is about all. So we were surprised to be called there on Saturday. We knew something bad had happened when we looked through the letterbox, but I wasn't expecting an OD. Inside we found the two girls, the sisters, very close to each other. Decent and respectable girls by all accounts. It was obvious they had both died some hours before; they were cold, rigor mortis had set in. There were signs of cocaine use in the flat, but nothing major or habitual. There was a plastic envelope on the floor with sizeable traces of a white powder, a small mirror, a rolled-up fiver. There was also another bag, which seemed not to have been opened. It's not usual to find a spare hit of coke at an OD site. And then there was the kiddie, the little boy. I've got one the same age. The poor lad was distraught, but he looked like he had been well cared-for up until then.

"We're still waiting for lab tests on the powder, and the post mortem on the girls is set for later today. The case is being dealt with as an unexplained but not suspicious death for now, so we're the investigators until someone else gets interested. My guess is that there was something wrong with the coke the girls took. It was cut with something nasty maybe.

"I had a quick look at Mercy's phone, and her sister's, just recent calls. Mercy doesn't use hers much, but there's a number for a 'Charlie C' that she calls about once or twice a month. I reckon that'll be her dealer, but he or she isn't going to retire early by selling small hits to a council admin worker once every two or three weeks. They weren't big users, ma'am. In my opinion they were decent young girls who liked to have a little blow every now and then. They just got unlucky."

"Thanks, Kevin," said Julia. "Could you let me know about the test results, and let Raj have Mercy and Chantelle's phone numbers and the number for the dealer. Don't worry, I am interested but I won't be getting involved in the investigation, at least not for now. You are doing a good job, and thanks for coming in. I think you can both get off home now if you want."

They stood. The second officer who hadn't spoken hesitated.

"Yes, Alwin?" asked Julia. Name badges were so useful.

"Sorry, ma'am, I just want to say that I knew Mercy McMorrow. We went to the same school, but she was a couple of years behind me. She was a bit of a handful for a while, truanting and running with a bad crowd, until she had Etienne, her little boy. Then she settled down. I spoke to her recently. My folks are planning an extension and she works, worked, in the council planning department. We spoke on the phone and she remembered me; she was very helpful with the application, very professional. I just want to say that I'm shocked that she died like this. She wasn't a risk taker, and she adored Etienne. She wouldn't have taken anything from someone she didn't know, so it must be some really bad stuff."

"Thank you Alwin, that's interesting," said Julia. The patrol officers left.

Julia continued with the meeting. She politely instructed Central Drugs and Community Policing to work together with SIB to bring her a report, ideally within two weeks, outlining the circumstances of all apparent cocaine overdoses and looking for common links in the supply chain. If there was adulterated cocaine in circulation in London she wanted to know where it was and where it came from. Did they have any questions? They didn't.

Chapter 3

Tuesday evening. Mel Dunn arrived at the St Ermin's Hotel bar first. She hadn't seen Jake since she had come back from her holiday in France. It seemed a long time since the dramas of Alan Ferdinand, the arrests, the deaths. Summer had been and gone. Mel had asked Jake if she wanted to go with her to France for some sun, but Jake had declined. She said she was of good Scottish stock and if she lay in the sun she would turn from pale and interesting to barbecued red in 20 seconds. Instead Jake had gone to Scotland to see her parents and get eaten by midges. Her loss.

She saw Julia Kelso walk in. Her short blonde hair was stylish, as ever, and she was discreetly but expensively dressed in a tailored woollen jacket and trousers, with one of her 'working clothes' fine cotton blouses. As usual, she wore no make-up and her skin shone with health and vigour. She smiled when she saw Mel. The friends hugged each other.

"You've had your hair cut," Julia stated.

"I only had it shortened a bit. I do it about twice a year, but it always grows again." Mel was smiling.

"It looks good. You should keep it a bit shorter. But not too much. Gin and tonic?"

"I've already ordered for us. How was your Scottish safari? Cold, wet and itchy I hope."

"That's not nice. It was windswept and beautiful, with just a bit of chilly moisture. Mum and dad are doing well, and it was great to spend some time with them, and to catch up with some old friends."

"Was it itchy, though? With the midges?"

"A bit, but you get used to it. What about you?"

"La belle France. I drove down to Aquitaine – I told you I gave in a bought a car, didn't I? I went with a friend and we found a little B and B near Mimizan and spent a gorgeous week on the beach. Then we joined the rest of them at a rented villa with a pool for another week. It was blissful."

"Was this with your weirdy-pervy mates?"

"I wish you wouldn't call them that, but yes. I drove down with Cadi and we did the beach thing together, then we met up with Jilly, Frank and Sven in the Lot valley. Jilly and Frank booked the villa, but we all chipped in."

"I want all the details, but not now."

"I'm not sure you do, but never mind."

"Down to business," said Julia. Their drinks had arrived, and they clinked their glasses together. "It's good to see you, Mel."

"You too, Jake. OK, so I asked around. No one has really noticed any huge increase in cocaine overdoses. I spoke to the Coke Intel Unit but as usual they're focussed so far upstream they aren't the best people to know what's happening here on the ground. Then I called round our regional offices. There are some pockets, some spikes, but they are very localised. Just a few here and there, but numerically on the increase. Not many overdoses are being thoroughly investigated, but they have done quite a good job on a couple in the North West and the Midlands. What these cases show is that some overdoses have been a result of extremely high-grade cocaine, well over 90 per cent purity. This is strange. Most ODs happen because the gear is rubbish and it's cut with all sorts of crap, more Harpic poisoning than overdosing. Virtually pure cocaine never reaches the streets, in fact it doesn't often reach the UK. It's normally been cut down by the time it gets here, down to about 70 or 75 per cent purity. By the time it has been through the wholesalers to the retailers it's been cut again. Good, and I say 'good' advisedly, middle-class party-grade coke is around 50 to 60 per cent pure and it is very expensive. Most of the stuff that's sold retail on the streets and to addicts, other than the stuff cooked up into crack which is seriously strong, is anywhere between 25 and 40 per cent pure, sometimes less if the market is weak and the punters are poor, on benefits or students. The really cheap stuff is sometimes called monkey dust.

"So, to get virtually pure coke up someone's nose is not right, not usual. But there isn't enough data to form a workable hypothesis yet. Sorry, that was a bit analyst-y. Why are you asking?"

"There was a double overdose over the weekend," said Jake. "Two sisters, late teens and early twenties – the older of the two had a three-year old. They were in the elder sister's flat, and it seems that they are in the habit of having a few lines of coke every couple of weeks, just for the buzz. No hint that they were addicted or heavy users, and not the types who could or would shell out on high-grade cocaine. The older girl was a local authority worker, the younger one a trainee beautician, neither was a big earner. I'm waiting on lab tests on some powder that was found in the flat, and on the post-mortem results. There's just something about this that doesn't sit right. I did some checking in the Met and surrounding forces. There does seem to be the beginnings of a trend indicating a possible spike in cocaine ODs – very localised pockets of twos and threes, but overall numbers are up quite a lot. I'm keeping an eye on it.

"I'd like to know a bit more about the cocaine trade, the supply chain and the economics of it all."

"I know the very person to educate you," said Mel. "Fix a lunch and I'll bring him along. He's the head of the Coke Unit, a customs officer. A proper coke nerd, if you get my meaning. He knows the trade inside out. He used to be one of the liaison officers in Venezuela and then in Spain. He can fill you in."

"Thanks, Mel. I'll do that through you if I can. Let me know if he's available on Friday, would you?"

"Sure."

"Have you heard from Alf?" asked Jake.

"Ferdinand? Not for a while. I must admit I haven't checked the mailbox since I got back. I'll do it tonight. Why?"

"Just curious. The inquest returned a verdict of suicide on him and murder on Banbury. He might want to know he's really properly dead now."

"This is so weird. I'll let him know, assuming he's still looking at the email account he set up. Do you want another drink?"

"I shouldn't, but I will," said Julia. "It was a long week and I didn't get a huge amount of sleep, but I can have one more. Are you up for a work-out at the weekend, at Dolphin Square? I should have some spare energy by then."

"That would be good. I haven't been exercising much since I got back. A gym session and a swim will be painful but worthy."

The two women chatted on for another thirty minutes before they hugged again and said goodbye. Jake walked back to her apartment in Dolphin Square while Mel walked to Waterloo to get a train back to her flat in Raynes Park.

On the way Mel thought about Alan Ferdinand. Her friend and occasional bed-mate, a former Detective Chief Inspector in the Metropolitan Police and a Branch Commander at the National Crime Squad. Alf, as he was known, had been the victim of an attempt to frame him for corruption, but he had (with hers and Jake's help) unearthed the real corrupt actors and had engineered their downfall. Alf had personally killed four people in the process, including a senior police officer who was running organised crime across the south of England. He also staged his own suicide. He would be pleased to know he was now officially dead after the inquest verdict. The information he had given to Julia, again with Mel's help, had been all she needed to build a strong case against two very senior police officers and three other more junior ones, all of whom were now serving long, very long, jail sentences having been fast-tracked through the courts.

Ferdinand had set up a communication channel between himself and Mel, an email account they could both access and leave messages as drafts. Nothing was ever sent. She would check it when she got home, maybe leave a quick hello if he hadn't left a message.

At home she logged on. Nothing from him. She typed a short message. 'Suicide verdict. All good. I've been away but back now. J says hi. x" She saved it as a draft and logged out.

After a warm shower she had a light supper and went to bed early. She was still relishing the afterglow of two weeks with nothing but sun, sea or pool, good food and conversation, and of course some gorgeous sex with her group. There were five of them, including Mel, who liked, trusted, and cared deeply for each other. They were close friends, one married couple and three single people, who had a strange and complex sexual connection between them. It was hard to explain. Jake was always probing and one day Mel supposed she would tell her more about it. One day, maybe. Now she drifted off to sleep, her mind wafting between memories of her friends and the image of Jake Kelso's cool grey eyes, perfect skin and beautiful face. Life could be worse.

In Pimlico in her apartment at Dolphin Square Julia Kelso was trying to relax in a warm bath. Her phone was in the other room, the first time that it had left her side in more than a week. Another officer had taken over as senior on-call, and she had asked another Commander to cover her department just for the night. She needed to unwind. As she lay in the bath she thought about Mel. She was curious about Mel's relationship with her group, her playmates as she had once called them, curious about her ability to disregard gender when it came to sex and still remain discerning. She envied her friend's ability to separate her physical and sexual self-indulgence from emotion and conventional relationships, but she didn't understand it, any of it. Jake knew that Mel fancied her. They had seen each other naked often enough in changing rooms and she had seen the way Mel looked at her. They had also shared a bed from time to time, but Mel had never tried to seduce her or try it on in any way. Jake wondered how she would react if she ever did. She had never had sex with another woman, although at boarding school there was the inevitable fumbling with other girls in the dorm, and once in a while races to see who could come the quickest, loudest or longest, but all that was just growing-up stuff. As an adult she had had sexual partners, always men and always with the thought that this one might be 'the one'. She had never found 'the one', although she thought she had come close once. Since she moved to London she had found herself isolated, and for the first time in her life with almost no social life and few friends. Only Mel, in fact, apart from some of her father's old mates.

She hadn't had any sex at all, at least not with anyone else, since she arrived in London. She corrected herself; she had almost forgotten the one-nighter with an old college boyfriend she bumped into in Edinburgh just a few weeks earlier. After a reasonably enjoyable dinner they ended up at his hotel for a nightcap and she had stayed the night in his room. The sex wasn't particularly memorable, or even enjoyable. In fact the whole thing had been awful and empty. She had deleted his number already. It dawned on her then that the one night stand in Edinburgh had been the act of a lonely woman. She shuddered.

So, she thought, the next time there was a chance with Mel maybe she should take it? Mel would be discreet, and no doubt she would help her overcome her uncertainty and reservations. She was also very attractive, both physically and personally. And with Mel if it didn't work out or feel right there would be no broken hearts or wailing. Jake liked Mel a lot, maybe more than that. There certainly wasn't any prospect of any sex anywhere else on the horizon, let alone a potential husband or life-partner. Julia shivered despite the warmth of the bathwater. She lay back and let her mind wander.

Chapter 4

On Wednesday Julia Kelso received an email from PC Nelson, or Kevin as she knew him. Kevin wanted to tell her he had chivvied up the lab tests on the powder recovered from Mercy McMorrow's flat. It was extremely high-quality cocaine, over 90 per cent purity. He had preserved the bag as an evidential exhibit, along with the lab report. In all his time as a patrol officer he had never come across cocaine of that purity, and there was no way Mercy or Chantelle could have afforded it. The second bag was also cocaine, but of low purity, less than 30 per cent. Neither sample was cut with anything toxic.

Julia replied immediately, thanking Kevin and asking for the exhibit reference. She also asked him to email her the lab report in full, if possible. She then called the pathologist for the area in which Chantelle and Mercy's post mortems had been conducted. She got through after some polite persistence. The pathologist had just finished the examinations. Initial indications were that Chantelle had suffered a massive cerebral haemorrhage brought on by a cocaine overdose. Death would have occurred rapidly within minutes, if not seconds. Mercy had had a heart attack, a cardiac arrest also brought on by cocaine. She would have taken a bit longer to die but would have been doomed from the moment she inhaled the drug. Toxicology tests wouldn't be back for a few days, but in the pathologist's experience neither girl's body showed any signs of prolonged drug abuse of any kind, especially not cocaine. There were no traces in their nasal passages of any foreign substances that could have been used to adulterate the cocaine they had taken, and in any event the pathologist was not aware of any contaminant that would cause a heart attack in one user and a brain haemorrhage in another at the same time. In the pathologist's view both girls had been killed by inhaling a small quantity of almost pure cocaine, more than either girl would have been used to or able to deal with physically. The pathologist would know more when the tox report came back.

Julia thanked the pathologist and asked if she could be copied on the autopsy report when it was ready. She hung up.

She called down to Brian Kearney and asked him to come and see her. She told him the outline of what the pathologist had said, and also gave him the gist of what Mel had told him about the national picture, such as it was.

"So, Brian. We may have some very dangerous and very pure cocaine in circulation. I would really like to know where it is coming from and who is distributing it. Mostly I really want to know why. From what little I know about the illegal coke trade dishing out 90 per cent plus purity cocaine makes no sense at all. It must be costing the suppliers a fortune in lost profits. I also want to try to understand the geographical spread of the deaths. It can't just be one supplier or a simple accident, can it? Not in four or five London Boroughs and in the North West and in the Midlands? Any ideas?"

Kearney thought for a while. Julia could see him puffing on an imaginary pipe. Eventually he spoke.

"Last time I saw anything like this, not the same but a bit similar, it was a turf war between two Jamaican firms working the North Kensington area and fighting for market share. One firm tried to put customers off the other one by adulterating gear or interfering with its purity and getting it to their punters. They were basically poisoning people or giving them a really bad experience. Maybe nine or ten died in total, over a couple of months. But it was local, just two rival firms. The aggressor had bought a couple of the other firm's runners so was able to substitute the poisonous stuff for regular coke. The bought runners didn't last long, obviously, and the whole thing ended in a shoot-out on Shepherds Bush Green. A few of the gang members were banged up, but once honour was seen to be restored the bosses agreed on boundaries and everything got back to normal. This was eight or nine years ago, as I recall. But multiple locations using 90 per cent pure cocaine? No, that's a new one on me."

"Which firm has the territories where the recent spate of ODs happened?" she asked.

"No particular one. Things are a bit fluid these days, but there is still a sort of territorial divide. Sometimes it's just on postcodes and a street-gang gets to control a few streets or an estate. It's possible that they could be buying from the same supplier, but it doesn't seem likely.

"What we can do is send out some Test Purchase Officers to get samples from as many street-gangs as possible, and if we get a lead on who has the very pure stuff we can work out an undercover operation to find out where the supply is coming from. Just a thought, ma'am."

"A good one, Brian. Let's do it. Start the TPOs running a soon as you can and report back by the end of the week. Is that too soon?"

"Monday would be better, ma'am. It will give us the weekend. Peak shopping time and all that. Can I use your budget?"

"Yes, do. Raj can give you the cost-centre code on your way out. Thanks Brian."

Test Purchase Officers, TPOs, were police officers who had been trained for limited undercover roles as drug buyers. They were a vital tool in understanding drug supplies, availability, purity and pricing, but sadly they tended to be under-valued and used simply to prove that individual street-level dealers were selling. Kelso liked the idea of using them for a more strategic purpose.

She called Mel. "How are you getting on? I've heard back from the investigators looking into the McMorrow girls and the coke that seems to have killed them was very pure indeed, 90 per cent plus. I also spoke to the pathologist doing the PMs. No toxicology reports back yet but she seems to think that it was a small-quantity, high-purity overdose. Mercy had a heart attack, Chantelle a brain bleed. Nasty. How does that sit with what you have from the North West and the Midlands?"

"You're too quick for me, Jake. Maybe being called a Commander makes things move faster than being called an analyst, senior or not. It might help if you spoke to the DG and got him to support you, then I'd have more resources to work with. I'll call in a few favours to try to get some additional stuff to support you with the DG – you know it's always better if a problem is cross-border and not just the Met's. No offence."

"I'm getting used to being offended, don't worry. Is Friday OK with your cocaine man? "

"I hope no one listened to that! Yes, he's on. I said 12.30. Shall we do St Ermin's again, in the restaurant?"

"Are you trying to sabotage my expense budget, Miss Dunn? I'll have Raj book a table, and I'll get an appointment with your DG for Monday or Tuesday next week – I should have more to go on by then. See you Friday."

Julia hung up. She found herself smiling.

******

Friday came around soon enough, it had been a busy week. Julia Kelso arrived at the St Ermin's slightly rushed just after 12.30. Mel was already seated at a table with a middle-aged, slightly overweight man with thinning hair. He was wearing a department store suit that had seen better days.

Mel stood up. "Julia, this is Andy Connaught, head of the Cocaine Intelligence Unit. Andy, Commander Kelso."

"Call me Julia. Good to meet you Andy. Mel tells me that there is nothing you don't know about the cocaine business," she said.

"True enough, sadly. My folks had me destined for the mines when I was a boy, and then when the pits folded they wanted me to be a teacher. Instead I joined the Customs. It drove them crazy!" Andy had a Welsh lilt, and his eyes sparkled. Shrewd intelligence lay beneath the shabby surface.

"Have you had a chance to look at the menu? Would you like a drink, some wine maybe? I won't as I have to see the Commissioner later and I don't want to fall over in front of him, but you carry on if you want."

Both Mel and Andy declined alcohol and chose fizzy water. Julia was amused when both her guests opted for low-calorie healthy stuff, which she did too. She had seen Mel looking hungrily at a steaming rib of medium-rare roast beef on the carving trolley, and at the heaped Yorkshire puddings alongside it.

They chatted politely until the food arrived, then Andy started.

"How can I help you, Julia? What do you want to know about cocaine? Just one thing though, before you ask. I'd like to know why you want to know what it is you want to know."

"Fair enough, Andy. It looks like there is some very high-purity cocaine in circulation at street-level. It's killing people. I'm almost certain about two cases in London, and I'm looking into another twenty-odd, all fatal overdoses. It may be that there is a similar pattern elsewhere in the UK, I don't know yet. What I would like to get from you is an understanding of how the cocaine business works, and also your thoughts on the feasibility of 90 per cent plus pure cocaine ending up being sold to punters on the streets of London and elsewhere."

"Fair dos," said Andy. "Second part first, I don't think it is feasible at all for 90 per cent pure cocaine to be sold to punters. Cocaine is an expensive and high-risk commodity. Nobody who has any is going to give it away. On current street prices a gram of 90 per cent pure cocaine, in the unlikely event that you could get hold of it, would have cost a dealer around £120. It would have cost the importer – who is the one taking a massive risk – at least half that amount. A street seller has to get half as much again, if not more, to make any money for himself once runners and gang-members have been paid. So, by the time it gets to street level it has been cut back to anything between 18 and 50 per cent purity. A gram of 55 or 60 per cent pure coke can be sold to a city slicker for £85 to £100. A gram of 18 per cent can go for £40. That way the street level dealer is making around £200 to £225 per gram of pure coke. The end-user purchase price has a limit. No one actually wants 90 per cent plus cocaine. It is generally dangerous, if not downright deadly. The end-user, the consumer, the punter, won't pay more than about £80 or £100 a gram, max. It follows that there's no market for 90 per cent plus pure cocaine and no dealer capable of the job is going to sell at a loss. When the price goes up or down the purity of the cocaine is adjusted rather than the price. It is a market that depends on retail buyers, and no dealer wants people getting used to strong cheap cocaine. Sometimes it might go up to 65 to 70 per cent, but that is quite unusual and it starts to get difficult for users to handle that strength. It can do strange things to mind and body."

"You know your stuff, Andy," said Julia. Mel was listening but said nothing.

"As for getting the product to market, how much do you already know?"

"Let's assume I know nothing." Julia threw a quick glare at Mel, who was failing to suppress a smile.

"Fair dos," Andy said it again. "Cocaine has been cultivated for thousands of years in the foothills of the Andes, mostly in the North West part of South America. The main producing countries are Colombia, Bolivia and Peru. Historically the coca plant was grown to produce a warm drink, a sort of tea, to help with altitude sickness and fatigue, and also as a leaf mixed with small bits of lime, calcium oxide, for travellers and others to chew on. In its raw form it is mildly, very mildly, narcotic and analgesic – pain-killing. Medicinally speaking, as a refined pharmaceutical product it is a very good anaesthetic, excellent for optical surgery and dental work. Of course, these days cocaine has been replaced by synthetic substitutes, novocaine, procaine or increasingly lidocaine. Anyway, at the beginning of the last century extracts from the coca plant became internationally and commercially traded when Coca Cola used it in the fizzy drink. They don't any more. Before that refined products from the coca plant were popular recreational stimulants, and quite legal. Queen Victoria is said to have offered cocaine pastilles to guests at Osborne House, as well as heroin or opium mixed with alcohol as laudanum. You could get that in suckable lozenges. Lovely.

"The twentieth century changed the image of refined coca products. Prohibition of alcohol in the US showed ordinary people how easy it was to evade the law and make big bucks, and when narcotics like cocaine and heroin became widely banned organised crime saw a way of making an awful lot of money from it, just as they had from alcohol during Prohibition.

"Politicians don't learn, though, do they? Cocaine was made illegal just about everywhere and the criminal trade in it took off. It's a very nasty trade too.

"Production of cocaine starts on the slopes of the Andes, like I said. Ordinary hill farmers are often coerced into planting coca illegally alongside other, regular crops. Many don't like doing it, but it can make a bit of money for them. You can harvest up to four coca crops a year, but with legitimate alternatives like cocoa beans you can only harvest one, so coca is better for cash flow even with its challenges. It is high-risk, both growing coca and refusing to if the squeeze is put on you. If you plant and grow coca the *federales*, the feds as the police and the army are known, could find it and burn you out of your farm and maybe kill you. If you don't plant and grow coca the cartels could burn you out of your farm and maybe kill you. Coca is easy to see. It is a very distinct light green colour, unmistakeable from the air.

"It takes roughly 100 kilos of dried coca leaf to make 1 kilo of coca paste. If the end-market wholesale price of cocaine is 100 units a kilo, the grower will get paid about one-tenth of a unit for his 100 kilos of dry leaf. The cartels have labourers, often slaves or prisoners, who collect and amass the dry leaf and start the 'refining' process.

"The leaf is shredded, dusted with dry cement and soaked in chemicals, including gasoline, caustic soda and various acids, and the labourers have to tread it like grapes to extract the coca juice. They do this is a canvas pool about one metre high, two thirds full of chemicals and coca leaf. The treading is done by bare-foot labourers. Many get sores and ulcers on their legs, some lose their legs, some die of infection. Sometimes the 'refineries' catch fire and the labourers in them at the time are burnt alive.

"When the treading is done the liquid is separated out from the residue. What's left is a sludge. The sludge is rinsed in water and air dried. This becomes coca paste – part-refined cocaine still bearing a lot of sulphuric acid, benzine and all sorts of nasties. At this stage a kilo of paste is about 70% pure cocaine. One kilo of paste is worth about one unit on the scale – ten times the amount the grower was paid for it. The coca paste can be consumed as it is, but it is really cheap, nasty and dangerous. You find a lot of it in the *favelas*.

The cartels gather the paste and further clean it up, refine it into almost pure cocaine hydrochloride and pack it in kilo or half-kilo blocks. In the control of the cartels a kilo of the refined cocaine becomes worth 5 or 6 units on the scale, and they will have accumulated hundreds and hundreds of kilos. The clever cartels have their own 'marketing teams' and they can control transport of the cocaine either to the appropriate border or to the end-user destination. For example, the cartels control cocaine moving from Colombia up to

Jamaica or Mexico, or across to West Africa. Sometimes the better organised and ambitious ones control it right across the Atlantic to Europe. Europe is the most lucrative cocaine market, and the UK the absolute top destination with the highest end-user price. The cartels want to get as much profit as they can.

"Your 5 or 6 unit kilo will be worth about 20 units by the time it reaches the coast of Colombia or Venezuela. It is worth 30 after the short run up to Jamaica, 40 when it reaches West Africa – São Tomé or Cape Verde or even Nigeria. Once inside the US border it is worth up to 50 units – 500 times what the grower was paid for his 100 kilos of leaf. Crossing the Atlantic is expensive and relatively high-risk, so it can jump to 60 or even 70 units by the time it gets to Spain or Italy or Holland or Albania, depending on the final destination. Movement inside Europe to get to the end-user market is the most risky part of the trade for the cartels. The chances of interception are relatively high, so a lot of effort and ingenuity has to go into concealing the cocaine, bribing officials, transporting the gear in the right amount to reduce the risk and scale of losses and so on.

Importing to the UK is said to be the biggest challenge with the highest rewards, which is why so many people try to do it. A kilo arriving in the UK hits 100 units, one-thousand times the price the grower was paid. Often the traffickers will use couriers from the Caribbean, Jamaica mainly. We have seen up to 20 or 30 couriers on one flight from Jamaica to London, each with between a half and one kilo in their stomach or up their bum, they are called stuffers and swallowers. They know that the border control can only handle two or three stuffers and swallowers at once, and then they can't detain anyone else, even if they are suspected. If their 'cargo' bursts inside them the couriers die. The border control can't have that on their plate, so if they catch and deal with two or three that means the trafficker still gets 20 plus couriers through – 10 to 20 kilos. That's still plenty of profit.

"It's no wonder all the old-fashioned villains are all into drug trafficking. Sure, the penalties are steep, but the risks are relatively low compared to more traditional criminal activities.

"Cocaine has a relatively short shelf-life, though. Unlike heroin, which is a stable substance that won't change much once it's refined, cocaine goes off. It gets weaker over time, not in days or weeks, but it doesn't take too many months for it to deteriorate. This is where we, the authorities, have our only advantage. The traffickers need to get their gear to market and quick, or just like fresh milk or fruit it steadily loses value until it is eventually worth nothing. They need to take more risks, need to speak to more people, make more deals. Each contact leaves a trace and gives us a chance. Isn't that right, Mel?"

She nodded. Andy had been eating steadily throughout his monologue, not a pretty sight.

"So Julia, in a nutshell that is cocaine 101. Going back to 90 per cent pure coke being flogged retail, you can see why it isn't a realistic scenario. Not one that I've experienced anyway, and I've been doing this a long time."

Julia asked a few clarifying questions before looking at her watch.

"Sorry, Andy. I do have to go. Thank you so much for your time and sharing such knowledge. I wouldn't know where to start finding all that out myself. I'll give you a call if I need more. Do stay and have dessert if you want. They'll send the bill to my office."

Julia stood to leave, making the 'I'll call you' gesture to Mel behind Andy's back.

"Thanks again!" she called over her shoulder as she walked out.

Her mind was racing.

Chapter 5

Julia's meeting with the Commissioner had just finished, and it had been a puzzling and pointless one. He gave her some tea and they chatted inconsequentially for about 20 minutes. Then he said that she was doing a great job and he had high hopes for her. His door was always open, he said. Then he shook her hand and showed her out.

As she entered her own office Raj handed her a sheaf of messages. The top one was from Andy Connaught at NCIS. Could she give him a call.

"Andy, it's Julia Kelso. You called?"

"Thanks for calling back, Julia, and thanks for lunch too, fabulous it was. I hope I didn't go on too much. You mentioned some OD cases in London. I was wondering if you had any lab analysis of any cocaine samples connected with any of them? You see, we keep a database of cocaine sample analysis and sometimes we can link them to a particular consignment, or more usually to one of the cartels back in Latin America. No two batches of cocaine are ever identical, chemically speaking, or at least it's very unusual."

"Bear with me, Andy." Julia opened her email inbox. There was a reply from PC Nelson, with attachments. One of them was a GC report on the sample from Mercy and Chantelle's case.

"Andy, I have a Gas Chromatography report in front of me. It's from a double overdose last weekend. Give me your email and I'll send it to you. I'll have someone check if there are any others." She hung up.

Twenty minutes later her phone rang. It was Andy Connaught. "Good news and bad news, Julia," he began. "The GC report is an exact match for a consignment that was recovered from a small fishing boat on a beach in Kent about four months ago. No one was arrested. I would imagine that the boat had been beached, either on purpose or because of some emergency, and the traffickers were keeping an eye on it to see if we were on to them. As it happens someone had called the coastguard, and they turned up with the police so the haul was abandoned. The boat is in one of our yards. It was bought for cash in France last year and it's forensically clean. I doubt it was actually intended to land in the UK, not with that level of purity. It may have been going for further refining or cutting somewhere like Ireland.

"The cargo recovered was 100 kilos of top-grade cocaine, wholesale value 12 million pounds or 22 million on the street. It would have cost the trafficker who owned it around 6 million, so not exactly small change. Surprisingly we don't have any intelligence on where it came from, who owned it or where it was going."

"And the bad news, Andy?" Julia asked.

"Bad news is that the entire cargo was officially incinerated – destroyed – a month ago. So the cocaine that killed your two can't be from that shipment, unless….." he paused.

"Unless what?"

"Unless the shipment wasn't destroyed, or the stuff we recovered was only part of the shipment. Neither case is likely."

"Who manages the storage and destruction of seized narcotics, Andy?"

"We used to, Customs and Excise. We had secure warehousing and furnaces, but a few years ago the Home Affairs Select Committee in Parliament got all arsy with us and the police. Seems that samples of cannabis that were being found on suspects had already been through the system, sometimes more than once. The labs were complaining that all the old fingerprint powder on the packaging was contaminating their facilities. Some enterprising coppers, and in fairness some customs officers too, were either nicking evidence and re-selling it or borrowing it to plant on people they wanted to bang up. Either way, the politicians decided enough was enough and we weren't to be trusted, so they ordered an independent storage and destruction system to be established. It's been outsourced, don't ask me who to, or where the storage and destruction takes place - I don't know. It's Top Secret. No one on our side ever asks. We just follow the process."

"What is it? The process, I mean?" Julia asked.

"Once the gear is no longer needed physically for court evidence an email is sent to someone in the Home Office. They arrange for the stuff to be collected. If it's high-value, and this shipment would certainly be classed as high-value, they send armoured vans and get armed escorts from the MOD police. It's not unusual for them to send three or even four identical convoys, one real one and the others as decoys. There is a system of code words and numbers that have to match, and if they do the gear is given over to the couriers and off it goes. We don't see it again. Just get a receipt off the person in charge of the convoy. The destruction site is rumoured to be somewhere east of London, but I don't know."

"Thanks, Andy. I'll get any other lab reports to you as soon as I get them. I'm coming over to see your DG on Monday. I expect we'll be doing more on this. Have a good weekend." Julia hung up.

She thought for a while, then called Brian Kearney. He arrived in her office a short time later.

"Hello, Brian. Do we have any lab analysis of any samples recovered from the other suspected ODs, the twenty-three you mentioned?"

"I believe so. It should be standard procedure. I'll get on to it, but as you know ODs don't get much priority for lab time or forensics budgets."

"I would like these prioritised, and you can offer my budget if you need to."

"Can I ask a question, ma'am?"

"You just did. Is there another?" She smiled at him.

"Just this, ma'am: Why?"

"It could be, Brian, that the cocaine that killed Mercy and Chantelle was already in official custody and had been destroyed a month before it went to work on those two girls. If that's correct, someone is recycling seized cocaine. Which is a bad thing, I think you'll agree. I need to know if the other ODs come from the same batch – NCIS think they can tell me if they have the chemical analysis. But Brian, please don't mention this to anyone else for now. Just hurry the lab reports up and use my budget to sweeten Boroughs; say it's for strategic statistical research or some such phrase that sounds good but means nothing."

Brian Kearney allowed himself a slight smile. "Of course, ma'am. Right away."

By 5pm Julia had three other analytical reports relating to samples from other suspected overdoses in front of her. She quickly read them, comparing the numbers with the Mercy and Chantelle McMorrow analysis. She needed Andy Connaught to confirm it, but as far as she could see the numbers were identical. So, four separate overdose cases in four different parts of London in the past month, at the least, all caused by the same high-purity cocaine. Cocaine that had been seized and destroyed by the State. She called Mel.

"I'm surprised you're still in the office, Miss Dunn," she started.

"I've got my coat on and am half-way out the door," Mel lied. She was deeply engrossed in an intelligence analysis study relating to people trafficking.

"Those overdoses, Mel, the ones in the North West and the Midlands, do you have Gas Chromatography analysis for any samples recovered?"

"I'm not that sort of analyst, Jake. Why?"

Jake told her. Mel said that all the regional offices would be down the pub by now so she would get on to it on Monday.

"What about tomorrow, Jake? Are we still on for a bit of sweating, and not in a good way?" Mel asked.

"Sure. Why don't you come over in the afternoon, say between two and three, then we can do the sweating before a drink and some dinner."

"Bliss, a lie in! See you then, Jake. Have a good evening." Mel hung up.

Distracted, she put away the reports she was reading and locked her cabinets up. If Jake was onto something it could be another big one. From what she knew about the seized narcotics destruction system it was theoretically impossible to remove anything from it once it had been put there. It was in the same league as the Bank of England's security for banknote destruction. She made a mental note to call someone she knew at Thames House on Monday, someone who would probably know something about it.

Mel made her way home. In her flat she checked the email account that Ferdinand had set up. The draft had been changed.

"Never thought I would be glad to hear about a suicide verdict. I am between places just now but will check this every few days. Keep in touch. x"

She closed her computer. She sat with a glass of chilled white wine and watched the telly until she fell asleep on the sofa.

Chapter 6

Mel left for Dolphin Square around 1.30pm. She had her sports bag, and as an afterthought she had added clean underwear, a long tee-shirt and a washbag to her gym kit and swimming costume. An afternoon with Jake Kelso could easily turn into an all-nighter. She phoned Jake when she emerged from Vauxhall station and said she would be there in 15 minutes. Julia was waiting for her in the reception, dressed for her work-out in the tight knee-length Lycra running shorts and white tee-shirt she liked. Mel tried not to look at Jake's pert bottom.

Jake sat on a bench while Mel changed into her kit. The two friends had long-since stopped being awkward dressing and undressing in front of each other. An hour and a half later they were back in the changing room, red-faced, sweating, hair slicked wet across their heads. Donning one-piece swimsuits they showered quickly before going to the pool. They swam steadily for 30 minutes until Jake decided she had done enough. They rested with their backs against the side of the pool, which they had to themselves.

"I heard from Alf," Mel started.

"Oh. How is he?"

"He said he's glad to be dead. He also says he is between places, whatever that means, but he will be checking for messages every few days. I expect he's quite lonely. Do you think I should go and see him?"

"It's up to you. It might be a bit strange, and maybe it would be better to let him put it all behind him and get a new life for himself," Julia mused.

"Does that mean you've gone off your daft idea of saving the world from corruption using him as your secret weapon?"

"You didn't think it was so daft when you agreed to help. But no, I haven't gone off it. In fact it may be starting sooner than you think."

"You mean the cocaine thing?"

"Possibly. It's developing quite fast. We may need some unorthodox insights to make sense of it. Let's get showered."

In the showers Jake admired Mel's refreshed all-over tan. "Clearly you weren't staying in the shade in France. Look at you! Even your nipples have a suntan!" she commented. "Can you do my back? I think I've still got midge bites and they're itchy."

Mel squeezed shower gel onto her hand and soaped Jake's back slowly, stopping at the top of her buttocks. There were no midge bites; the skin on Jake's back was as flawless as the rest of her. "And just as clearly you didn't take off a single stitch in daylight up in Scotland. The only colour you have is a bit of rust!"

Julia's skin was pale, even the faintest tan she had had a few months before had gone, now she was a uniform pale pink, almost white. Julia turned suddenly and Mel found herself with her hands on Jake's rounded breasts. She drew them away.

"I do have some colour!" Jake protested, nodding down towards her rosy pink and decidedly proud nipples. "You haven't finished my back yet." She turned again and Mel continued washing her back, glad that Jake couldn't see the longing in her eyes.

Later, dried and changed, Mel waited for Jake in the bar while she took their sports bags up to her flat. Mel sipped a gin and tonic. She had ordered one for Jake too.

Jake appeared and the two friends sat together in a quiet corner.

"What did you mean, about the cocaine thing needing some 'unorthodox insights'?" Mel asked.

"Well, if someone has been able to circumvent the storage and destruction system, which is supposed to be utterly secure, I can think of only two ways they could have done it. One is by being technically cleverer than the system designers so they can defeat the security system through exploiting any flaws it has. Or they could buy their way in. Which would you do?"

"I suppose buying my way in would be more likely to get the result I want, whatever that is."

"I agree. If someone is recycling seized cocaine I think it likely that there is some significant corruption involved. Especially in that particular system."

"Do you remember Simon Waterson?"

"Of course," Jake replied.

"Well he's back at Thames House now, although he's looking for another job. He's decided that organised crime and MI5 aren't for him, not after his experiences with the Carlton family. Anyway, I had a drink with him a while back and for now he's doing stuff with their protective security people, designing and inspecting security systems at key national facilities. I am pretty sure his department will have something to do with securing narcotics storage and destruction facilities. Do you want me to give him a call on Monday?"

"Is there anyone or anything you don't know, Mel? Go and see him, see what he knows," she smiled. Mel smiled back.

There is one person that I might not know as well as I thought I did, she thought, recalling the way Jake had engineered things in the shower so that Mel was touching her breasts. Girls just don't do that by accident.

******

While Mel and Jake were enjoying their drinks in the bar at Dolphin Square, just over a mile away three men were deep in conversation in the corner of a gentlemen's club smoking room. The Club, although in St James's, was not one of the traditional ones, nor was it particularly reputable or picky about its membership. It was, however, very expensive and therefore afforded a degree of privacy.

The clear alpha male of the group was tall and slim. In his 60s, he was wearing expensively tailored weekend clothing, namely a sports jacket, lightweight wool trousers, an open necked shirt and a crimson cravat. His flowing grey hair was slightly too long. The man he was talking to in low earnest tones was a little younger, paunchy, with thinning hair. His clothing was neither stylish nor costly. A standard grey office suit, rumpled, an off-white shirt and an imitation old school tie. His shoes were scuffed. The third man was saying nothing. He was soberly attired in a tailored suit that barely concealed his bulging muscles.

48

"So, Geoffrey," the alpha male said, "the trials seem to have gone well. The method is effective. I think it is time to ramp it up a bit, move towards the result we are looking for."

"Are you sure, Sir Charles? We did agree that something needs to be done about illegal drugs, but this seems excessive. Eliminating drug users? Is that the best way to defeat the narco-traffickers? I don't think I want to be involved in this anymore."

"I do hope you're not getting cold feet, Geoffrey. You are involved in it, irrevocably, whether you like it or not. You've been a vital part of getting us this far. It would be a pity to have to throw you to the wolves."

Geoffrey looked at Sir Charles in horror. The man was threatening him! But Geoffrey knew that he was right. He was in it up to his neck. He had used his position at the Home Office to get access to the seized cocaine, the cocaine that Sir Charles, his son and his intimidating assistant had used to see if casual drug users could be killed off in sufficient numbers to eliminate the drugs market.

"We have been generous to you so far, Geoffrey, don't you agree? You've been rewarded handsomely for your good work for our cause. Let's not spoil it now. Phase 2 is coming. You know what you need to do. We need to get a further four kilos out there onto the streets, then we need another twenty kilos from the same shipment. It is exceptionally good quality and has been very successful so far. The one kilo we have used so far has disposed of at least 50 parasites, multiply that by twenty-four and you start to have an impact. The value of cocaine in this country will be reduced to nothing within a month! Now, drink up, and Artur will show you out."

Sir Charles stood, and nodded at the silent Artur, who also stood. Artur followed the trembling Geoffrey out of the room. Once they were alone Artur seized Geoffrey by the throat and growled "You do what you have been told, or I will be coming to see you. Understand?"

Geoffrey nodded, barely able to breathe. The taciturn Artur terrified him. Geoffrey was lifted off the floor, he squealed, his legs flailed, then Artur let him drop. He fell to the floor. Geoffrey had wet himself. "Get out!" growled Artur.

Artur currently worked for Sir Charles Murston, chairman of Murston Asset Management and the sitting member for a safe seat in the Shires, at least until the next election. Sir Charles had had enough of constituents. A former Home Office Minister, he still served on the Home Affairs Select Committee, which was where he had come across the mousy Geoffrey Appleton, a Principal Officer in the Home Office responsible for drafting illicit drugs policy. Sir Charles had watched Geoffrey being torn apart by an overly indignant member and he saw an opportunity.

After the session he sought Geoffrey out, took him to the Tea Room and sympathised about his brutal treatment at the hands of the aggressive committee member. Sir Charles asked pertinent questions about drugs policy and listened carefully to the answers, praising Geoffrey for his insights and wisdom. Within 45 minutes Geoffrey Appleton would have crawled over broken glass for his saviour, which was precisely what Sir Charles wanted. He collected people like Geoffrey, people of low worth to most others, but potentially of great value to Sir Charles. Sir Charles survived in the City by manipulating people and situations. He had dozens of Geoffreys dotted about the place, and they all paid a price for his support and affection in the end.

Chapter 7

They decided to eat in the restaurant. Jake ordered pasta, Mel had a steak. She was starving, she said. They drank red.

When the food arrived Jake started. "How did you get into it, the thing with your group? I'm curious. I mean, how does that sort of thing happen, and why?"

Mel noted that Jake hadn't used her usual 'weirdy-pervy' description. She paused. Part of the convention of the group was to not talk about it too much to outsiders, people who wouldn't understand and who might try to spoil it. But she had decided she could tell Jake something about it, if she asked again. The experience in the shower had moved things on a bit, and it might help if Jake knew and understood more about the way Mel was about sex.

She started. "Let's do the 'why' first. Most people, almost everyone I know, are normal. They have rounded, complete lives. One partner, a job, kids, house, likes and dislikes, stability and routine, and I'm happy for them. I'm different. I can't understand why or how one person can be everything to another. I know I can't be everything to someone else. I've tried being normal, boyfriends and stuff, and it didn't work for me. I like sex, good sex, I physically need it like I need exercise or food or sleep, but in moderation. I'm not promiscuous, I won't hire people for it, I need to like and trust someone who can do it for me sexually. And there aren't many of those about, I can tell you. So I've experimented with different types of sex in different settings, not very successfully. Getting sex is very easy if you're not fussy. Finding good sex is not easy at all.

"When I first came to London I enjoyed the vitality of the city, but after a while it got a bit lonely and a sex life was just a distant memory. I really don't like sharing living space, and in London most people's friends seem to be the people they accidentally live with. So I went looking for people I didn't have to live with, not to be friends with so much as just to know, to talk to and be interested in. I'm usually quite happy on my own, I don't really need to have other people around me, but I'm not actually that antisocial and I find people interesting.

"Anyway, at Uni they taught us to draw when we were out on archaeological digs. The tutors said cameras are all well and good, but they are too quick. They don't encourage you look at what you're finding. If you draw it you have to really examine the site, and you end up concentrating on what interests you. I enjoyed drawing, I still do, so I signed up for a course at a local further education place. I went along on a Wednesday with about five or six other people and we drew things. It was good, I liked it. I got to know the others a bit. After a few weeks two of the people in the class asked me if I wanted to go for a drink. They were clearly a couple, my sort of age, and I went along. They were, are, Jilly and Frank. We had a drink and chatted. I liked them. They asked if I was looking forward to next week. I asked why. Jilly said we would be doing life drawing, with a model. In fact we would be doing that for the next two weeks. I said oh good, that'll be different. Of course, I was being a bit dim and didn't realise that 'life drawing' means nudes. Jilly said Frank was going to be the model next week, and she would be doing it the week after. They both hoped I would be there for both.

"The next week I went along. Jilly and Frank were there. We had the usual coffee and a chat, then Frank disappeared. He came back after a few minutes in a dressing gown. He said something about giving clothing marks time to fade. Then it dawned on me. I was a bit flustered. The class started. Frank took off the dressing gown and arranged himself as the tutor wanted. He kept smiling at me, and every time I looked up I could see Jilly looking at me. I concentrated on my drawing. It was quite good, if I say so myself. Afterwards, when Frank had dressed, Jilly asked if I wanted to go for a drink again. I went with them. All Jilly wanted to talk about was Frank's body, especially his cock. Did I like it? Was it big enough, or too big? Did I think that it would be more beautiful if it was circumcised? Did his pose show his cock off to best effect? Would it be better if it was hard? And all the time Frank was just sitting there looking at me, smiling. Not at all bothered that Jilly, who is actually his wife, was discussing his penis in a pub with a virtual stranger.

"The next week it was Jilly's turn. She lay on a couch, nude, and I swear she just stared at me for two hours while I drew her body. Afterwards she asked to see my drawings of her and Frank. She said they were excellent. In the pub it was Frank's turn to ask me what I thought of Jilly's body. Her proportions, her boobs, her cunt – that's what he called it, but affectionately – could I see her lips clearly enough? Were her boobs firm enough? Did I think her nipples looked good standing up as they had done? It was weird.

"Then it was the final week of the course. We all had to draw someone's face, someone in the class. I drew an older man who hadn't said a word for at least six weeks. Jilly and Frank both drew me. I could feel their eyes on me, but I wasn't freaked out – it wasn't creepy. Afterwards we went for a drink, the three of us. Jilly and Frank became quite serious. They said they were a married couple and they loved each other, but they sometimes liked to have sex with other people. Always as a couple, so no secrets or surprises. They asked me straight out if I'd like to have sex with them. They'd seen the way I looked at them, and I'd seen the way they looked at me. They gave me a piece of paper with their address and both their phone numbers and said to come round on Friday evening if I wanted to – but only if I wanted to. And that's how it started."

"That's mad!" said Jake. "What did you do?"

"I went home. I was in a rented flat then. I had a bath. I had a drink. I thought about it. In one way I really wanted to go, in another I was terrified, or maybe just very excited. I kept thinking about Jilly and Frank. Their bodies, and Frank's cock of course. Which was quite beautiful, really; it still is. Things had been extremely lean, or rather absent, on the sex front since I got to London, it seemed that my only options were either commitment to a heavy relationship or becoming an indiscriminate slut and shagging anything with a pulse. I wasn't interested in doing either, but as I said I do like sex. I need it from time to time and I wasn't keen on giving up on it altogether. I went to bed thinking about it but I couldn't sleep. I just kept imagining Jilly and Frank and what it would be like to have sex with them. After a while I treated myself to the mother of all wanks and when I had calmed down I decided to go."

Jake choked on her wine.

"Then I started worrying about the etiquette of it all," Mel continued, "what to wear. Personal hygiene. Should I take a bottle of wine. I mean, what *is* the form when you are invited to come round and have sex with a married couple you hardly know? No one teaches you this stuff, so I called Jilly to ask. She told me to relax. No need for wine. Just dress comfortably. We would all have a shower anyway, and they had loads of condoms and lubricants so nothing to worry about. Friday came. I couldn't concentrate at work so I said I was ill and went home early. I was outside Jilly and Frank's for twenty minutes getting my courage up, then I rang the bell.

"They couldn't have been sweeter. We sat down. They thanked me for being there and then, and this is important, they asked me if I really wanted to do it. They said they wouldn't try to seduce me or persuade me. I could stop it and leave any time I wanted, and they would be fine with it. They wouldn't be taking my clothes off, I would be the only one doing that. The whole thing had to be wholly voluntary, with a willingness. They said that in their book consent alone was not enough; a sex partner had to be an eager,

56

active participant. That's one of the group rules, the main one really. We can't, mustn't, seduce people. It's a rule I stick to, totally. Except I might have broken it with Ferdinand the first time we did it."

"How?" Julia asked.

"Well, basically I stood in front of him with no clothes on and said I'd shag him if he wanted me to, or words to that effect. Where I come from in East Yorkshire that counts as seduction."

"I think you'd have a defence. Go on."

"We took turns to shower. Jilly went first, then me, then Frank. He complained that we'd used all the hot water. Then we sat round in towels and had a glass of wine – we aren't supposed to use alcohol or any other substance to disinhibit people either - then Jilly stood up and dropped her towel. She walked into the bedroom. I took a deep breath and did the same. I got onto the bed with Jilly. Frank came in, also naked, and it started. It was amazing. They were so gentle, so caring, asking all the time if I was OK, would I like to do anything, or did I want them to do anything to me? They spent ages just exploring me with their eyes, their hands and their mouths. I felt so special. The first time I came with them it felt like I was being electrocuted. I realise for them it must have been a bit tame, but for me it was utter heaven. I had come home. This was the sex I wanted to have. Not necessarily with this particular married couple, but informed, gentle but passionate accomplished physical sex. No inhibitions, no cruelty, not competitive like sex nearly always is. And most of all no expectations, no being

57

owned or possessed by anyone. Are you OK, Jake? You've gone a bit pink."

"I'm fine, it's just the wine."

"We stayed in bed until noon the next day, only getting up for food and drink and the bathroom. I lost count of my orgasms. They had to call a taxi to get me home in the end; I could barely stand. They took me down to the taxi and Jilly and Frank kissed me goodbye on the doorstep. Then Jilly said that I had wonderful delicious boobs, but maybe one should have a pierced nipple. I would enjoy it, she said. Frank said he adored my gorgeous cunt, he said it felt and tasted wonderful. I said his cock was the best I had ever had, it felt and tasted great too, as did Jilly's lovely cunt, which I also adored. Not your usual after-party thank you speeches, I'll admit, but sincerely meant. I'm going to stop there. You don't look too good."

"Let's go up," said Jake, "I need gin."

In Jake's flat Mel poured drinks. Jake disappeared into her bedroom for a few minutes and came out in a bathrobe.

"That was quick! I assumed you'd gone for a..."

"...mother of all wanks?" Jake interrupted, with a slight smile.

"Blimey, Kelso, you must have needed it badly!"

"Don't be like that, Mel. This is very difficult for me."

"I'm sorry, I didn't mean to be flippant. Come here." Mel held her arms out. Jake came over and let herself be enfolded. She rested her head on Mel's shoulder. She looked up, her eyes slightly red.

58

"Let's take these drinks to bed and talk some more," Mel suggested.

Jake nodded.

They cuddled together. Mel let Jake stroke her body tentatively through her tee-shirt, but she didn't return any caresses, not yet, not until Jake was sure.

"Who else is in your group, Mel?"

"Well," Mel replied, "you know about Jilly and Frank. They asked me if I would like to meet some friends after we had been together a few times. They introduced me to Sven. He's Swedish or maybe Norwegian, an alternative therapist, and to Isabelle. Isabelle had already left the group, but she started it with Sven. Her biological alarm clock had gone off and she felt a need to rush away and have babies. She grabbed the first available rich banker who passed by and was married inside two months. She told me she hadn't had an orgasm since leaving the group. She also said that pregnancy and childbirth had left her with boobs like two socks full of wet sand and a fanny like a trouser-leg. She hadn't had an adult thought in months, and she wouldn't have her life any other way. She said I'd enjoy the group and she could see I would fit in. Sven is into meditation and all sorts of strange stuff. He really likes slow, prolonged sex - he can go for hours. He once kept me on the edge of an orgasm for six hours just by stroking and licking my clit and kissing me gently. When he eventually let me come I thought I was going to die. I told Alf about it once. I said I didn't stop shaking all weekend and couldn't construct a sentence until the following Tuesday."

"Alf knows about the group?"

"No, not really, not like I'm telling you."

"Go on." Jake was idly teasing Mel's nipple-stud with her fingers. Mel was trying to suppress her excitement.

"The other group member is Cadi. She's Welsh and was brought up a very strictly. For years she felt guilty about being naked under her clothes, and she hadn't even kissed anyone until she got to university. To look at her you'd think butter wouldn't melt. She's a librarian in one of the colleges, and by day she looks the part. She is sweet and pretty and looks very innocent, but she can suck a lad inside out and lick the top off a mountain. I've seen her exhaust Sven and Frank one after the other, which is no mean feat, and then want me and Jilly to have a go at her. Jake?"

"Mmm?"

"Unless you stop twiddling my nipple stud we are going to have to have words."

"What words? Words like 'would you like me to fuck you Jake?' 'Do you want to have sex with me Jake?' Those words?"

"Yes. That sort of thing."

"I've never done it with a woman," Jake whispered, "I don't even know if I can. I haven't had any sex at all since I came to London, except for that lousy one-night stand in Edinburgh a few weeks ago. I hated it. The way you talk about how great and simple, straightforward, sex is for you makes me jealous, I envy you. I am not whinging, but being a single, senior female cop is not so good for dating.

"I want you to, Mel. Please? Will you?" said Jake, softly.

60

Mel took Jake's face between her hands and kissed her mouth the way she had wanted to since she first saw her. She peeled off their tee-shirts. She put her hand between Jake's hot moist thighs and stroked her silky blonde pubes. She bent to kiss her again.

"Oh, alright then," she said.

Mel treated Jake with utmost gentleness, exploring her body with her fingers, lips and tongue. As she led her towards orgasm Mel knew that it would inevitably the best Jake had ever had. She wasn't wrong.

Chapter 8

The sun was up when they awoke on Sunday morning. They were still in each other's arms. Mel's hand rested on Jake's stomach. Jake opened her eyes. She reached for Mel and kissed her fully on the lips, her tongue darting inside.

"That was wonderful! The best ever," she said.

"No regrets?" Mel asked.

"No, none at all. I think you might have ruined me though. I'm not sure I want to have a penis near me ever again!" Jake sighed.

"No regrets is good. There are still some good penises out there, Jake, so don't write them all off just yet. Now, I have to say this, and it may sound harsh after last night. We are friends. Friends and colleagues. The fact that we've had sex together does not make us girlfriends or partners. I loved having sex with you, and I hope we can do it again, a lot. I've wanted to for ages, as I'm sure you guessed. But we aren't going to be a couple. Is that OK with you?"

"Yes, I think...It was magic, and I'm glad we've done it; it's cleared the air, there was a tension between us. I don't want to be with you as a girlfriend or lover or partner or whatever, but all this is very new ground for me. I think I like us as we are. So, I guess we're cool."

"Good." Mel kissed her.

"Coffee?"

When they were both showered and dressed Jake checked her emails as they shared coffee and toast.

"Jesus!" she exclaimed.

"What?"

"More ODs, twelve incidents between Friday night and now, with twenty-five fatalities. All over London. Can you get anything nationally at this time on a Sunday?"

"I can call the duty room and ask them to find out."

Mel made a call and waited. "I'll need to call you back, Mel," said the duty officer after a few minutes.

Some moments later Mel's phone rang. She answered and listened, her smile vanishing. "OK, thanks. No, the Met will be seeing the DG tomorrow morning, I was just trying to verify some information."

She turned to Jake. "Lots of them, Jake. All over. In every region. No numbers yet, but a lot of fatalities."

That put paid to a leisurely Sunday. They headed to their respective offices and agreed to speak later in the day.

"Thank you, Mel," said Jake, as they were leaving, "I didn't know how much I needed last night."

"Me too, you daft cow! What took you so long to ask?"

"I'm just a wee Highland lassie, not used to your sophisticated big-city ways." They parted with another kiss.

Chapter 9

In his Jacobean pile in Hampshire Sir Charles Murston was enjoying a late and leisurely Sunday breakfast with his family. His eldest son, another Charles but known to everyone as Charlie, had brought his two children over to play in the pool while he caught up with his father's news on the operation. It had been his idea, after all.

They left their respective wives to clear up the breakfast debris and adjourned to a quiet corner of the huge terrace. There they could talk privately but also keep an eye on the children as they splashed about.

"So, Phase One is going well, Pa?" Charlie started.

"So far so good. The first kilo was a resounding success as a tester. The rest of the first batch is being released into the system as we speak. Some went out on Friday, so we should hear about it on the news during this week or next. I've got the civil service chappie working on another twenty, and that will probably do it," Sir Charles replied.

"Excellent! By my reckoning that should eliminate the most profitable part of the market, the interesting bit. I've given Artur all the key dealer phone numbers I've been gathering from up and down the country. He and his boys can muscle in on them and get our stuff to their clients. It seems to have worked well so far. I don't want to know how they persuade the dealers to hand over their customers, though!" Charlie laughed.

"A clever idea of yours, Charlie, shorting the cocaine market! Just because it's an illegal and underground one doesn't mean it behaves any differently to any other. A sharp price reduction means we can buy up a lot of the commodity for next to nothing and cash in when the consumer market bounces back."

"As it will, inevitably; amazing underground marketing! If you consider the illicit drug trade and how it works - without advertising or promotions or showrooms it still generates billions in revenue. I'm drawing up a list of contacts to reboot the market after the price crash, which should happen within about four weeks of the Phase Two mobilisation. How much are you going to put in, Pa?"

"Personally, or through Murston Asset Management?"

"Both, how much in all?"

"I can raise three million myself, without making too many waves. MAM can do twenty, maybe twenty-two. So Twenty five in all. What about you?"

"As you know, Dad, my cashflow isn't brilliant just now. I can re-mortgage, as long as Serena doesn't find out, and put up about one point five, but that's all. But I *am* doing most of the hard work, so that should be worth something."

"Oh, it is Charlie, it is. You'll get ten percent of the profits as your fee, on top of a percentage of the rest depending on your investment. With a thirty-five million total investment, say - I can probably get a few others to chip in - we should be able to clear, conservatively, a 300 percent profit, depending on how low we can force the price of the commodity. That means you should clear between ten and twelve. And it won't be going near any accounts or the Revenue. Not a bad return, eh?"

"And you'll get the lion's share, as always."

"I *am* putting up most of the money. That's how it works, you know that."

"Sorry, Pa. I didn't mean anything by it. Just a bit stressed at the moment."

"Fancy a livener, Charlie? It's gone 12. G and T?"

******

At his much more modest home in Croydon Geoffrey Appleton was not enjoying his Sunday at all. He had spent a sleepless night worrying about the mess he was in. He had even shunned his ritual visit to the pub for his three pints of real ale and a bit of banter with his fellow beer and cricket nerds before lunch. Sunday lunch these days was a solitary affair, since Karen upped and left. A pre-cooked roast dinner for one from the supermarket and a half-bottle of red in front of the telly. Maybe with a bit of cricket or a documentary about something interesting if there was one on. Not even that today, though. He just wasn't in the mood.

His life had been going reasonably well. He had never been an upbeat optimist, but he was doing OK. He had just about scraped through to become a Principal Officer in the Home Office. He knew that that was it for him, as far as he would go. It gave him a decent amount to live on as long as he remained careful, and there was the promise of a pension when he crossed the finishing line. The work was quite interesting too, or at least it had been before his recent posting, when he was in the Home Office proper working on Policy issues, real civil service work. Then he was moved across to manage the secret narcotics storage and destruction facility out in the Essex marshes, bloody miles away in the middle of nowhere, out of sight and out of mind. The job had been sold to him as an important career move, a step towards another promotion, but it had turned out to be a dismal chore and, in career-terms, a dead-end. And just when things couldn't get any worse Karen walked out of his life and Sir Charles bloody Murston walked back into it.

He had kept in loose contact with Murston since their meeting after he suffered a particularly nasty interrogation in front of the Home Affairs Select Committee. Geoffrey should never even have been there. The designated Principal Officer had called in sick and he had been sent along instead, an ill-prepared lamb to the slaughter. Murston was all charm afterwards. Then a few months ago Murston had emailed him out of the blue and asked him to come for lunch. He had accepted. Another misjudged error.

Murston had his son with him, the fat and greasy Charlie, and the two of them grilled him, over Dover Sole and a rather good premier-cru Meursault, about the UK's illegal drugs trade. They were especially interested in middle-class professionals' cocaine usage. A second bottle of Meursault was produced, followed by cognac in the Club lounge. Geoffrey told them everything he knew, and invented a few things that he didn't. He also let slip that he had just been nominated for the lead role in the storage and destruction of seized illegal narcotics. He was trying to impress Murstons senior and junior by exaggerating his importance in the UK's war on drugs, although for the life of him he couldn't say why.

Two weeks later there was a repeat performance. This time the Murstons expressed their disgust at the way criminal drug traffickers were flaunting the laws of the United Kingdom, and wasn't it time that upstanding citizens like the three of them did something about it? Geoffrey agreed wholeheartedly. This time it was pink roast lamb carved from a joint on the trolley – Geoffrey had had his cooked a bit more by the kitchen so it looked more 'English' - two bottles an excellent Médoc, and more cognac of course. Then they said they had a plan and that he could help; he could be part of it.

Charlie, the son, started explaining that the essence of the plan was to persuade the middle-class casual cocaine users to give it up. They were the ones who paid top prices and made most money for the traffickers, a bit like the business-class travellers on trans-Atlantic airliners. If they could be persuaded to stop using cocaine, or at least seriously reduce their consumption, the traffickers would lose money and have to go somewhere else.

Geoffrey should have recognised this as simplistic nonsense, but to be fair he was quite pissed. Then Charlie hit him with it. All they needed was a small sample of cocaine that they could lace with an irritant and get into the supply chain feeding the professional and middle-class users. If enough of them became temporarily unwell they would put two and two together and stop buying cocaine. But where to get hold of some cocaine, without putting their own good money into the traffickers' pockets? Of course! Geoffrey had control of lots of cocaine destined for destruction. Who would miss a little bit of it, for a good cause? Geoffrey had mumbled something about difficulty and checks and security. Sir Charles said a man of Geoffrey's calibre could get round all that. If he needed to oil a wheel or two Sir Charles would provide the wherewithal to do that. In his alcohol-fuddled state Geoffrey agreed.

The following Monday Geoffrey went to withdraw his weekly cash from a hole in the wall money machine. As always, he checked his balance. He checked it again. It was much higher than it should have been, higher to the tune of a full month's salary. When he got to his office he called the payroll people. No, no additional or erroneous payments had been made. His office line rang – no one was supposed to have the number. It was Charlie Murston. Just checking to see that everything was alright and that he had received the donation towards expenses.

Geoffrey had made no attempt to return the money, which he transferred to his savings account. Maybe it could go towards a nice holiday to the Caribbean the next time there was an England / Windies test match there. He was snared.

Chapter 10

A month later Geoffrey's bank account received another unexpected deposit, and yet another the month after that, but no requests or demands came from the Murstons. Then one evening there was a knock on his door in Croydon. Charlie Murston was there, with the thick-set and muscular reptile Artur. Charlie asked politely if they could come in. The visitors pointedly ignored the dated décor and poor furnishings of Geoffrey's shabby little house, clearly a sad bachelor's hang-out. They didn't sit. In the hallway Charlie outlined what he wanted.

Geoffrey was to identify the purest cocaine he had under his control at the storage and destruction facility. It had to be at least 85per cent pure, and ideally over 90per cent. There had to be at least 20 kilos, but the more the better. Geoffrey was to find a way to falsify the paperwork to show that the cocaine he had identified had been destroyed – Charlie assumed there had to be certificates and so on – and then move it somewhere within the facility to a place where it wouldn't attract any attention. Was that clear? Geoffrey started to protest that this was not possible. Charlie gave a slight nod to Artur, who darted forward and gripped Geoffrey's testicles through his baggy trousers and squeezed. Geoffrey squealed. Artur let go. His free hand now held a large knife.

"I can twist them off, or I can cut them off. I don't mind which. Now you remember that nothing is impossible. You will do what you are told!" Artur had a strong foreign accent, Geoffrey later guessed he might be Russian, but for now, with his throat full of bile and an excruciating pain in his groin, he was thinking of nothing at all.

"Artur puts it succinctly, Geoffrey," said Charlie. "You had better be nice to him as he will be the point of contact between you and me until this is over. You will be seeing a lot of him. He does have a short fuse, as you have just experienced, and he does have complete freedom of action, operationally speaking. Just saying."

Artur said nothing, but softly and slowly drew the knife across Geoffrey's throat, drawing just a slight trickle of blood.

"I am glad we understand each other, Geoffrey," said Charlie. "Artur will be in touch in a day or two to see how you are getting on. Oh dear, your collar's getting marked. You'd better put some styptic on your neck."

The visitors left. Geoffrey went to the bathroom and looked at his neck in the mirror. Then he started shaking and vomited violently into the basin.

The next day he made the journey to the facility with more than a little unease. It was so far out of the way that he had been forced to buy a car for the commute, and he didn't like driving at all. By the time he arrived at the plant there was a strong easterly wind blowing across the Essex marshes, and although winter was still a few months away the light rain felt bitterly cold on his cheeks as he stomped across the car park to the reception area. Even he, as the plant manager, had to pass through the security checks to get into the facility. As always he had his civil service briefcase, which he slid into the x-ray machine alongside his mobile phone and glasses case. Bizarrely, nothing was ever x-rayed on the way out. He had been planning to remedy that and re-write the security procedures but hadn't got around to it yet. In light of his current predicament he was grateful for his own laxity.

Alone in his small office he pulled out the file that was used to record the deposit of seized drugs and their eventual destruction. The file was just a digest. There was extensive paperwork for each deposit, as it was termed, including laboratory reports on quality and quantity of each consignment, photographs, a brief history of how and where the material came into the possession of whichever agency had seized it, court orders for destruction, and so on. There was also a detailed record of each consignment's destruction, which was carried out in the facility's own very high-temperature incinerator furnace with special exhaust filters at the back of the site. Usually he witnessed the destructions himself and signed the certificates. The procedural orders stated that at least two people had to be present, apart from the incinerator operator, and each had to sign the destruction certificate. Before destruction, each consignment was photographed and weighed, and the weight compared to that recorded when the consignment arrived in the facility.

In order to avoid unnecessary down-time for maintenance the incinerator was only fired up on Mondays and Fridays so that servicing and cleaning could be done mid-week on a planned, and therefore more economical, basis. Geoffrey had learned to be very frugal with public money.

Geoffrey studied the file. As usual, there were more than fifty separate deposits in the facility. They varied from a few hundred grams to several tonnes, and they included heroin and synthetic drugs as well as skunk, cannabis resin and cocaine. He looked for high-purity cocaine deposits over 20 kilos and narrowed in on one in particular that was 100 kilos exactly. He noted the reference and called up the details on his computer screen. 100 Kilos of very high-grade cocaine recovered from a beached fishing vessel in Kent three months ago. He looked at the pictures of the deposit. It comprised half-kilo blocks wrapped in black plastic film, unmarked. A few blocks had been randomly selected for testing and had been opened, these had white sealing tape on them. There had been no arrests or prosecutions and the deposit had been cleared for destruction, but no date had been set.

Geoffrey then looked at the destruction schedule. He saw that the coming Friday had two very large deposits listed for incineration, each over a tonne, as well as several smaller ones. They would take the entire day to work through. Every now and then work would have to stop to allow the furnace to cool, so it would be relatively easy to slip another 100 kilos into the list. Geoffrey made his mind up.

Deposits were periodically moved around the facility to manage space and to place things in the right position for destruction. Geoffrey pulled up the next day's movement list and inserted the deposit he was interested in. The deposit was to be moved to the low-value storage area. This was the part of the facility where items not deserving of priority destruction could be stored for longer periods. It was in a separate building. Geoffrey looked at the listing of contents in the low-value area and selected a 100-kilo deposit of low-grade cannabis resin. He inserted instructions for the day after tomorrow to get that deposit moved to the space to be vacated by his deposit, and a further instruction for the following day to transfer 'his' deposit to the bay that had previously held the cannabis load. The fork-lift driver was not the brightest of creatures and was unlikely to question the deposit movements, which happened all the time anyway. Finally, he slated the transferred (cannabis) deposit for destruction this coming Friday, in between the two large deposits and along with the smaller ones. He didn't change the records of what was stored in the numbered locations around the facility. So, to all intents and purposes the high-grade, high-value cocaine currently in Bay 74B would be destroyed on Friday, whereas it was actually now in Bay 176C. Bay 74B would contain 100 kilos of cheap and nasty cannabis, but no one would know that but him. By Friday evening he would have control of all the cocaine that the evil Murstons and that animal Artur could want. He just had to find a way to get it out of the facility. He felt physically sick.

Chapter 11

In her office that Monday morning Julia Kelso felt more alive and alert than she had for a long time, thanks to her Saturday night with Mel. She marvelled inwardly at the therapeutic effect the Demelza Dunn experience had had on her. She focussed on the task ahead – she needed to try to make sense of the surge in sudden unexplained deaths that had happened over the weekend. She called all the Borough commanders in the areas where deaths had been reported and asked that they treat the cases as a priority and copy her into all scene reports, post-mortems and lab analysis. When questioned on a few occasions as to why she responded that there may be some deliberate adulteration going on, and that each case could actually be a murder. The Borough commanders who had posed the question groaned out loud and said they wished they'd never asked.

At 10am Julia was in the office of the Director General of the National Criminal Intelligence Service, NCIS. They had met before and were on good terms. He congratulated her on her recent promotion and asked how he could help.

"In the Met we've had a significant increase in the number of sudden deaths that seem to be caused by cocaine overdoses. My understanding is that there are other spikes up and down the country as well. In London there were twenty-five deaths last weekend alone. Analysis of samples from two deaths the weekend before, and at least three others, all suggest that the overdosing is being caused not by adulteration of the cocaine, but by its very high purity. I think the cocaine that's killing people is above 90 per cent pure. The same analysis indicates that the cocaine residues found at each of four scenes has an identical chemical composition, and I mean identical, to that of a shipment recovered on a beach in Kent some months ago. That shipment was destroyed last month at the Home Office facility that no one is supposed to know about.

"Mel Dunn, who is both a colleague and a friend of mine, is doing some research this morning to see what the national picture looks like. I expect she will have found that there have been a large number of similar deaths over the weekend.

"My concern, obviously, is that someone may be deliberately killing off, murdering, cocaine users. I have no idea why. If, and it's a big if, the cocaine in circulation has been extracted from the destruction facility it would suggest that some high-level, or at least very influential, corruption is at work."

"Dear me, not again! Shall I call Mel over?" The question was rhetorical because he was already on the phone.

"Mel? Richard here, the DG. Could you come over? I have Commander Kelso with me. Excellent. See you in a minute." He hung up.

Mel arrived a few moments later. She smiled at Julia and nodded. "Good morning, DG," she said.

"That remains to be seen, Mel. Julia has been telling me about her cocaine problem. Oh dear, that came out all wrong, but you know what I mean. What have you found out?"

"Nationally there seems to be a similar problem to the one the Met has identified," Mel started. "Initial reports, and these aren't complete, show that there has been a marked increase in the number of fatal cocaine overdoses over the last three days. They tend to be centred on the major conurbations, and most of the fatalities seem to be casual users rather than hardcore addicts. You could say middle-class or professional types mostly. The numbers are worrying. Julia told me that there were twenty-five deaths in London over the weekend. Nationally we are looking at double that number last weekend alone. My rough estimate is that in the last month there have been around 125 fatal cocaine overdoses that we know about. If someone is doing it deliberately that could be 125 murders." Mel paused. The DG had gone pale.

"And do you? Think it is deliberate?"

"I'm sorry to say I do, DG," Mel continued. "The vast majority of cocaine related fatalities are caused by adulteration or contamination, predominantly among addicted and less affluent users. The current spate seems to be caused, based on the limited evidence available, by consumption of very high-purity cocaine - very unusual and expensive cocaine. Cocaine of above 90 percent purity is never seen in circulation at street-level, even among the wealthy weekend users. There is no logical way it could be on the streets unless someone has put it there on purpose, for whatever reason."

"Are there any rational reasons, Mel?" the DG asked.

"None that we've seen before. In the past, targeted adulteration has been used as a weapon in turf wars, but not flooding a section of the market with top-grade wholesale gear. The coke trade is economically driven, and it makes no sense to use top price stuff to kill off your best paying customers. The only thing I can come up with, and even I think it's completely bonkers, is that someone is trying to skew the cocaine market completely. I think that idea is too speculative to develop at this stage. I'm trying to keep an open mind."

The DG was silent for a moment or two.

"So, what do you want of us, Julia?"

"Firstly, urgent national research. Is this a national problem and if so, how big is it? Secondly, anything and everything about the seizure in Kent. Third, a good extended analytical look at the user of a telephone, one that belonged to the dealer who may have supplied two of the victims. Fourth, comprehensive analysis of the dealer networks for every identified overdose victim who has been killed by very pure cocaine. Finally, I think it would be best if no one knows about the possible corruption at this stage."

The DG raised an eyebrow.

"It's OK, Richard, Mel knows about it already," Julia said.

The DG's eyebrow stayed up but he said nothing.

"That all sounds doable. Can you get it in motion Mel? Copy me on your file note to kick this off, whatever resources you need are at your disposal. If you get any whinging send it my way. The wheels of

NCIS are starting to roll for you Julia. Good luck with this, and let's hope you are wrong about the Big C. We really don't need another corruption scandal, not so soon after the last one! Now, let's fix a date for lunch one day soon."

The meeting was over. Julia and Mel left the DG's office together.

"Are you OK with all that, Mel?"

"Of course. It's what I do. In the daytime." She grinned. "Now, I'm going to be busy for a bit. I'll give you a call in a day or two."

She squeezed Julia's hand fleetingly and turned on her heel.

In fact, she called Julia the following day.

"Jake, it's Mel. I think we have a problem. We need to meet. St Ermin's at 6?" Jake agreed.

Mel was there first and was already half-way through a large gin and tonic. A second was on the table waiting for Julia.

They brushed cheeks. "What is it, Mel?"

"The dealer networks. I looked at all the victims that I had data on, and it was easy to identify their suppliers. Most of them are pretty well known known and low-level, or they were. In the last couple of months there have been some quiet but significant changes. Contact numbers for dealers used by the victims have changed. Some of the dealers have vanished, not just from phone records, but completely. Not entire networks, just the dealers supplying certain groups of customers, the wealthier ones. Strangely, the only anomaly is the case that flagged this up in the first place – Mercy and Chantelle McMorrow. Mercy's dealer, who's been lifted by the way, swears blind that he only ever dishes out crap stuff and as far as he knows no one else ever sold to Mercy. There's no reason for him to lie about it, so where their overdose came from is still a mystery.

"I spoke to the source units, the people who run informants - the Covert Human Intelligence Sources. The word is that in various parts of the country some smaller dealers with very specific client lists have been taken out of play, no one knows how or why or by whom. They are being replaced by 'foreigners' - nothing more specific. Other dealers, but not the 'foreigners', are continuing to buy from the bigger dealers who supplied the displaced ones, so everyone is still reasonably happy - apart from the ones who have gone missing.

"Now, this sort of thing happens from time to time, the odd hostile takeover of a lucrative patch or contact book. But there's normally some identifiable reason behind it. A crime group trying to grow its territory, an individual dealer who has pissed off his supplier or been taken out of play by us, that sort of thing. It isn't usual to see a sort of cherry-picking approach. The bigger dealers don't tend to like or tolerate it.

"To me, this suggests that the replacement dealers could be part of something that the bigger suppliers are wary of. One of the cartels, maybe, or an international organised crime group like the Mafia. None of the people I've spoken to today, and that's a lot, have a clue about what's happening or why. And now the bit that really concerns me.

"The new dealers, the 'foreigners', are invisible. Apart from the numbers they have for customers to call to order stuff, they have *no* apparent means of communication with anyone. Not their supplier, not each other, nobody. That *never* happens! Street-level dealers, whoever they are, are never off their phones. It's how they tick. These are not everyday street-level dealers. We won't be able to get a grip on them."

Julia was thinking. "Has anyone tried surveillance?"

"It's been tried a couple of times, but no joy. One team told me that a 'foreign' dealer they tried to follow - it was in Manchester - behaved like a trained professional. He lost them just when he wanted to, probably after he had identified the whole surveillance team." Mel stopped.

"We need to infiltrate them somehow. In the meantime, we need to get anything we can glean on the new dealers, descriptions, accents, photos, anything. And you try to do that magic stuff with cell-site that you do, start around the known dates, times and places where fatalities have occurred. I think we might need to make use of a bit of that unorthodox help I mentioned too, but at this stage I have no idea how." Julia paused.

They looked at each other. "Alf?" they said, simultaneously.

"I'll contact him. I think we should meet. I'll see if we can get hold of him next weekend." Mel finished her drink but declined another. "My head's full, Jake. I need to think."

Back in her flat she opened her laptop and the Alf email account. There was nothing new in the draft message. She deleted everything and typed 'we need to meet urgent. you say where. can you do this weekend? x" she added the date, for clarity.

Mel sat in a chair for hours, mulling things over. Having ideas and then dismissing them. As her eyes became heavy she checked the email account one last time before bed. The draft had changed. It said 'gualdo cattaneo sat 11 am. be outside caffe in piazza. do not speak but have something on table to show me where you are staying. X'

She wrote down the content and deleted it, then she wrote 'gualdo what? X'

She logged out. In the morning the message had changed. 'cattaneo. it's in umbria. look it up!'.

Mel called Julia. "Jake, it's Mel. Do you like Umbria? It's in Italy."

Chapter 12

The two women sat sipping their coffees outside the tiny *caffe* in the piazza in front of the church. The hilltop village of Gualdo Cattaneo was medieval, quaint and almost silent. Crickets clicked and birds sang as the already warm air heated up. The women were obviously British. The blonde one was wearing a long linen dress and a white straw hat, with large sunglasses. She was reading a guidebook about Umbria. The one with light brown hair wore long shorts and a loose tee shirt, but also a white hat. She looked up at the church and enjoyed the sunshine. On the small table between them was a room key from their hotel in Bevagna, the walled city just a few miles down the hill. It was 11am on a sunny Saturday morning.

A tired grey Fiat with Turin plates wheezed into the piazza and docked next to the small fountain. A man, the only occupant, got out and stretched. There was a damp patch on the back of his shirt. He was medium height, muscular and lean, with short grey-flecked hair. He hadn't shaved and had a grey stubble. His face was handsomely chiselled, and despite the bags under his eyes he looked healthy. The woman with the light brown hair was smiling to herself. She hadn't seen him in a long time. The blonde didn't look up from her book.

The man walked towards the *caffe*. He was wearing sawn-off denim shorts and espadrilles beneath an old faded cotton shirt. Like most people who live in sunny places he shunned sunglasses.

"B'n giorno," he mumbled to the women.

The one with light brown hair nodded. He glanced down and went into the *caffe*. At the counter he ordered an espresso and a cornetto, the small buttery croissant so popular with Italian men in the mornings. He didn't talk to anyone. Once he had finished he bought a bottle of water and left. As he passed the British tourists the blonde one was doodling with her finger in a small pile of sugar that had spilled onto the table. She formed the number 2 with her finger before brushing the sugar off the table. The man didn't acknowledge the women. He got back into his battered grey Fiat and chugged off.

The women finished their coffees and talked for a while. They had a look around the church and chatted about it, then they found their hire car and the blonde one drove them back to Bevagna. They parked outside the walls and strolled through the cobbled streets to their hotel. They had time for a light lunch and a rest.

At 2pm precisely the handle of their hotel room door moved, it was not locked. The man entered. The woman with the light brown hair leapt off the bed and ran towards him, throwing her arms around him and kissing him firmly on the lips.

"Don't mind me," said Jake, "shall I leave you both to it or go get another room?"

"Hello Julia," said the man, "you look well."

Julia smiled "You too, Declan or whatever your name is today."

"I've missed you!" said Mel to the man, kissing him again.

"Put him down, Mel, we don't have much time. We may have a job for you, Declan."

"Sorry Jake." Mel sat down on the bed, her hands folded in her lap.

"How have you been?" Julia asked.

"Not so bad. I quit Spain and came here to Italy a couple of months ago. Too many Brits in Spain. Here there are still loads of them but they're easier to avoid," Ferdinand replied. "What's up?"

"Someone seems to be trying to flood the UK drugs market with very pure cocaine and killing off a lot of people, pushing two hundred at the last count. So far, that's my problem, but…," Julia paused.

"But?" Ferdinand prompted.

"The cocaine being circulated had already been seized months ago and it looks like it has been diverted from the Home Office's supposedly secret and very secure storage and destruction facility, where it's officially listed as having been destroyed. Corruption seems the most likely cause for that to have happened. Plus there's something sneaky about the dealers who are supplying the stuff to their customers. Mel?"

Mel took over. "There are intelligence reports saying that 'foreigners' have been displacing selected dealers with the right sort of clientele, the wealthier professional and media types or predominantly weekend users, not your hard-core potless addicts. Some areas have tried to identify these 'foreigners' and one or two have tried surveillance. They've all failed so far. One surveillance team described the dealer they were on as a trained pro. There are no communication patterns for the 'foreign' dealers, which is so far off usual for street-dealers it's ringing my alarm bells. They don't seem to talk to anyone. The phones we can identify are used only to take orders from customers, not to make any calls or contact suppliers up the chain. Established supplier / dealer networks are letting this happen, which suggests to me that the incomers are pretty powerful or scary people, possibly international organised crime."

"Like cartels or the Mafia?" Ferdinand asked. "Why would they be interested in street-level supply in the UK?"

"I have no idea, but we need to find out. Which is where you come in."

"We need to know what's going on, Alf," Julia said, "and why. There are some avenues that we can explore conventionally, but I expect there will be others that we won't be able to follow. I want to try to infiltrate the supply-chain of this virtually pure cocaine to find out if there is a corrupt conspiracy, and if there is one who's behind it and what they want. I also want to know who these 'foreigners' are. Are they Mafiosi or Colombian gangsters? And how did the stuff get out of a secure place - where it should have been destroyed - and onto the market?"

"OK," said Ferdinand, "a couple of questions. What do we know about the secure facility?"

"Do you remember Simon Waterson?" Mel asked. He nodded.

"Well, he's back at Thames House doing protective security while he's looking for another job outside the service. He wasn't too well for a while, after that business with the Carltons, so they gave him something less stressful. I spoke to him a few days ago and he's arranging a spot security audit of the facility, which he confirmed is out in Essex. I have the grid reference. Thames House oversees its security. Simon says there have never been any issues there. Everything is properly logged and recorded, there are cameras rolling pretty much all the time. The place is staffed by people who don't really knows what it does – it's badged as a chemical waste management plant. The only people who do know all about it are the site manager, who is always a career Home Office person on a two-year assignment, and the site foreman who needs to know what they're handling for health and safety reasons. Simon's going to give me all the details after the audit next week."

"Second question. It sounds like you know something about the cocaine that's being used. What can you tell me about it?"

"There was a find on a beach in Kent a few months ago," Mel said. "A hundred kilo load of 97 per cent pure cocaine was recovered from an abandoned fishing boat that had been beached. A dog-walker spotted it and called the police and coastguard. Customs think that whoever was going to collect it was spooked and abandoned it. I've trawled through all the intelligence I can get my hands on and no one is squealing about losing 12 million quid's worth of gear. I've been onto our Drugs Liaison Officers in France, Belgium, Ireland and the Netherlands to see if there are any signs it came from an OCG in those countries – it could have got lost or blown off course or something. So far absolutely nothing. It could be a cocked-up Customs job that they aren't owning up to, but I doubt it. Just a thought, Jake, but could you ask your mates at Vauxhall Cross if they know anything about it?"

Jake nodded. Alf was silent for a while.

"OK. There are things I'll need to do, and there will be a lot of reading for me to catch up on. I'll have to come back to the UK, and I can be in London by Tuesday. Can I use your place as a base, Mel, just for a couple of days until I work out a game plan and what I'm going to need?"

"Sure, for a couple of days. If it drags on I might need to go and stay somewhere else – nothing personal, just a practical thing." Mel glanced at Jake.

Ferdinand noticed it. He had detected a change in the relationship between Kelso and Mel. It was clear that they were sharing the room they were in, and there were frequent glances between the two of them. He may have been imagining it, but Kelso also seemed much more at ease than she had been on the few occasions he had met her before.

"Don't worry, Mel. I'll get out of your way as soon as I can. It could be bad for everyone if I get blown and I'm associated with you – either of you."

"What should we call you, Alf?" This was from Julia.

"I think Thomas Donohue will be coming back for this, then he'll need to vanish. Call me Thomas."

They talked for a further half-hour. Then 'Thomas' said he had to get on. He kissed Mel good-bye, and offered his hand to Kelso. To his surprise she stood and kissed him too.

"See you Tuesday evening, Mel," he said. And Thomas was gone.

Chapter 13

Julia and Mel spent the night in Bevagna before driving back to Rome on Sunday morning. On the plane back to Heathrow in their business class seats - Jake had insisted and paid - Mel squeezed Julia's hand. "These last two nights have been lovely, thank you. It was good to see Alf, or whatever he calls himself, but it's all a bit surreal, isn't it?"

"Just a bit." Julia was pensive, but she squeezed Mel's hand back. "Sorry, I'm just thinking about what might be coming. I checked my emails at the airport. There have been more deaths in London. It's going to be a long week. Do you mind him staying at your place? We can always insist he goes to a hotel or something."

"A couple of days will be fine. I get edgy if anyone stays longer than that – even family. Especially family." Mel smiled. "If it gets too much, I can always find a bed at yours, can't I?"

Julia chuckled. "Yes, but we would only be sleeping, I can assure you. My week is crammed already."

"Seriously though, Alf and I will be doing a lot of talking about the case and doing lots of data crunching. It's how he works. It won't do any harm to reconnect with him either, make him feel we are in this together."

"Reconnect? Is that code for what I think it is?" Jake asked.

"You're not jealous, are you?" Mel asked.

"Not jealous, no. Or I don't think I am. I'm just trying to get used to the idea, to get used to you. You'll need to give me some time to do that, to get over my 'conventional' ways. You do what you want with Ferdinand, just spare me the details for now. This last week has been a massive change for me – you've had years of practice." Jake leant over to kiss Mel's cheek.

"Let's get a drink." Mel pressed the call button.

At Heathrow they got a taxi and Julia dropped Mel in Raynes Park. Mel called Jake later to say goodnight. They were both tired but neither slept particularly well, however nice it was to be back in their own beds. Both of them felt trouble coming.

******

Monday morning came around soon enough, and Mel made her way to work. From her office she called Simon Waterson. He told her he was going to do the audit himself over two days, starting today. He would give her a call that evening to go over what he had found and to see if there was anything she wanted him to follow up on Tuesday. She thanked him and set about reviewing the weekend reports. They weren't good. The death toll was continuing to climb. Police services all over the country were issuing warnings to cocaine users saying there was a contaminated batch in circulation, which was about all they could do.

Mel co-ordinated a team of analysts crunching communications data for as many of the victims as possible, trying to identify, or at least count, as many of the poison coke dealers as possible. By mid-afternoon she thought there were up to six separate 'foreigner' dealers, based on analysis of communications at virtually the same time in different locations. Mapping the calls showed that each dealer had two or three territories in the same general area. The territories seemed to have been carefully selected along socio-economic lines.

Mel called Jake's office, but she was out. Her assistant Raj picked up. Mel asked if the Met had done any communications analysis on their overdoses, and if so, could she see it? Raj was noncommittal. Could Commander Kelso call her back when she had a moment?

Around 5pm Simon Waterson called Mel's mobile. He was on his way home but needed to drop a car at the Security Service garage on the way. He suggested they meet for a quick drink somewhere near Raynes Park or Norbiton, where he lived. Mel gave the name of a wine bar not far from Raynes Park station and said she would be there around 7.

Waterson had no idea of the turmoil he had left in his wake. When he arrived at the facility he had shown his identification and asked to see the site manager, Geoffrey Appleton. The security guard phoned Geoffrey and informed him that there was a visitor from the MOD, that being the department specified on Simon's identification. Geoffrey took fifteen minutes to get from his office to the reception area, the delay being caused by an extended visit to the bathroom where he vomited loudly for quite a while. He tried to compose himself, but barely managed it. He excused his tardiness to the visitor, saying he had a bug and wasn't feeling too good.

Simon produced an official letter of notification of the 'inspection' for Appleton's records and explained the purpose of his visit – a snap audit. Nothing to worry about, just part of a new security awareness regime. It was a sensitive facility, after all. Simon started with a full tour of the site making sure he looked into every storage bay, locker, office and cupboard, photographing everything he saw. He couldn't examine the furnaces as they were fired up awaiting that day's destructions. Simon watched 200 kilograms of Afghan heroin combust and saw the recording process in action.

After lunch - Simon had brought his own - he asked for use of an office and he spent the next few hours on his own going through ledgers and records. He made copious notes on a laptop. He left at 4pm and headed back into London, calling Mel on the car phone along the way.

As soon as Simon left the facility Appleton made a call on his mobile to the loathsome Artur. He told him that the Security Service was conducting a spot check on the facility, a snap audit, and that the officer would be back the next day to complete the task. Yes, just one officer on his own. He said it was just routine, but Geoffrey was worried that he might ask questions about the cocaine hidden in the low-value cannabis store. Artur for once was conciliatory. He told Geoffrey not to worry. He asked about the officer. What did he look like? Did he arrive and leave in a car, what was the car? What time had he left? What time would he be back in the morning? Geoffrey answered each question. Artur told him to go home, come back as normal the next day, and not be concerned about anything.

Simon met Mel as planned and he talked her through the facility. He showed her diagrams and photographs he had taken on his phone – he had one of the fancy ones provided by the Service that had an inbuilt camera. He emailed the pictures to her NCIS Inbox , along with the notes he had made. Thus far he hadn't found anything amiss, but armed with the knowledge of the missing 100 kilos of cocaine he would do some proper ferreting tomorrow. Mel described the packaging of the cocaine that had been seized. Andy Connaught had shown her pictures earlier in the day. Plain black plastic wrappers, very tight. Each block weighed 500 grams and was about the size of a slim paperback book. They agreed to meet again the next day, but near their respective offices.

Mel made her way home alone. Simon went back to his wife and kids just up the road in Norbiton. He was glad to be able to repay Mel, and Julia Kelso, at least partially, for making it possible for him to escape the clutches of the Carlton crime family.

Julia Kelso had had a rough day. There was mounting panic among the upper echelons of the Metropolitan Police. The Mayor's office was on the phone to the Commissioner every hour, as was the Home Office. She asked about the communications data that Mel wanted and had barely controlled her anger when a hapless Detective Superintendent told her he hadn't thought it necessary to do any and was conserving budgets. She told him icily to forget about the budgets and get people working on the analysis.

Right now - and all night if necessary. She wanted a report on her desk at 8am the following day, a report that told her how many dealers they had to find, and where and how they were operating.

It was almost 8pm when she called Mel to tell her that she was at least two steps ahead of the Met, and that the data she asked for would be, or should be, available the next morning. Mel asked if she could call in at the Yard in the morning to see the data herself. And maybe get a decent coffee. They agreed on 8.30am.

Alan Ferdinand, aka Thomas Donohue, aka Declan Walsh, spent Sunday and Monday driving up through Italy and France towards the English Channel. He left Bevagna as soon as he could, finding it quite a strain to be so close to Mel Dunn and not be alone with her. Apart from his now ex-wife, widow even, she was the only woman he had slept with in more than 20 years, and she was amazing. Not just in bed, but in every way. He knew she would probably kill him if he said so, but he had no doubt that he was in love with her.

All he owned, apart from several million Euro in various bank accounts, was in the battered grey Fiat. Just one small case and a backpack. He liked it that way. He hadn't gone back to his rented flat in Perugia, he just turned his car north and started driving. It wasn't a fast car so it took him until Monday night to make it to Dieppe. He stayed at a Formula One motel on the outskirts, and on Tuesday he drove into Dieppe town. He parked in a beachside carpark and stashed the keys up the exhaust pipe, just in case. He put a few coins in the parking meter as a gesture and got a bus to the ferry terminal. A few hours later the cliffs of Beachy Head came into view. He got the irony, being as that was the place where he had 'died' a few months earlier. He hadn't seen the cliffs since. A slow train took him to Victoria station in London. He had chosen the route via Dieppe because it usually had fewer checks and officials covering it, unlike the Calais – Dover ferries or the Eurostar. He had no reason to think that anyone would be interested in him, but old habits die hard.

From Victoria he took the tube to Morden via Stockwell and walked to the newsagents where he had a rented post box. It took just a few moments to put the identity of Declan Walsh in the box and swap it for that of Thomas Donohue. Wallet, money, driving licence, bank cards, everything. All that done, he took a bus to Raynes Park and sat in a pub over a couple of pints of proper Guinness, which he had missed, while he tried to calm his nerves as he waited for Mel Dunn to come home.

Chapter 14

They didn't know it, but Mel and Simon Waterson had been on the same train into London early that Tuesday morning. She changed at Clapham Junction for Victoria, while Simon got off at Vauxhall and took the tube to Stockwell to collect his car from the Security Service garage. He had been allocated the same vehicle as yesterday, a run of the mill Mondeo.

Mel walked from Victoria to St James's Park and New Scotland Yard. Jake came to meet her and escort her up to her office. Inside, with the door closed, Jake kissed her softly on the lips.

"Sorry," she said, "I just wanted to do that. Coffee?"

"Fine with me, and yes, white no sugar." Mel was smiling.

They sat at the conference table and Julia pushed a slim file across to Mel. "Make of it what you will. It might as well be in Mandarin as far as I'm concerned."

Mel studied the file and pulled a notebook out. She sheepishly donned a pair of glasses, a recent acquisition. Jake smirked.

"I hate bloody spreadsheets, Jake. They mess with your eyes," she complained.

After a few minutes she took the glasses off. "Can I have a copy of this? It's interesting. It looks like you only have two dealers operating across London, based on the call traffic. But they're working together as a team."

"How do you work that out?"

"The locations of four phones called by your victims - they're nearly always in the same place. It looks like two pairs, so one dealer has two phones, not two SIM cards, but two actual phones. One dealer is taking orders north of the river, the other south. You have customers in North London calling phones south of the river, and vice versa, placing orders. The phones are moving around, but nearly always together - I can send a mapping chart over later - and deliveries are being made within a few minutes many miles away. Maybe one takes the orders, the other delivers, but they must be in touch, they have to be talking."

"How can they talk, if not by phone?"

"They could be using radios. Call boxes are highly unlikely. They could be using computers, voice over internet, they could be using satellite phones. In any event, it's too clever for your average street-dealer. It looks professional, organised, and really quite sophisticated. When I get back to the office I'll lock myself in a cupboard and have a think about it."

Julia summoned Raj and asked him to copy the file for Mel. He hadn't even taken his coat off yet. He was looking forward to the day he got into the office before his boss. One day. He delivered a sheaf of paper a few minutes later, which Mel stuffed into her bag. Raj was hovering, so she and Julia shook hands. "I'll send that mapping to you and give you a call if I come up with anything else from this lot. Thanks Julia."

As Mel walked across Lambeth Bridge towards the NCIS base Simon Waterson was pulling off the A13 just past Rainham. Going against the traffic made for quick progress. He was in a good mood, things were looking up. He had a job interview lined up next week, he was going back to banking. His well-intentioned adventure with the Security Service had been harsh, and he owed it to his wife and children to provide a more stable and financially secure future. He adjusted Radio London to get the 9.30 news. The facility was only a few minutes away, a mile or so down this narrow lane. He rounded a bend and swore loudly. A massive tipper lorry was heading towards him at great speed. There was no way it was going to stop. He leant on the horn, his last futile gesture. The huge truck, fully laden with gravel and weighing over 30 tonnes, ploughed into the Mondeo and flattened it. A young squat man in a black boiler suit climbed out of the wreckage of the truck, pausing only to drag the lifeless body of the truck's previous driver back behind the wheel and thrust it through the shattered windscreen. The driver had died some minutes before the crash with a broken neck.

The man in black bent to peer inside the destroyed Mondeo. The Mondeo driver's body was smashed and he was clearly dead. A large Mercedes car had pulled up behind the wreckage. The man in the black boiler suit climbed in, and Artur drove them both away.

At the facility Geoffrey didn't know whether to be pleased or perturbed by the non-appearance of the Security Service officer. It was only when one of the security guards mentioned that there had been a terrible crash in the lane, two people killed, that Geoffrey really started to be frightened.

In the Special Branch control room at New Scotland Yard the alarm on an old fashioned teleprinter

99

bleeped. It was a Marker message. All vehicles used by the Security Service, and indeed many others, are flagged with a Marker with a code number. Whenever a 'Markered' vehicle is checked on the Police National Computer a message is automatically sent to Special Branch in London. The Marker code number tells the Special Branch operator who to call to advise that vehicle registration ABC was checked at Y time by whoever. In this case it was a Security Service vehicle checked by Essex Police around 10am. A call was made to the Security Service duty officer, who looked up the vehicle and saw who it was allocated to that day. Not especially sensitive. A message was sent to the Essex Police Security Service liaison person, a local Special Branch officer, with a request to find out discreetly who was interested in the vehicle and why. As a routine matter it wasn't until the afternoon that the Essex liaison called in to Thames House to say that a terrible thing had happened, and that they better get someone out to Essex as soon as possible.

Simon's boss went out, and her voice was shaking when she called the office to say that Simon Waterson had been killed in a vehicle collision, along with a lorry driver. Welfare was dispatched to the Waterson household to break the news and convey Mrs Waterson to the hospital mortuary in Essex.

Mel Dunn called Simon's office number at 5.30 to arrange their meeting. The phone was answered by a young woman, who sounded in a tearful state. Mel asked for Simon and was told that someone would call her back. Someone did, someone who wanted to know who she was and why she wanted to speak to Simon.

Mel told them. In return they told her that Simon had been involved in a very serious road accident in Essex that morning, and he had not survived.

Mel hung up, shocked. She liked Simon; he had once made a bad decision and had been through a lot, but he was essentially a decent bloke. He was also very careful, and not the type to have serious road accidents. She made herself a coffee and called a contact at a National Crime Squad branch based in Essex. She asked if anyone could find out the circumstances of a fatal collision that morning involving Simon Waterson, possibly just east of Rainham?

Twenty minutes later her desk phone rang.

"It's a bit strange, Mel," said her Essex NCS contact, who was also an Essex Police officer. Your man's Mondeo was flattened by a tipper truck full of gravel on a side road off the A13. He was killed outright. The truck driver was also dead at the scene, but the traffic guys aren't convinced that he was killed in the collision. Wrong sort of injuries and not in the right place. The truck driver did have injuries, a broken neck for one. Traffic are asking for a post-mortem and a full investigation but are struggling to get the resources."

Mel thanked him. She called Jake and explained what had happened. Julia listened in silence.

"It's starting Mel. This isn't a coincidence. I'm going to call in a few favours in Essex to get the post mortem done and a full investigation underway, but we need to talk, you, me and Thomas. I'll come to yours later."

Mel's head was reeling as she made her way home. She felt exhausted and overwhelmed. Her pleasant anticipation about seeing Alf, or Thomas or whoever he was today, had evaporated. She hoped he didn't have any great expectations. Thomas had seen her from the pub. He saw that her tread was heavy, and she looked worried. He gave her twenty minutes then made his way to her street door. She buzzed him up. He climbed the familiar stairs and saw her door standing open. She was inside, slumped in a chair.

"What is it, Mel? What's happened?" he asked.

"Simon Waterson has been killed. It may have been deliberate, he may have been murdered. He was helping us out by doing a snap audit at the narcotics facility in Essex. He was there all day yesterday and was going back today to finish off. His car was hit by a truck near the facility this morning. Both he and the truck driver are dead."

Thomas wanted to hold her, to comfort her, but she stayed in her chair so he couldn't touch her. He went to the kitchen and found a bottle of red wine, and the remains of the Scotch she had bought for him last time he had been in the flat. He poured them both a drink.

"Jake's coming over. We all need to talk. If you were expecting a welcome back party tonight it's not going to happen. Sorry, I'd been looking forward to it."

Thomas didn't comment, but inwardly his heart soared. "Don't even think about it, Mel. Drink."

She did.

Kelso arrived around 8. Mel buzzed her up. Kelso closed the door behind her and leant back on it, exhaling. She took her coat and jacket off, and to Thomas's surprise kicked off her shoes too. "I need gin, Dunn." She said.

Mel looked at her, then gave a wry smile and stood up. She went to the kitchen and made Jake a massive gin and tonic. Jake pointedly gave Mel a kiss on the lips as she thanked her for the drink. She sat down next to Thomas on the sofa.

"Fuck me, what a day!" she said.

Chapter 15

Once she had her drink in her hand Julia filled the others in on her conversation with Essex Police. The new Assistant Chief Constable had been at Bramshill Police College with her. Once Julia explained that the Mondeo driver was a Security Service officer who had been conducting an 'inspection' of a drug storage and destruction facility the ACC was all ears. Julia told him that she had suspicions that the facility was involved in some way with the supply of a lethal batch of cocaine that was killing people by the score. The ACC had no idea that the chemical waste management plant on his patch was a secret Home Office facility. He promised that the apparent road accident would get the works - full forensic investigation, reconstruction, post-mortems on both drivers, the lot. He would be in touch.

"You saw Simon yesterday, didn't you Mel?"

"Yes. We met near here. He told me about his first day at the site over a drink. He emailed me some notes and the pictures he had taken, but they're on my work computer. I can transfer them tomorrow and show you. He said that on the face of it everything seemed in order. The site manager was behaving a bit strangely, he kept disappearing to the loo to throw up. Simon said the guy claimed to have a stomach bug, but he just seemed really scared about the audit. Simon said that the ledger entries confirmed that the cocaine recovered from the beach had been destroyed, 100 kilos in half-kilo bricks went into the incinerator. Curiously, the CCTV on the furnace was down that day so there isn't a photographic record, just the certificates signed by Appleton, who is the plant manager, and his foreman. The bay where the cocaine had been stored was empty. Simon did take pictures of all the storage bays, but I haven't had time to look at all of them yet."

"Did you get the Appleton's full name?" asked Thomas.

Mel looked at her notes. "Yes, Geoffrey Appleton. He told Simon he lives in Croydon, but I don't have an address. He was moaning about the commute to Rainham. He's about 45 to 50 years old. Simon described him as 'unexciting'. Why?"

"I think he needs a visit," said Thomas. Julia said nothing.

Julia's mobile rang. She answered it and listened intently for a couple of minutes.

"That *is* interesting Stuart, thanks for that. I'll call you tomorrow." She hung up.

"That was the ACC from Essex. He's really onto this thing now. He's had all the ANPR, the Automatic Number Plate Recognition system, checked for a five-mile radius around the facility. At around 9.40 this morning a dark coloured Mercedes was clocked going onto the A13 westbound, towards London. No images of anyone in it, but the interesting thing is that it was on false plates. I'm going to get all the other ANPR cameras on the A13 checked."

Julia made a call to Special Branch on their 24-hour number. She identified herself and asked for urgent checks to be made on ANPR, initially on the A13 but then London-wide for a dark coloured Mercedes. She gave the registration number, and her own mobile number. They would call her back.

Mel outlined the results of the research and analysis she had started on the dealer phones.

"I'm pretty confident we aren't looking at a large network, maybe six dealers nationally. They must be pretty busy. Their communications are secure; all I can see is contact between the customers and the dealers. I can see roughly where the dealers' phones are physically located. They seem to be in two or three distinct areas. The more communication data I get the narrower the parameters will be. In London it looks like there are two bases in use, probably by the same two people, one in Dulwich and the other in Hornsey. Quite posh. I'm mapping the others, the cells and phone masts aren't so plentiful outside London so it takes a bit longer to pin the phones down. What I don't have is any other communications from the dealers, nothing upwards or sideways. I've requested a load of historical data going back a few months focussing on the displaced dealers to see if I can find an entry point for the 'foreigners'. It could be a long job. Finally, I have a call booked with GCHQ in Cheltenham tomorrow to see if their wizards can give any pointers."

"Alf, sorry, Thomas, any thoughts?" Julia asked.

"I want to get my hands on Geoffrey Appleton first. If I can, I'll follow him home tomorrow evening and have a fireside chat. I have a feeling he's been got at by someone. I might be able to persuade him to tell me about it. The communications set up is interesting. It's not the standard stuff you get with regular street-level dealers. Their phones are red hot all the time, you can't shut them up. This lot seem disciplined and professional. It's not home-grown organised crime, Mel's lot would have heard about it if it was. I've had some dealing with the cartels. They don't do subtle or disciplined, so it looks like Mafia or something. If it is Mafia, it's also a bit strange. They like to stick to their own turf. When they expand into a new territory it's usually through investment, buying in rather than having a physical presence. They only tend to move operational people to a place when it's really necessary. So I'm thinking this could be a mercenary outfit, trained thugs for hire. Maybe East European or Russian, ex-special forces types."

"Could you ask your friends at Vauxhall Cross, Jake?" Mel asked.

"Yes. I already asked if they can throw any light on the cocaine shipment. They can't. They might be better on foreign mercenaries."

They talked on for a further hour, discussing possibilities. Julia's phone rang. It was Special Branch.

"Evening, ma'am. That Mercedes you're interested in was clocked by ANPR on the A13 westbound at Beckton just after 10am, and again in the East India Dock tunnel. It went into Canary Wharf but it didn't come out again. The Wharf has its own CCTV and ANPR, so we can't get at it without a production order. We have one image, not a very good one, of two front-seat occupants, which I've emailed to you. Just a thought, ma'am, if this vehicle is on false plates it probably disappeared into the underground roadway at Westferry Circus to change them over. We've seen it done like that before. We can look at whatever CCTV we can get hold of tomorrow if you want, but you'll really need to speak to our Commander first."

"Is that you, Niall? Niall Morton? I thought so. I'll call Tim tomorrow. This is very helpful, thanks." Niall Morton was one of the Special Branch team that had helped Julia with the previous corruption case that the then DCI Ferdinand had been tangled up in. Morton and his team were very good. Julia hung up.

"Curiouser and curiouser," she said.

Mel yawned. It was nearly midnight.

"I'm off to bed," she said. "Are you staying Jake? You're welcome, but I'm not in the mood for sex tonight. With *either* of you." Thomas raised an eyebrow.

"I want to chat some more with Thomas, so yes please, I will stay."

"One of you can come in with me. I'll get a duvet and the other one can stay on the sofa. It's up to you who goes where."

Mel went off to the bathroom and re-emerged a while later in one of her long tee-shirts. She plonked a duvet and a pillow on a chair. She kissed Thomas on the mouth, then did the same to Jake.

"G'night both," she said.

When Mel's bedroom door had closed there was a slight tension between Jake and Thomas.

He broke the silence.

"You're sleeping with her, then?"

"Blunt but to the point, Thomas."

"Sorry. It's none of my business."

"It's probably best we don't have secrets if we're working together. It's a recent thing, no more than a couple of weeks. Mel and I have come to know each other well, we've become close friends since the Carlton business. We meet for a drink or a meal, work out, swim together. Once in a while we've shared a bed if we overdid the gin and tonic, but nothing sexual until very recently. Mel told me about her views on consent, how consenting to have sex with someone isn't enough. You have to want it actively, to participate fully. Then I realised she had been waiting for me to initiate something. I'd never done it with a woman before, and it had never occurred to me that I might want to. So, long story short, we've started sleeping together, having sex as she insists on putting it. It's incredible."

"You know she's fancied you from the moment she met you, don't you, Julia?"

"Has she? She told you? I know you've slept with her too, excuse me using the less explicit term. I'm a bit old fashioned and I'm still trying to get used to her."

"Yes, a few times. You're right. It's amazing with her."

"Stop talking about me!" Mel shouted from her bedroom.

Jake and Thomas laughed.

"We need to get to know each other better, Thomas. Understanding how we both feel about Miss Dunn is a start. She's made it clear that nobody has any rights over her, not you or me, or her group of playmates."

"She told you about them?"

"Oh, yes!"

Julia stood up and stretched. "What's your preference, Thomas. Here or there?"

"You go in. I'll be fine here. I've slept on this sofa before, and I'm bushed. I don't think I'd get a wink of sleep anyway if I was in a bed with Mel."

"OK."

Julia undid her skirt and stepped out of it, oblivious to Thomas's gaze. She folded it neatly and put it on the back of a dining chair. He saw that she wore self-supporting stockings, not tights. She removed these too. She walked to the bathroom and he watched her taught bottom move in its white pants. When she came out, she was wearing another of Mel's tee-shirts, a shorter one that barely covered her thighs. Thomas was standing. Julia put her arms round his neck and kissed him, stretching up to do so. He saw the reflection of her now naked bottom in the bathroom mirror.

"Good night Thomas. Sleep well."

"You too, Julia."

"I think you should start calling me Jake," she said, turning away from him and going into Mel's room. She left the door open, and Thomas watched as she peeled off the tee-shirt and slipped into bed beside Mel, who was already asleep. He watched Jake kiss Mel gently and fold her arms around her. Thomas pulled the door closed.

"Jesus!" he thought, "what was that all about?"

After he had showered, Thomas fell asleep on the sofa. All he dreamt about was Julia, Jake, Kelso's stunning body, and about it being entwined with

Mel's equally gorgeous form. He wasn't sure if the dream was heaven or hell. He just knew he wasn't in it.

In the small hours Jake emerged from a dream, a dream in which her lover was kissing her nipples and stroking her thighs.

"I thought you weren't having sex tonight," she whispered to Mel.

"I'm not, you are. You were twiddling me again; I'm doing this to shut you up. What do you expect when you're naked in my bed tweaking my nipple-stud?" Mel stopped talking and resumed kissing Jake's breasts. Jake's thighs parted to allow her access.

From the sitting room Thomas heard the unmistakeable sound of a woman trying to have an orgasm very quietly. It didn't sound like Mel. He smiled.

Chapter 16

Despite Mel's nocturnal ministrations, Julia was awake and in the shower at 6am. She dressed quickly. Before she left the flat she kissed the sleeping Mel, and as an afterthought Thomas as well. He was stirring. Outside she was lucky to find a passing black cab on its way into town. She feigned sleep to deter conversation with the cabbie. She was at home in Dolphin Square before 7. After a change of clothes, some much-needed coffee and a bowl of muesli she was at her desk by 8.

In Raynes Park Thomas placed a steaming mug on the bedside table next to Mel. She was waking up.

"It's alright," he said, "it's tea."

Mel lifted the duvet and nodded that he should get in. The bedclothes smelt of Julia Kelso. Mel hugged him to her.

"I missed you, Alf, Thomas, whatever. How have you been?"

"Not as busy as you, it seems. I never had Kelso pegged as, well, you know."

"Gay? I don't think she is. She's just experimenting, a late developer. She's had quite a tough time since coming to London; she's feeling very isolated. It was quite a thing for her to do, come to bed with me, but she does seem to have rather taken to it. I do adore her, and you too, of course."

Thomas started stroking her stomach through her tee-shirt. She shook her head.

"Not now," he stopped immediately, "but lie back and close your eyes," she told him.

It was over in a few exhilarating minutes. He lay back, breathing heavily, while Mel wiped her hand with a tissue.

"That was a little something to keep you going until we can say hello properly. I did the same for Jake last night so it seems only fair," she said.

"Now, I've got things to do, and so do you."

She leapt out of bed and disappeared into the bathroom. An hour later she was in her office.

She had given Thomas a spare key to the flat, saying firmly that she wanted it back on Friday. After a shower and a light breakfast Thomas fired up her laptop and searched for used motorcycles. There was a dealer in Worcester Park specialising in courier bikes, not pretty but reliable and mechanically sound. He phoned them using Mel's landline - he hadn't yet acquired a UK phone. Did they have anything available immediately, to buy, not rent. His bike had been nicked and he had jobs lined up. He needed some wheels urgently to keep him on the road until the insurance was settled. The bike dealer had one that had been prepped, serviced and MOT'd for someone else, but he had vanished. He could have it for five hundred and fifty, on the road by 10am. Thomas said yes.

He collected the bike, an aging but still serviceable Honda 500cc with a courier-sized top box on the rear luggage rack. He added a helmet, gloves and a waxed cotton jacket and parted with £680, but he was mobile. He needed somewhere else to stay, but that would keep for a day or two. By lunchtime he was on the A13 near Rainham. He had looked up the grid reference on

113

Mel's laptop and knew where the facility was. He circled the area, scouting out a suitable place to wait. The police cordon from the day before had been removed, but there were still traces of the crash on the surface of the lane. He found a patch of waste ground that had a few old cars and vans on it. It would do. He went to find some lunch and was back by 4pm.

At 4.40 he saw the facility gates open and a small Ford hatchback drove out. The driver fitted the description of Appleton, the 'unexciting' man. He was clearly an anxious driver and he took no notice of anything going on behind or beside him. Thomas followed him easily through Dagenham towards the Blackwall Tunnel and onward into South East London. It took a little over an hour to get to the small terraced house not far from Crystal Palace football club where the little Ford slowed to a halt. Thomas watched the driver emerge. He looked pale and ill, clutching a black civil service briefcase to his chest. He opened the front door and went in. Thomas hung back. It was just as well he did.

Not ten minutes after the door closed a stocky, very muscular man in a dark suit approached it and knocked. Appleton let him in quickly and closed the door. The man emerged less than a minute later with a supermarket carrier bag in his hand. He walked from the house away from where Thomas had stopped his bike. A hundred yards or so down the road the man opened the passenger door of a large, dark-coloured Mercedes saloon and he was driven away. Unlike Appleton, the Mercedes driver was clearly very aware of what was going on around him and Thomas quickly abandoned any notion of trying to follow it. He made a mental note of the registration.

Thomas went back to Appleton's house. Keeping his crash helmet on he rang the doorbell. Appleton opened the door and started to say "What now..." when Thomas shoulder charged his way in and flattened the startled civil servant against the wall. Thomas slammed the door behind him.

Appleton was squealing. Thomas could smell urine. This was not a brave man. He relaxed a little.

"Calm down, Geoffrey. I just want to talk to you."

Geoffrey cowered, sobbing. "Who are you? What do you want?"

"Let's sit down in the kitchen." Thomas guessed where it was and led the way. He pulled out a chair and told Geoffrey to sit. He complied. Thomas removed his helmet. Appleton looked at him uncomprehendingly.

"What do you want?" he stammered again.

"I want you to tell me what's going on. I mean with the cocaine."

Appleton started to cry. Christ! thought Thomas.

He made Appleton a cup of tea and brought him some kitchen roll to wipe his nose.

"Now, Geoffrey, tell me."

"Who are you? Are you Security?" Appleton asked.

"That's not something for you to worry about at the minute," Thomas was letting his Belfast accent loose. "My friends want their cocaine back. Where is it? I know you didn't destroy it, like you said you did."

"How do you know that?"

"Where is it, Geoffrey?"

"It's still at the facility, but in a different place."

"Why?"

"Why what?"

"Why did you move it, not destroy it like you certified?"

"How do you know about the certificates?" Appleton's voice was rising; he was about to cry again.

"I know far more that you'd think. Now tell me why?"

"I can't! They will kill me!"

"If you don't, I might kill you." Thomas stated calmly. This set Appleton off again and Thomas waited five minutes for the man to calm down again.

"The thing is, Geoffrey, they - whoever they are - are not here. I am. So at this moment who do you feel it best to try to please?"

"You..." he muttered.

"Very good, Geoffrey. Now, tell me."

"They said it was for a good cause. To beat the traffickers. Just a little from the facility to get things going, only a few kilos. I didn't know they would want all of it, all one hundred kilos, which they're now demanding. I didn't know they would set that animal on me. They said the money was just to cover expenses, not a bribe. But they send it every month now. I can't get out of it."

"Who are you talking about, Geoffrey?"

"I can't tell you that. I really can't. Do whatever you want to me, but I can't tell you who they are. They are ruthless!"

"Did one of them come to the door just before me?"

Appleton nodded.

"What did you give him?"

"The other two."

"The other two what?"

"Kilos. They've already had three, they wanted five in total to start with, so I gave them the other two. I smuggled it out."

"What do they want it for?"

"They want to kill the parasites, that's what they said."

"There's ninety-five kilos left. What are they going to do with that?"

"I don't know. They said it's for Phase 2, now they know it works."

"What works?"

"The idea. Killing off parasites with very pure cocaine."

Thomas's blood froze.

"Geoffrey, listen to me. Give me your mobile number. I'll send you a message tomorrow, give you a way to contact me. They won't do anything to you until they've got what they want, so just go along with them, but try to stall for time. I can help you."

"Who are you?" Appleton scribbled a number on a scrap of tissue and passed it to Thomas.

"That's something you don't need to know. Just listen for my voice, mine only, no one else's, even if they say they are working with me."

With that Thomas walked swiftly from the kitchen and out of the house. He waited a few moments. As he expected, Geoffrey didn't open the door to see where he had gone. Thomas rode back to Raynes Park to wait for Mel.

117

Chapter 17

Thomas paused on the way back to Mel's flat to buy a pay-as-you-go phone. It was only a cheap one and would do the job. He let himself into the flat and sat with the lights off in silence, thinking through everything the frightened man had told him.

He heard a key in the door. When Mel turned on the light she let out a yelp.

"For fuck's sake, Alf! What are you doing sitting there in the dark? You scared me half to death, idiot!"

He stammered his apology. "Sorry. I was just thinking stuff through."

"Can't you think with the lights on?"

Mel went to the kitchen and poured herself a gin.

"Drink?" she called. Without waiting for an answer, she poured a whisky and handed it to him.

"Yes, I will, thanks," he said.

Mel kicked off her shoes and sat on the sofa.

"So? What have you been up to?"

"I went to the facility. I followed Appleton home. I saw him hand over two kilos of cocaine to a very nasty looking gangster who was driven away in a dark Mercedes. The registration number of which I have written down on the pad stuck to your fridge. Appleton's address and mobile phone number are there too. You might want to do something with them.

"Then I had a longish conversation with Appleton, who is not very robust and cries a lot. He won't tell me who, but someone is about to unleash another two or three kilos of very pure cocaine on the sniffing public.

118

Apparently this is an experiment to prove the concept that if you give people almost pure cocaine some of them, maybe most of them, will die when they inhale it. They, whoever they are, have proved it to themselves and are about to go to Phase 2, which involves anything up to a further 95 kilos of cocaine. What about you?"

Mel stared at him.

"You *are* fucking kidding, right?" she drained her glass and went to the kitchen for a refill.

"No. I think that's what Appleton believes, that that's what he has been told."

"But, why? Why would someone want to do that? Christ, at the same kill-rate of about 50 to 70 deaths per kilo that's 5,000 to 7,000 bodies! 5,000 to 7,000 murders!"

"You'd better call Jake," he said.

She looked at him. "You called her Jake."

"She told me to."

Mel picked up her phone. "Jake. Thomas has been busy. You need to come over. Don't bring your toothbrush." She hung up.

Jake Kelso arrived less than an hour later. She looked business-like.

"What's up?"

Thomas told her. She paled.

"I've checked the ownership of the Mercedes through NCIS. It comes back to a leasing firm in Leeds. We can't find out who it's leased to until the morning," said Mel.

"What did the guy you saw look like, Thomas?" Jake asked.

"Stocky, very muscular, close cut grey / blond hair."

Jake pulled a notebook out of her handbag and showed Thomas a grainy print from an ANPR camera. A picture of two men in the front of a large Mercedes.

"Could either of these be him?"

"I think it could be the driver, but not 100 per cent. It's the same model of Mercedes that I saw, though."

"Thanks. I have to stop this. I am going to bring Appleton in. I need to go to make arrangements."

"You might want to get a warrant to search the facility." Thomas suggested.

"That would be an interesting application. The Met Police getting a warrant to search a bit of the Home Office! But yes, I'll get on to that too. Thanks Thomas, Mel." Jake left and hailed a cab.

Within two hours she had an arrest team lined up and had finalised the warrant application. She had briefed one of her senior team to be at Chelmsford Crown Court to see a judge before the sessions in the morning. She dialled the ACC in Essex, but his phone was engaged. As she put her phone down it rang. It was the ACC.

"I've been trying to get hold of you, Julia. The Home Office place that you are interested in has been attacked. An armed raid, several fatalities among the night security team. All of whom are, were, unarmed and mostly past retirement age. It's still patchy, but we're responding. Now, what the fuck is all this about?"

"Sorry, got to go." Julia hung up and called the Information Room, the emergency call centre. She

120

identified herself to the Inspector and instructed that an emergency armed response team be sent to Appleton's address where there was an imminent threat to life. If the occupant, one Geoffrey Appleton, was present he was to be detained and taken into protective custody.

Fifteen minutes later her phone rang. Information Room.

"Sorry ma'am, we were too late. The door was off its hinges and one male body, white, late forties to early fifties was found inside, multiple stab wounds, blood everywhere. Definitely deceased. A murder investigation team is being assembled."

Geoffrey Appleton was dead. No doubt the remaining ninety-five kilos of almost pure cocaine would be what the raiders at the Essex facility had wanted. They no longer needed Appleton. It was lucky that Thomas had been able to speak to him, but a bit of a puzzle as to why the gangsters hadn't dealt with him when they visited earlier. There could only be one reason. Appleton must have told the gangsters about Thomas's visit, spooking them into the raid – which was obviously already planned for.

Julia made a list of things that needed to be done. When she had finished she called the Commissioner's staff officer and her own Assistant Commissioner. They agreed to meet in the Commissioner's conference room at 8 in the morning, and they decided who needed to be there, and who most certainly didn't.

The next call Julia made was to the head of homicide. She briefed him succinctly and suggested that priority actions might be to examine Appleton's bank accounts and his phone records. She had intelligence that Appleton had a corrupt relationship with persons unknown and had been getting paid for smuggling seized drugs out of the facility he managed for the Home Office. It seemed very likely that his killing had been timed to coincide with an armed raid on the facility in Essex, during which several people had been killed. The homicide Commander groaned. He missed the old days when homicide was just drunk people stabbing each other. Julia told him about the briefing the following, no, this morning and said she would see him there.

Finally, Julia called the Territorial Support Team commend centre and stood down the arrest team lined up for the next morning. Sadly, now no longer needed.

All that done she walked home through the quiet streets to Dolphin Square. She had a cool shower and fell into bed, hoping to get at least a few hours sleep before the alarm went at 6. It didn't work.

By 6am she was back in her office, as ready as she could be for the turbulent day ahead. The leads that Thomas had identified the day before were now mostly redundant. All they had was the Mercedes.

She called Mel to give her the news. She was still in bed. Thomas was on the sofa, snoring softly. She listened intently as Jake itemised the bad and worse news. Jake said she would be busy all day but would try to keep her up to speed on developments. In the meantime, could she wake Thomas up tell him what had happened, and ask him what the fuck to do next?

Mel was stunned. This thing was moving fast. She was used to being in control, up to a point, or at least able to make sense of what was going on. This was in a different league. She shook Thomas until he awoke. He looked at her, bleary eyed.

"What do you want first? The bad news, the very bad news, or the really awful news?"

He was wide awake in a moment. Mel told him about Appleton, the attack on the facility and the evaporation of the leads he had established the day before. Except the Mercedes. He thought for a few moments.

"You've got Appleton's mobile number. Check it to see if it made any calls after 5pm yesterday, if so to whom and also where the recipient was located if you can get it. Then we need to see who leased the Mercedes, which will no doubt be found burned out sometime this morning. The details will be false, but it may tell us something. I know the murder team will be doing all that anyway, but it will take ages to go through the HOLMES system, and we don't have any time.

"I want to know who was paying money to Appleton. I want to see his diary, if he has one. As Simon said, he isn't, wasn't, an exciting man and would probably make some kind of note of anything unusual, probably in some weird code.

"Jake needs to get the images of the two guys in the Mercedes to the Spies. An armed assault on a Home Office facility is looking more and more like mercenaries than organised crime. In which case someone will have found them and hired them. That's the sort of thing Six might know about." Mel had been writing it all down.

"What are you going to do now?" she asked him.

"I'd quite like to have a pee, actually."

Mel had been sitting on the duvet on the sofa, pinning Thomas down.

"Oh, sorry," she said.

Chapter 18

Mel's mobile rang again. It was Jake.

"You said you had photographs that Simon took at the facility. Could you print off a copy of them, two copies, and bring them over to the Yard? I'm going out to the facility after the Gold Group briefing to try to make peace with my ex-friend the Essex ACC. I'd like you to come with me if you can. It'll be a bit gruesome, all the bodies are still there, but I'd like your help to work out what happened. I'd like to take Thomas too, but that would be stupid."

"OK. I'll be over as soon as I can get the pictures printed. I'm on the train to Vauxhall now."

In the office Mel opened the emails that Simon had sent her on Monday evening, before he was killed. Christ, how many more bodies would there be? There were several emails, and about thirty images in all. She loaded some photographic paper in the printer and set it in motion. It took almost an hour, during which time she had pulled Appleton's phone records, such as they were. He hadn't had many friends. Only one call had been made yesterday, around 5.28. It was to a mobile number, an unregistered pay-as-you-go. Mel managed to cell-site it to the Dulwich area. She saw that Appleton had called the same number on Monday, after Simon's visit to the plant. She did a search on it but got no hits on any of her databases, so she flagged it to herself in case it came up in future. Then she sent it down to Cheltenham and asked if they had ever come across it.

She decided to walk to the Yard. On the way she called Thomas - she was still finding it hard to call him that - and told him what she was doing. She told him about the number Appleton had called and the Dulwich location. He didn't say much, but she could have sworn she heard him thinking.

She had to wait for Julia, Raj escorted her up, and although she was gagging she declined a coffee, remembering Jake's disparaging comments about her assistant's coffee-making abilities. Mel was startled when Jake came in in her full Commander's uniform, something she hadn't seen before.

"Did you think I was making it up?" Jake asked, "being a Commander and everything?"

She was smiling. Raj closed the door. The friends hugged each other and Jake gave Mel a sensual kiss.

"That was nice! I've not been snogged by a lady policeman in full uniform before. Not unless you count that time at a rather strange party at Uni. But I don't think she was a real lady policeman, not with the fishnets and the platform stilettos and everything. Have you got those too, as part of your dress uniform?"

"Shut up. Let's go," said Jake.

Seconds later they were in the lift. Julia had an official car waiting. Although she was entitled to her own car and a traffic-trained police constable to drive it, she chose to use the pool cars instead. She valued her privacy too much to want a driver knowing everything about her life, especially now.

The drive to Essex was tediously slow, and Mel was feeling a bit apprehensive. Julia looked at the pictures and listened as Mel told her about the call Appleton had made, almost certainly to his killer. She had flagged the number but would share the flag with the murder team as and when they wanted it.

There was no mistaking the hitherto secret Home Office facility as they approached it. Several TV news vans were present; a police helicopter hovered overhead. The entire area had been taped off, and the boundary fence had been shielded with blue tarpaulin sheets to deter the cameras.

Julia showed her identification, as did Mel. They were directed to the command centre, a large blue van, where they would find the ACC. He looked stressed. Julia could charm an angry bear, and soon they were friends again. He walked them through the scene. The attackers had rammed their way through the main gate in a truck at around 6.30 pm and had shot the security guard in the access control post. The stolen truck they had used had been abandoned, burned out, near the flattened gates. Then they blasted their way through the main door, probably using solid-slug shotgun shells. Both of the security staff inside were shot dead, one with a solid slug, the other by several 9mm rounds. The shell casings had all been retrieved by the attackers, but so many had been fired that it was possible that one or two might still be found. The final fatality was the plant foreman, who hadn't been scheduled to be there but was working late. He had been shot once in the head. There were no survivors or witnesses.

The bodies remained where they had fallen. Jake noticed that Mel was looking a bit green. She promised herself that she would make it up to her. Jake asked to be shown the storage and destruction areas. The ACC knew less about the facility than she did, so using Simon's photographs she and Mel pieced together the layout with the ACC. Everything seemed undisturbed, except one thing. Storage Bay 176C was now empty. Simon's photographs clearly showed that the bay had contained a pallet loaded with small bricks covered in black plastic, under a cling-film wrapping - allegedly cannabis resin. That was where Appleton must have stashed the cocaine!

The gangsters had their cocaine, enough to kill up to 7,000 people!

Mel took lots of photographs with the NCIS-issued digital camera she had thought to bring with her. Looking at the carnage through a lens made it less real and she was able to examine the scene with relatively cool detachment. She photographed tyre tracks in the yard, possibly made by the killers' vehicle. They would have needed transport to shift a ninety five kilo load. The tyre tracks were quite narrow and not too far apart, suggesting a small car or a van. That in turn suggested that the assault team was not large, two people, maybe three, no more than that. Mel made a note to check any phone activity in the area at the time of the assault, and the period before and after it happened. She knew Jake was thinking along the same lines, but she still made a note to check CCTV and ANPR footage for anything interesting.

In police investigations there are normally two strands of activity. The first is getting the evidence, proof of what had taken place that can be put before the courts. The second is getting the intelligence, knowing what happened and why, but not necessarily being able to prove it. The search for evidence is of necessity methodical, painstaking and can be quite slow. The quest for intelligence can be more agile and intuitive, blind alleys can be followed freely, as well as intelligence highways. Lateral thinking had a big part to play in intelligence work, which is why people like Mel Dunn were very good at it.

Julia Kelso offered the Met's full support to Essex and said that they should merge the HOLMES accounts (HOLMES was the Home Office Large Major Enquiry System - an automated database that generated investigative actions and nagged endlessly until its daft questions were answered. Everyone who had ever used it agreed that it was a massive pain in the arse) for the attack and murders at the facility and the murder in Croydon, which were undoubtedly linked.

In the car on the way back into London Jake asked Mel if she was OK. Mel had been quiet, but she said she was fine, just thinking.

"We should go and see your friend at Vauxhall Cross, and soon," she said to Jake.

"Hugh Cavendish? I'll call him now."

Cavendish could see them immediately after lunch. Julia gave him both their names so that passes could be organised. The car dropped them back at the Yard. Julia changed in her office, swapping her uniform for her 'normal clothes', as she called them, one of her business suits. They walked down to the river and had a light lunch at the café by Lambeth Bridge, and then continued on to Vauxhall Cross. Mel told Jake that NCIS people called the strange-looking muddy brown and green MI6 building on the south bank of the Thames Tracy Island, after the old Thunderbirds puppet show on TV. They also called Thames House, MI5's headquarters on the opposite riverbank, Toad Hall and consequently its tale-spinning occupants were known as The Toads. Jake found it amusing.

They were escorted to Hugh Cavendish's spacious but functional office. He revelled in the title 'Controller Global', but insisted he didn't control anything, global or otherwise. He had been a protégé of Jake's father and had known Jake nearly all her life. They greeted each other fondly.

"Hugh, this is Mel Dunn, a senior analyst at NCIS and a very good friend. She knows all about the Declan Walsh business and she's helping me on it. He's back in the UK, by the way, Walsh. He's working with me on a very major problem."

"Oh good," Cavendish said, unenthusiastically, "a very major problem?"

Jake explained the cocaine poisonings, saying that the use of almost pure cocaine to kill off users made no criminal, financial or business sense. She said she had brought Declan Walsh into play because it seemed highly likely that corrupt forces were involved or were responsible and it might take some unorthodox methods to deal with them. The death toll was now nearing 200, not counting yesterday's five murders. She said she agreed with Declan Walsh's assessment, based on his knowledge of the UK drugs trade and the people involved in it, was that whoever was

130

masterminding the poisonings was being supported either by international organised crime like the Sicilian Mafia, or more probably by mercenaries with a Special Forces background. Intelligence reports mentioned the dealers distributing the high-grade cocaine were 'foreigners'.

She gave Cavendish a copy of the grainy image of the two men in the Mercedes. "I think this picture shows two of them. It was taken on Tuesday by an ANPR camera, shortly after they had probably murdered a Security Service officer. He studied the image closely. He had served extensively in Russia, Ukraine and the Central Eurasian 'Stans'.

"You could be looking at ethnic Russians, but it is hard to say from this image. Could you bear with me while I call someone?"

He picked up his phone and dialled an internal number. A few minutes later a very fit looking man in his early forties appeared at the door.

"Jake, Mel, this is Major Evans from the SAS. He's attached to us for a while, poor chap. Justin, Jake Kelso from the Met and Mel Dunn from NCIS. Jake is an old family friend."

"The Rake's daughter?" Evans asked. "How is he? I haven't seen him for ages."

"He's doing very well thank you. He's up in Scotland, Edinburgh mostly, researching things," Jake answered.

Hugh Cavendish repeated what Jake had told him, practically word for word. He passed the image to Evans, who studied it.

"The driver looks a bit familiar," he said. "Can I take this, run it through the albums?"

"Of course," Jake said. "Who do you think it might be?"

"I can't say for definite. He does look a bit like a Captain who was fired from the Ukraine Security Service, the FSU. He was in charge of one of the Alpha teams, the special operations bods, but got kicked out for being 'over-zealous', which is polite code for being a psycho. The Alpha teams call themselves Special Forces, but we might disagree. There are Special Forces and Special Forces, the FSU Alpha groups are a bit second division. If it *is* the guy I'm thinking of his name is Artur Kuznetsov, or that's the name he uses. It's like 'Arthur Smith' in English. He's ethnic Russian, from Crimea. The rumour was that he was in the pay of the Russians, the GRU, and that now he's out of the FSU he's on the market for hire. I think I have a few photos of him somewhere. Let me go and have a rummage."

"Thanks, Justin," Cavendish said. "Justin is currently heading up our team keeping tabs on mercenaries, soldiers of fortune and the like. They're not always bad types, some just don't or can't fit in with normal society and aren't happy unless someone's shooting at them. Some of them can be quite useful to us, but others can be very bad indeed. Ukraine is a wonderful country, but sadly it produces some of the craziest people on the planet."

Evans left and said he would call Jake as and when he had something.

Chapter 19

After their meeting with Hugh Cavendish Jake and Mel parted company. Mel went back to her desk to do more digging into phone records and things like that, Jake went back to the Yard to check on the progress of the Croydon murder investigation.

Jake's phone rang as she was crossing Lambeth Bridge. It was Hugh Cavendish.

"Justin is 70 to 80 percent sure that it *is* Kuznetsov driving the car. He also thinks the passenger may be ex-FSU Alpha, an NCO who served under Kuznetsov. He's going to do some more research and get our main man in Kiev to see if there is any current gossip. He's also going to check on port movements and suchlike to see how long Kuznetsov's been here, and who else might be around as well. It's a start at least. Good luck, Jake."

She thanked him and hung up. A start indeed, and a good one! She called Mel and shared the news. Within moments GCHQ was scanning the cybersphere for mentions of Artur Kuznetsov, and for any connections to the phone he or one of his people may have been using when the late Geoffrey Appleton called it on Monday afternoon and Wednesday evening. At last something to work with.

Mel focused on the phone, which she now called K's phone. From its call history it seemed to be reserved only for Appleton, so Mel started trawling cell site data for co-located phones. It didn't take her long to find two of the dealer phones used by London customers as being in close proximity to the K phone.

The cell-site mapping was narrowing in on Dulwich, specifically the boundary areas between Dulwich Village and East Dulwich, both up and coming trendy oases of affluence in the generally bleak desert of South London. Crunching the data Mel was starting to see other phones that could be related, but at present there were far too many to be overly optimistic. She put in billing requests for all of them, marking them urgent. She would have the data by the next day.

There was little more she could do that afternoon. She was feeling strained and tense so bunked off early and went to her gym club in Wimbledon to run, sweat and think.

Thomas, meanwhile, had been out on his motorbike. With a few hours to kill he rode back to his old house in the suburbs out of nothing more, he thought, than idle curiosity. The street looked the same, but his old house had a 'Sale Agreed' sign outside it. He pulled up near the end of the drive and sat there for a few minutes. Joanne's little Mazda had gone. In its place was a dark grey Mercedes E-Class convertible with a red top on the most recent London number plates. It was brand new. Also in the drive was a Volvo Estate with logos advertising interior design and bespoke kitchens and bathrooms. As he watched the front door opened. A man aged around 40 emerged and put a briefcase in the Volvo. He turned back to the house and Thomas saw Joanne, his, or rather Alan Ferdinand's, wife in the doorway. She looked terrific. She had lost a bit of weight and her hair was stylishly spiky. She was in a dressing gown, despite the hour. The man went to her. He tugged at

135

the knotted belt of her dressing gown and slipped his hands inside. Joanne put her arms around him and kissed him, giggling. After a few seconds the man stepped back, offering a fleeting glimpse of Joanne's bare skin as she pulled the dressing gown together. She kissed him again and stepped back into the porch, laughing. Thomas felt a flash of unwarranted and irrational jealousy, but it passed quickly. Why shouldn't she have found someone else? She seemed happy, which was a good thing. The Volvo pulled out into the street and drove away. The gravel where it had stood was dry. The man had been there overnight. Good for her, he thought, and rode away.

When she eventually arrived home Mel had almost forgotten that she had a temporary lodger. 'Thomas' was lounging on the sofa but leapt to his feet when she opened the door. Her momentary annoyance at finding another person in her space evaporated quickly, and she was glad to be able to tell Thomas everything she could about the day she had had, and to show him the images from the facility. He listened carefully, asking pertinent questions from time to time.

"So," Mel summarised, "on the face of it we may have a team of ex-Ukrainian secret police mercenaries running around poisoning people with very pure cocaine when they aren't butchering civil servants or mounting armed assaults on government facilities. We have one name, one possible name, Artur Kuznetsov, and we think he may be holed up somewhere near East Dulwich. Any thoughts?"

"Ukrainian mercenaries won't be coming cheap," he said, "so someone is putting up some serious money to do this. The big question is who, and why? The attack on the facility was high-risk, almost reckless, even with inside information from Appleton, as was assassinating an MI5 officer. It gave us the image of Kuznetsov, if it's actually him. That says there's some time pressure, and it also says they only have limited resources and people available to them. Depending on how they see the outcome of yesterday, they might be under more pressure now and they might be pushed into making more mistakes. I think their communications will be vital to them, and to us, now they'll have to multiply their efforts. Assuming they plan to flood the market with the other 95 kilos, that is."

"What are you thinking of doing?" she asked.

"Right now I'm going to East Dulwich for a sniff around. I'll be back late, so don't wait up. I'll try not to disturb you."

He retrieved his crash helmet and jacket from the cupboard where Mel had stashed them and left.

It didn't take long to reach East Dulwich on the bike, traffic was light. He trailed round the affluent streets looking for anything that might be a clue - but mostly to get a feel for the place. Most houses had lights on; streets were lined with modern, good quality cars, but no large flashy Mercedes saloons. This area had far better taste. He didn't find the Mercedes, but he did come across another car that looked seriously out of place. It was a light blue BMW M5 with blingy alloy wheels and blacked-out windows. It had the stripes, and the suspension had been lowered. It was on German plates and was left-hand drive. It had two parking tickets on it. Thomas parked his bike in the shadows under some trees between two lampposts and sat and waited. He noted the name of the street and the house numbers nearest the BMW. He was about to give up the wait when a stocky man, quite short but clearly well-muscled, approached the car. He had a cigarette on the go. Thomas hadn't seen where he had come from. He heard the man swear in a language he didn't recognise as he ripped the parking tickets off the windscreen. He threw them in the gutter. Thank you, thought Thomas. The man also threw his cigarette end in the gutter near the parking tickets, got in the car and started it noisily. He drove off. Thomas gave it a few seconds before gathering the debris the man had discarded. He found the cigarette end, still smouldering slightly, and once it was properly out he was able to put it in one of the plastic sleeves that once held a parking ticket. He put his finds in a pocket of his waxed cotton jacket and went back to the bike. He was fully aware of the risk he had just taken, he could easily have been spotted by an associate of BMW man, so he was ultra-cautious as he piloted the motorbike back towards Raynes Park. He did so many back-doubles that he was certain no one was following him, but he still parked a good half-mile from Mel's flat and stopped off in a pub before returning to her place at closing time. If it was a Ukrainian mercenary team he didn't want them anywhere near Mel Dunn.

She was still up when he let himself in quietly.

"You took a while," she stated.

138

"I went to the pub," he smiled, "just as a precaution."

"That's the first time I've heard that as an excuse, not that you need one. You can do what you like." There was no edge or rancour in her words.

"So, what have you been up to?"

"I skulked around East Dulwich for a bit, to get the feel of the place. I thought there might be an outside chance of spotting the Mercedes, but that's probably long gone. It's a tidy, respectable area, affluent and getting trendily tasteful. A big Mercedes would stick out like a sore thumb. I did find another sore thumb though, a very tacky looking BMW, a boy-racer's toy. It just didn't fit the area. I saw the driver, stocky, muscular, foreign-looking. Sound familiar? He ripped two parking tickets off the car, and obligingly chucked a fag-end in the gutter. It's all in here." He retrieved his finds from his jacket pocket. "Can you get these to Jake tomorrow? She'll know what to do with them."

Mel looked at the parking tickets.

"This is a German registration. I can get the NCIS Liaison Officer in Frankfurt to check it out fast-track in the morning. Now, do you want a drink or something to eat?"

Mel poured him a scotch. She should have been tired but was still unsettled by the day's events. Tomorrow would be another long day, she expected, and the following day Thomas would be moving out. So, she thought, if he wants to.........

He did, very much.

It reminded Mel of their first night together, when he was still Alf Ferdinand. She had been idly wondering if he had been with anyone else since he had been away, not that it was any of her business. She didn't ask, but she knew in her heart that she had been the last person he had been to bed with, all those months ago. She was glad, it did away with the need for fiddly condoms. As she had done the first time she took charge gently and after two hours they were both deeply satisfied and sleeping soundly in each other's arms.

The following morning Mel called Jake as soon as she woke up. They arranged to meet for a quick coffee and to hand over Thomas's collection from the previous evening.

Thomas had said he would find somewhere to stay that day and move out on Friday. Mel was both pleased and saddened.

Chapter 20

On the train on the way in to meet Jake Mel called the Liaison Officer in Frankfurt. She knew her well. After a few moments of idle chat Mel gave her the registration number and asked if she could check it out – it was official. The Liaison Officer said she would call back when she had something.

Jake was waiting in a small Italian café a short walk from Scotland Yard. Mel smiled at her and sat down.

"You look tired, Mel," Jake started, "but do I detect a spring in your step?"

Mel looked at her but decided to ignore the barb.

"Thomas went out skulking in East Dulwich last night, just on the off-chance. He didn't find the Mercedes, not that he was expecting to. He did get a bit of a feel for the area and he clocked a car that really didn't fit in. He watched it for a bit, and he saw someone who could be the passenger in the Mercedes get into it. It was a BMW M5, but tarted-up. It was / is on German plates. Our girl in Frankfurt is checking it out this morning. It may be nothing at all, but Thomas recovered a cigarette end that the BMW man threw away and a couple of parking tickets that he saw the guy touch."

She placed an envelope on the table. She had carefully gathered the samples and put them in a fresh envelope to try to preserve any forensic evidence.

"It would be amazing luck if there's anything in it. I'll get this stuff processed and see what happens. What's he going to do now?"

"He's going to find himself somewhere to stay. I did say my place was only a short-term thing. He should be gone by tomorrow. He's not much trouble, really. Quite well house-trained. He is concerned, though, about attracting unwanted attention. I think he means to me."

"He's right too. This Kuznetsov is a real nasty piece of work. I had Special Branch doing some research overnight. Kuznetsov is particularly ruthless. He's ethnic Russian from Tatarstan, in Crimea, so he's technically Ukrainian, but SB say that the Tatars are more Russian than the Russians. They want to be Russian. One reason why Kuznetsov was kicked out of the secret police was that he was getting far too tough on Ukrainian nationalists in Crimea, abducting, torturing and murdering activists. The government didn't want to make an ethnic Russian martyr out of him, so they quietly sacked him. By all accounts he flips backwards and forwards in and out of Russia, and he does work that's too dirty even for the dirty tricks department of the GRU. I've asked Hugh what they can find out about who might have hired him here in the UK.

"We'll need to be careful about how we use Thomas, if at all. I don't want him muddying evidential waters, and I'm worried about what could happen to him. Sure, he can look after himself, but against Ukrainian SF killers? I think we need to have a heart to heart with him. Could you keep him at yours until Saturday? I should be able to come over Friday evening or Saturday morning."

"I don't think that'll be a problem," Mel said, knowing full-well that Thomas would happily stay another night.

They finished their coffee and parted. Jake's comments about the spring in Mel's step when they met hung in the air between them. Mel wondered if she had made a big mistake by bringing Jake Kelso into her complicated and unusual personal life. She hoped not; she had become genuinely and deeply fond of the blonde Scot and would miss her hugely. She didn't think their relationship could be wound back to exclude the bedroom, not now. Oh well, she would just have to deal with that if and when the time came.

******

Sir Charles Murston was at his desk in the City early that day. He liked to avoid the manic traffic that blighted the square mile. One of Artur's men (Kolya, was it?) drove him in in the Rolls Royce from the Chelsea house. Kolya was taciturn, or maybe he just didn't speak English. Murston didn't know. His regular chauffeur was in Hampshire sulking, but Artur had been adamant that it had to be one of his men with Sir Charles at all times as long as the operation was in progress. Murston had no idea how many men Artur had, he just knew how much it was costing. Not cheap, granted, but if the 'operation' paid off as expected it would be money well-spent.

Sir Charles had first encountered Artur a few years earlier when a Moscow contact had hired him to provide some security and protection for Murston during a visit to the North Caucasus and the area around the Kerch Strait. Muston had been looking at

143

prospective purchases, which would be very lucrative for the Moscow contact, who really didn't want Murston to be inconvenienced, see the wrong things or otherwise be put off. Sir Charles had engaged Artur Kuznetsov himself on a few occasions since then, and he had learned a bit about him. To say he trusted the Crimean would be a step too far, but he did have an appreciation of the man's capability and complete absence of morality, hence his employment of the current outrageous 'operation'.

And the operation was going well. The fuss at that Home Office place had been a worry, but Artur assured him that it had been necessary. The extra cocaine they now had that would not now be needed for the revised Phase 2 would be very useful, and profitable, when Phase 3 started. When Appleton had told him about the visit from the stranger, presumably another MI5 man, Artur knew that the original plan to extract the commodity from the facility a bit at a time would need to be accelerated. He had already made contingency plans, which went into operation on Wednesday night. He now had direct control of the commodity, and any residual risk posed by Appleton had been neutralised.

Reflecting on his conversations with Artur, Sir Charles shuddered at his choice of terminology that made the venture sound so pedestrian. In some ways he felt the plan was sufficiently bold and audacious to warrant more dramatic language, but there would be plenty of that in the tabloids in the weeks ahead.

The boy Charlie had worked out the original details of Phase 2 with Artur. Sir Charles had decided he needn't be too involved in day to day operational matters, so he hadn't been too sure of the exact details of what was going to happen. Now that he had intervened and adjusted the Phase 2 plan with Artur he knew that shock waves would rip through the weekend snorting community as they came to fear the fizzy little drug that had previously perked them up and repressed their inhibitions.

Phase 3 was still in the planning stage. This was the acquisition of as much cocaine as he could afford that was already in the supply chain and heading for the collapsing markets, not just in Britain's major cities but in several European ones as well. Phase 3, and the project as a whole, depended on him being able to buy up unwanted cocaine shipments very cheaply and then rapidly rebuild confidence in the middle-class market as quickly as possible. For Phase 3 he would need an emissary. He knew that Artur and his boys weren't right for the job, and indeed their very public sacrifice was needed to start of the market rebound, which Sir Charles called 'Phase 4'. For Phase 3 he needed a negotiator, someone who knew who to deal with in the drugs world, and how. Murston was determined not to get tied up in the drugs business for any longer than necessary, just this one big hit.

To the world Sir Charles appeared cool and calm, a man in charge of his destiny and his empire. Inside, however, he was seriously worried, close to panic. He knew that the venture he had gone into with Charlie was risky, but really he had no choice. When he met with his Finance Director a few months ago a bomb had fallen on him. The FD said that a full regulatory audit of Murston Asset Management was being scheduled, and he had heard from a contact in the Financial Services Authority, which Sir Charles still thought of as the Securities and Investments Board - its old name, that it would happen with very little notice in the next couple of months.

What the FD didn't know was that Sir Charles Murston had been plundering the company accounts to fund his own lifestyle and some of the less conventional investments he had been making. Many of these hadn't paid off. Sir Charles had been adept at hiding the losses from the FD, who hadn't been appointed because he was the brightest of accountants, and he had always intended to repay the money, which he termed a loan, before its absence was noted. He wasn't a common thief for God's sake, but he was a bit short at the moment. Several million short. That was why he was pinning everything on Charlie's madcap scheme. If it worked all would be well, if it didn't his world and life would come tumbling down once the audit started.

******

Julia Kelso instructed Raj to get Thomas's finds to the lab and to invoke her name and rank to get their examination prioritised. She wanted any fingerprints from the parking tickets and their plastic covers, and DNA from the cigarette end. She told Raj to wait for the results, and to wear his thickest skin. To his credit he reported back within two hours that the lab had found some partial prints on the outward facing parking ticket covers, as well as full prints on the front

146

and rear. The lab thought these must belong to the traffic warden, while the partial ones were likely to have been left by the person who ripped the tickets off the windscreen. DNA had been recovered and was being sequenced as he spoke, but it would take a bit longer to complete and then search through the databases. Could he come back now, please? The lab people were giving him filthy looks. The prints arrived in Julia's inbox. They didn't match any in the British fingerprint collection, so she immediately forwarded them to Europol to see if they could find any matches, adding that DNA would follow.

Over at NCIS Mel took a call from her friend in Frankfurt. The German registration was false. No such plate had ever been issued. The BKA had started a national search for sightings of the car anywhere in Germany, and the Liaison Officer had added it to the Europol database.

Mel called Jake.

"Seems like Thomas's instincts are working. That German registration is false." Mel said.

"Too true," replied Jake, "I've just had a call from Europol. They've a hit on a partial print off one of the parking tickets. They found it on the ICTY database."

"ICTY? The war crimes lot in The Hague trying to prosecute people from the Yugoslav civil war?" Mel asked.

"The same. The prints were lifted from bullet cases at a scene near Srebrenica, where the massacre happened in 1995. Forensic teams went in afterwards to see what evidence could be retrieved, then the pathologists went in to identify and recover the

147

bodies. It was the Serbian military that was responsible, but there were a lot of reports of foreign soldiers from Russia and all over fighting with them. Mercenaries. We don't have a name, but whoever it was that Thomas saw in Dulwich last night was firing a gun in the Yugoslav civil war. I've sent out an 'all cars' message to find the BMW. I want it stopped and the occupants arrested. There's also a surveillance team being deployed now on the street in East Dulwich where Thomas found it."

"Nothing on the DNA yet?" Mel asked.

"They said I would have it by tonight. Now, how are you doing on the communications stuff?"

"There are a lot of mobiles in that part of London, several could be, or could have been, collocated with the dealer phones. I'm churning through them looking for the oddballs. I spoke to Cheltenham about other types of communication, specifically around the time and location of the incidents on Tuesday night in Croydon and Essex. They're only allowed to hoover up international stuff, so nothing UK to UK without a warrant. But they can and do gather communications data. I can do that too on phones, so I got them to look for weird stuff – satellite calls, encrypted email, encrypted anything, radio.

"They haven't got anything very specific, but one of the boffins said they'd been seeing a lot of steganographic emissions."

"That sounds quite revolting. What is it?" Jake asked.

"Steganography. It's from the Greek *'steganos'* meaning 'hidden' and *'graphia'* meaning writing or drawing – my degree wasn't totally wasted. There are secret communications going on. Steganography has been around for ages, invisible secret messages written in lemon juice and that sort of thing, hidden in other texts or messages. With the internet it's now back in fashion in a very big way among techie people who don't want other people to know what they're saying or looking at. With digital steganography you can conceal messages or pictures within other messages or pictures. Paedophiles love it. Only someone with the correct key and the same encryption programme can see the hidden content. You only know it's there because the bandwidth it uses is far too big for the apparent size of the message. We're getting better at cracking some of it, but it's a race against organised crime and military development. Several countries are developing their own steganographic processes and programmes using massively complicated encryption. And guess what?"

"Don't tell me. The transmissions they have been picking up are military-grade stegano whatever it is."

"Correct. That's how the dealers are communicating - super-encrypted email, I'd bet on it. It all supports the Russian / Ukrainian mercenary theory, not that it's good news. But to communicate outside their closed network they will still need ordinary words used by ordinary people. I reckon one of the phones on my list will be a link between the dealers and whoever's paying them."

"Let's hope so, Mel. Let's really hope so, and hope you find it soon. We're braced for more overdose deaths this weekend. Apart from the fatalities there have been survivors. Some of them have life-changing issues now, they've had strokes, heart attacks, brain damage. A few are willing and able to talk, and we're starting to get a picture. As we expected, a customer calls a dealer with an order for so many grams for the weekend. The people who are talking to us say that their regular dealers vanished a few weeks ago, but they got text messages from their old dealers' phones telling them to call a different number, one of our dealer phones. Not so unusual in itself. Deliveries are made by male couriers, always dressed in black with motorcycle helmets. They collect payment in cash and hand over the stuff. They never speak. The customers are told how much money to have ready when they order the gear. There's a report from Manchester that a few local neds tried to intercept one of the couriers and rob him. It didn't end well. Even though it was three on one the courier wiped the floor with them. One dead, two in Intensive Care."

"Right," said Mel, "let's keep going. I'll talk to Thomas tonight and tell you anything interesting. Coffee tomorrow, same place?"

"I'd like that," Jake said.

Chapter 21

Thomas hadn't been idle. He had spent the morning in East Dulwich again snooping around the area, looking for clues. He moved on as soon as he spotted the first of the surveillance units doing exactly what he was doing. He left them to it.

He had been working out how he could best contribute to the efforts to combat the cocaine poisoning. So far he was feeling a bit of a spare part. He needed more of a steer from Jake as to what she wanted from him. In the meantime he thought about what he would do if he was completely on his own. He would want to get close enough to the dealers to find a weakness, one that would take him a step up the food chain towards whoever was behind this. So he might need to become a well-heeled weekend coke-head. He could do that. He just needed to look the part, have lots of cash and a decent address. Once he had made contact with the dealers he needed to develop an opportunity to get deeper into their organisation. That needed a credible back-story, and some props. He might need to call on Eugene in Dublin again.

Eugene Flynn was a good friend of Thomas's. He was an old IRA man who had become a very successful lawyer. He had retired but was still a wielder of great influence. Luckily for Thomas, he also relished a bit of underworld mischief, which he said reminded him of happy times in the old days. Thomas thought on. A good address would be a problem. Owners of expensive rental properties were quite

151

fussy about references and so on. Thomas could easily furnish credible references for a bed-sit or cheap flat, but not a fancy apartment in Kensington. He decided to move into an up-market West End hotel. That settled, he fired up his motorbike and headed for Jermyn Street. After a couple of hours in some of the better ready-to-wear outfitters he was all set. Suits, jackets, casual trousers, shirts, and shoes of course. All bagged up and paid for, to be collected in the next day or two. Money wasn't a problem. Thomas had access to more than he would ever need.

He headed back to Raynes Park. He would miss being with Mel but he knew he had to move on. He was starting to understand how she worked, how she needed people she cared about but also needed to be independent and have her own space at the same time. She managed to balance her needs without being selfish; she gave as much as she took. He could live with that, as long as he was able to stay somewhere in her life.

He was waiting for her. She was exhausted when she got in. He poured her a glass of wine and helped himself to a scotch. She filled him in on the day's developments. He said he knew about the surveillance team but had skipped out so he didn't get in their way.

"Jake wants to talk this through with us. Can you stay until Saturday? She plans to come over tomorrow night or Saturday morning. It's important that we all know what we have to do, and what we mustn't do."

"Message received. Sure, I can do another night, if it's OK with you. I've decided to move into a hotel. I'll explain when Jake's here, so as not to bore you to death."

They chatted for an hour or so over a plate of something that Mel rustled up from the depths of her fridge. Then she yawned and said she was going to have a bath and get some sleep. There was no invitation implied. He found the duvet and pillow himself. Mel slept alone behind her closed bedroom door, and she slept well. She was really tired. At 6 the next morning she was up and dressed. She made coffee for Thomas and kissed him goodbye.

"See you later. Have an interesting day." She left the flat.

She met Jake at the Italian café. Mel got there first and chose a corner table. She ordered coffee and croissants for them both. Jake arrived a few minutes later, all smiles and warmth.

"Sorry I was catty yesterday. I was stressed and the thought of you and Thomas being together was a bit much for me. It won't happen again, I promise, but I'm still trying to get my head around the way you do things." Jake wasn't finding this apology easy, so Mel moved things on.

"All forgiven and forgotten. Now, anything overnight?"

"I got the DNA result around 8 last night. I got it across to Europol and they're searching for traces. They're going to get it to ICTY as soon as they open, which is about now. Hugh wants to have a chat at 10 on a secure phone. I think he's got something back from Kiev. Surveillance have been out all night. The BMW came back in the early hours and they're on it.

They couldn't house the driver, but they know roughly where he is. Given the type of neighbourhood I don't want them breaking doors down and starting a massive shoot-out, so as soon as the BMW moves and is somewhere relatively safe they're going to do a hard stop and grab the occupants." Jake's phone rang. It was Europol.

"Julia? It's Willem in Den Haag. That DNA you sent over – ICTY have a trace. No name but the same DNA was recovered from a body – a woman who had been raped and then shot. Seems like your man is a rapist as well as a killer. Nice guy! Let us know who it is when you know. Ciao."

"The harder the better as far as I'm concerned," Jake said.

"Sorry?"

"That was Europol. Our BMW man likes raping and killing women as well as fighting in other people's wars. Our people won't be holding back when they get their hands on him!" Jake looked serious. "Got to go."

"Oh, Thomas is staying one more night. He's going to a hotel tomorrow. I think he's working up a strategy, god help us. Will you be able to come over tonight? The three of us do need to talk."

"I'd like to. Let's see how the day goes."

Things were happening. Around 9am the BMW driver was seen emerging from a house in East Dulwich. The team took pictures. The driver had a shoulder bag and a holdall. He looked like he was leaving. He was on his own.

Their instructions from Commander Kelso were to intercept the BMW as soon as they thought the risk to the public was manageable, or immediately if they thought there was a threat to life. The suspect in the BMW was probably armed and was a trained Special Forces operative, so no unnecessary risks and use the SO19 specialist armed team to do the stop when the time came. Under no circumstances was the suspect to be lost – if there was a chance he was getting away go overt and strike. The team understood.

The BMW only got as far as the South Circular Road when the surveillance team leader called in the strike. There was a risk that they could lose the target in the morning traffic. The surveillance team hit their lights and sirens, as did the three SO19 Range Rovers that were no more than 30 seconds away. The team blocked the busy road so that the BMW was isolated. As the Range Rovers approached at speed the driver of the BMW clearly made his mind up to go out in a blaze of glory. He leapt out and did a shoulder roll away from the car. When he came up, he had an MP5 machine pistol in one hand and a Makarov pistol in the other. He opened up with both weapons towards the nearest surveillance unit. It was all over in seconds. The suspect took at least 20 hits from SO19 as well as a few from the surveillance officers. They called it in. One surveillance officer with gunshot wounds – not life threatening. Suspect killed. Scene sealed and awaiting forensics and an explosives officer to check for bombs or chemical weapons or anything else that was nasty.

Julia thanked the surveillance officer when he finished telling her what had happened and she called the Commissioner.

The BMW was cleared by the Explosives Officer and loaded onto a truck to be taken away for examination. The dead suspect was searched. He had no identification documents on him, and all labels had been removed from his clothing. He had a packet of Marlboro cigarettes and a battered brass lighter. He also had a wallet with over three thousand pounds in 50s and 20s. In the holdall were two small bricks of cocaine, a few dozen wraps of white powder and a list of addresses with delivery times. In the shoulder bag there was a laptop computer with a power lead.

Julia ordered a search of the house the BMW driver had come out of. It had been kept under observation throughout the operation and there had been no movement in or out. An armed team put the front door in and stormed the building. It was unoccupied but clearly at least two bedrooms had been in use. More cocaine was recovered, some in small plastic containers and more weighed out in wraps or larger bags, along with another computer and piles of cash. There were two mobile phones plugged in to chargers in the kitchen. A quick check showed that there were no outgoing calls, just incoming. They were two of the dealer phones. Julia directed that the house be sealed for full forensic examination and placed under armed guard with no fewer than five armed officers there at all times. She authorised use of the Glock machine guns given the firepower demonstrated by the dead dealer.

The DI in charge of the house search called her. He explained what had been recovered and given the urgency of getting on top of the cocaine supply he had contacted the Met's forensic IT lab. They were saying it could take them up to two weeks to analyse the laptops properly, and then only if they could get into them. They suggested that GCHQ might fare better. Julia called Mel. Mel called back a few minutes later. Cheltenham would be thrilled to have a go. The Cheltenham courier left London between 5 and 6 pm, so if Julia could get the laptops to her at NCIS before 5pm she would make sure they went that evening and work could start over the weekend. Any steer on possible passwords would be handy, and yes, of course the chain of evidence would be intact. A traffic car on blue lights pulled up at NCIS fifteen minutes later and a rather sheepish Mel Dunn walked out to meet them and sign for the laptops and phones. By 8pm they were in the hands of the Government Communications Headquarters in sleepy Cheltenham.

Julia put in a call to Hugh Cavendish explaining what had happened. He didn't seem particularly disappointed that a suspected former member of the Ukrainian Secret Police had met his end on the South Circular Road.

"H-Kiev, our head of station, came up with some interesting snippets," Cavendish said once they had activated the secure facility on their respective phones, "your man Kuznetsov has been recruiting a small team of six men for an overseas operation. Good money, only a couple of months, and in Europe rather than Iraq or sub-Saharan Africa. We heard about it from someone who was approached but turned it down, an old friend of Kuznetsov. The guy who told us about it has terminal cancer and is racked with remorse for his past misdeeds, or so he says.

"Anyway, Kuznetsov told our man that he needed six operatives to do a job for 'a British Capitalist', only he used a very derogatory term instead. Our source doesn't know who it is, of course. That would just be too convenient. With Kuznetsov included, that means that there are seven Ukrainian mercenaries at large in the UK, or six if this morning's chap is or was one of them. Can I have pictures as soon as you can get them to me, Jake? I can get Kiev to confirm. Don't leave it too long, our source is really not very well at all. Oh, by the way, all Ukrainian FSU people have their blood group tattooed, usually somewhere on their right arm. Russian blood groups have numbers in Roman numerals rather than letters If they are, or ever have been, Alpha team people the blood group will be suffixed by a Cyrillic *OS* – looks like an upper-case OC – after it for *Osobyy*, 'Special' in Russian. Thus A Rh Positive would be *II+OC* on an Alpha trained operative. It's so the medics can prioritise Alpha trained people in a combat zone, and something to look for."

"One more question, Hugh. It's a long shot, but would your man have any idea what sort of passwords this team would use? We think they've been using some crazy encrypted email to communicate with each other. We've recovered two laptops which are with Cheltenham, but they may need a hint about passwords to get into them."

"I can but ask." Hugh hung up.

Julia called for a car and went to the mortuary in Southwark where the dead BMW driver had been taken. She examined the killer / rapist's dead body with the pathologist. She looked first at the right arm. The tattoo was there *I+OC* – O Rh positive, Alpha trained. The mortuary photographer took pictures as the pathologist worked. Julia asked for some facial shots for identification and she was told that they would be emailed to her as soon as the post-mortem had finished.

She looked at the face of the dead killer. It was unmarked and looked peaceful. Death had been too easy for him. His chest was a mass of wounds, entry and exit. He would have been dead before he hit the ground.

Julia went back to the Yard. The pictures were on her desktop. She emailed them to Cavendish with a note confirming the FSU Alpha blood group tattoo. Then she started making her notes. It took a while, especially to come up with a plausible reason why a Metropolitan Police Commander had come into possession of a couple of parking tickets and a cigarette butt that linked a brash BMW on fake German number plates to an unidentified Ukrainian mercenary who was wanted for war crimes, including rape and murder, and who was now full of police bullets in Southwark Mortuary.

Chapter 22

It was past 9pm when Julia arrived in Raynes Park. Mel had only beaten her by half an hour, but she was already on her second gin and tonic. She summarised the day's events for Thomas. Jake entered the flat as she had before, leaving a trail of outer clothing and cast-off shoes behind her. She extended her hand for a drink.

"The report I've just sent to the Commissioner should win me a Booker Prize! Great intuition, Thomas, but it was a bastard to explain how I came to get my hands on the fingerprints and DNA of an anonymous war criminal in East Dulwich. It may sound harsh, but the murdering rapist being dead instead of in the cells makes my life a whole lot easier. Cheers, both!" She drank.

Mel phoned for pizza and they got down to business. Thomas started.

"I've been thinking about how I can help. So far I've been able to add a bit of good luck and swift action, but I can see my involvement being a major problem going forward. I'm concerned that my visit to Appleton may have accelerated what happened to him, although I do believe he was a dead man walking anyway, and it might have brought forward the attack on the Essex facility. In fast-moving situations like this it's really not a good idea to have an active element doing things that can't be evidenced if and when it comes to it. There aren't any second chances."

"How do you mean?" Mel asked.

"What he means, Mel," Jake intervened, "is that everything that happens in a case like this is potentially vital evidence that could convict or acquit someone. If you have someone rampaging about the place who is technically or theoretically dead and if he wasn't he'd be a wanted killer, no offence Thomas, and who is the only person who can give that evidence the case is screwed. A point with which I do agree."

"Jake's right. I can only be of use as an intelligence source, one that isn't on any books or bound by any rules. So, what I think I can do is to start to infiltrate the dealers or try in some other way to work my way up the food chain until I can get to whoever is controlling this business. What happened today is a good pointer to what sort of people we are up against. These dealers won't be taken, and they certainly won't talk. We, by which I mean you Mel, need to get into their communications, but firstly we need to get to see them. Or rather I do."

Mel shivered silently. Jake was nodding her agreement. Silence followed. The door buzzer went and Mel nearly jumped out of her skin. It was the pizza.

"So, Thomas, how are you thinking of approaching this?" Jake asked.

"It may be best if I don't say too much. I'll need to keep my distance from both of you, but we need a way to keep in touch. We need to have an information flow. Mel has the number of a phone I bought, and we still have the email account."

"You'll be here though, in London?" Jake asked.

161

"For now. If it takes me somewhere else I'll let you know, if I can."

Mel had been in the kitchen sorting out the pizza and refreshing drinks. "Let her know what?" she asked Thomas.

"We've just been discussing arrangements for keeping in touch. I was saying I'll need to keep my distance from you, starting tomorrow. You've got my phone number, I'll get another as well, and we have the email account."

Mel looked a bit crestfallen. Jake hugged her and told her not to worry.

They ate. Serious talk became chat, which became banter. It was soon past midnight. Jake stood and yawned. "Time for bed. I'm knackered," she said. She did the thing with her skirt, just stepped out of it, and took off her stockings. Mel raised her eyebrows.

"Don't be too shocked, Mel," Thomas quipped, "she did that the other night too. She's shameless."

"It's only my knickers," Jake said, "it's nothing either you hasn't seen before!"

"What *does* she mean, Thomas?" Mel asked.

"I got to see quite a bit of Ms Kelso in Spain. The Miss Teeny-Weeny Wet Bikini number followed by a Walking Around the Room in my Underwear film clip."

"The wet bikini was an operational necessity to show you I wasn't recording the conversation, as you well know. It was very, very small. The underwear thing? Well, I just forgot you were there," Jake said.

"You never told me that bit, Jake. I'm seeing you in a different light!" Mel chuckled.

Jake stomped off into the bathroom, as dignified as she could be in just her white knickers and work shirt.

"What did you think of her bod, Thomas?" Mel asked him, teasing.

"Perfectly acceptable," he said, draining his scotch.

"Would you?" she asked.

"Would I what?"

Before Mel could answer him Jake came out of the bathroom. She was in the same shorter tee-shirt that she had worn last time. It barely covered her thighs, not that she seemed to mind.

"Would he what?" she asked Mel, but she had dived into the bathroom herself. Jake poured herself another drink and sat on the sofa, keeping one hand on the hem of her tee-shirt.

"She's a bit cross with me, Thomas. I think she thinks I'm jealous of you."

"Are you, Jake? Jealous of me?"

"I don't know. I haven't been in this sort of situation before, and I don't think you have either. I can't describe how I feel about her. I don't understand how she separates out parts of her life, but I'm trying hard. Are you jealous of me?"

"I shouldn't be, should I? But the other night I was, for a while. Until I heard you, whichever one of you it was, enjoying yourself. It made me smile and I was glad for both of you."

"It was me you heard. Mel did something to stop me fiddling," Jake said, with a slight giggle.

Mel emerged from the bathroom, tee-shirt donned.

"What are you two going on about?" She had the pillow and duvet under her arm.

163

"Your turn, Thomas," Jake said. He went to the bathroom.

He came out a few minutes later with a towel wrapped around his waist.

They all looked at each other.

"I'm having the sofa," said Mel, "you two can go in there. You can get to know each other better or just get some sleep, it's your choice. Have fun if you both want to. Otherwise, sweet dreams."

Jake and Thomas looked at each other.

"Not an outcome I was expecting," said Jake. She hesitated, then walked into the bedroom.

"Left side or right?" she called to Thomas over her shoulder.

Thomas said nothing, but got to his feet. He closed the bedroom door behind him. Mel settled herself on the sofa and allowed herself a little smile.

In the still bedroom Jake and Thomas lay in the bed, side by side, carefully not touching.

"This is weird, Thomas," she said.

"I can leave if you want, find somewhere to stay."

"No, it's alright. I want to ask you something anyway."

"What's that?"

"Why did you kill him?"

"Who?"

"Banbury. You could have turned him in, couldn't you?"

"When I got him in the car, that day in Putney, I really didn't know what I was going to do with him. I knew there would be options, choices. As things went on he told me too much too easily. By the time we got

164

to Beachy Head, where I had thought I could scare the bejesus out of him if he wasn't playing ball by then, I knew that if he ever got out of the car two things would definitely happen."

"What two things?"

"First, I wouldn't see the next sunset. Second he would walk away scot free. Banbury was the worst kind of criminal. He betrayed everyone, you, me, everyone who ever swore to uphold the law and protect the public. Everyone who has ever given evidence. Everyone who has ever turned informant. He killed people, he tortured people, he raped people, if not in person then by proxy. He let his minions do those things. And he did it all for money, nothing else. I couldn't let that happen, Jake. So I killed him. I didn't enjoy it. I didn't enjoy killing Vincent Carlton or Billy Ramirez, or the Anderson boy either, but I'm not sorry. Does that make me evil?"

"I don't know, Thomas," she turned towards him, laying her head on his shoulder. "I don't really know anything about you. I don't think you're a bad person, not deep down. But I do think you're troubled, and probably sad and lonely too."

"I'd agree, possibly. And you, Jake? Are you troubled, sad and lonely too?"

She propped herself on her elbow and looked at him in the half light. She thought for a moment.

"I wasn't troubled before, or sad, I might be now. But I am lonely. Mel's the only proper friend I have down here, apart from old family ones. I like being here with you, talking like this. Sleeping with her has confused me beyond belief. I mean physically it's

165

incredible, but I feel closer to her when we're talking through an intelligence chart than when we're in bed."

"Has she told you about her compartments? How she separates her life into boxes?"

Jake nodded.

"She doesn't do emotions like most people," Thomas continued, "I agree with you, about her physicality in bed and about being closer to her when we're talking. She's a strange one," Thomas sighed.

"We're all a bit strange Thomas, aren't we. Three misfits on some weird mission."

Jake snuggled into him. She raised her head and kissed him gently. He kissed her back.

The flat was silent apart for the sounds of contented breathing when Mel awoke. It was almost 8am. She put the kettle on and cleaned her teeth. Before making the coffee Mel opened her bedroom door. Jake and Thomas were on their backs, asleep. The duvet had slipped. They were partly covered by a sheet. One of Jake's breasts was exposed as was the top half of Thomas. Their hands were touching, and they looked adorable. Mel watched them for a few seconds. She thought for a fleeting moment about joining them, but quickly decided against it. It would be too much too soon, and threesomes were really difficult to do well. She fetched the coffee.

Mel put the coffee mugs on the bedside table. She covered the sleeping pair and knelt on the bed between their ankles. She let herself fall slowly forward to end up lying between them on top of the duvet and wriggling her way into the gap she had made.

166

"Good morning. Are we all friends now?" Mel asked. "Are we all happy and satisfied and relaxed? No more jealousies?"

Jake and Thomas looked at each other, exchanged smiles. Jake took Mel's hand and kissed it.

"Good morning to you too. No more jealousies," she said. Thomas nodded.

Then a cloud flitted through Mel's thoughts. They just had to get through this case. There had already been a lot of dying, and she couldn't bear to think of either of her friends not making it to the other end of the nightmare.

They decided that the week ahead was going to be tough, so why not make the most of their Saturday? Mel drove them all to Hampton Court where they hired a small cabin cruiser for the day, having bought food and wine on the way. A few hours on the river chatting and eating put them all in an even better mood than they had been in earlier. Jake was teased by the other two because she had had to borrow clothes from Mel, requiring a lot of rolling up of trouser legs and sleeves.

As evening drew in they went back to Mel's flat and after a light supper they all went to bed and spent their first full night together, but they only slept, peaceful and contented in each other's company.

Reality hit on Sunday morning. Julia's Blackberry was in meltdown with reports of overdoses. She had to go. Thomas left too, and Mel was suddenly on her own.

Chapter 23

As Jake Kelso arrived in her office Thomas was getting out of a taxi in Grosvenor Square. He had booked himself into The Millennium Hotel for a week. The motorbike remained in a Wimbledon side street. He had no idea if he would need it again. Once he had checked in he arranged to collect his new clothes.

He spent the rest of the day in his room, mostly catching up on his sleep and also reflecting on the bizarre turn of events between himself and the two women over the last couple of days. In his wildest dreams he had never imagined being in a bed alternately with Mel Dunn and Jake Kelso, or anyone else for that matter. Sex with Mel was earth-shaking, intense and really a bit scary; with Jake it had been warm and welcoming. He was in a strange state of emotional turmoil and utter physical calm, but he was able to think clearly and without the distractions of desire for Mel and wariness of Kelso. Now that they were all in it together, physically and mentally, he could concentrate.

Lying on his bed he was wondering how someone might go about contacting and hiring Ukrainian mercenaries to distribute lethal cocaine, attack a government facility and kill people? From his time in the police and from his undercover work he knew that the underworld most people thought of as fiction really does exist. There are people who will take money to do dreadful things to other people. There are people who will sell anything, drugs, weapons, people, for any imaginable or unimaginable purpose.

168

Access to this murky place was neither particularly difficult nor complicated, but it did entail high risks. The vendors in the underworld were wary and did not often give suspect new customers the benefit of the doubt. Declan Walsh had morphed into Thomas Donohue, who was going through a mental list of his old contacts.

A few years back Thomas Donohue, not that his police handlers knew him by that name, had worked on links between organised crime in the North West of England, Scotland and Northern Ireland. One focus of illegal activity was a seedy private members club on the outskirts of a Lancashire town. It was the sort of place you could go to, safe in the knowledge that what went on in the club stayed in the club. The clients were all male, sometimes someone took a girl in, but she was normally getting paid for her trouble. The few women who worked in the place doubled as barmaids and strippers, and for a fee they would put on a show for 'the lads'. Donohue had been a regular for a while. As he recalled there were a couple of ex-squaddies, former soldiers, who went to the club. It was said that they could get hold of guns for sale or hire when they weren't off somewhere working as Private Security Contractors. Thomas decided to pay the club a visit in the next few days to see if the squaddies were about.

Thomas went to bed early and slept like a log.

Monday morning dawned and after a session in the gym and some breakfast he strolled up to Oxford Street. In two different kiosks he bought two pay-as-you-go phones, complete with SIM cards and credit. He also bought a couple of dongles that would give him internet access via the mobile phone network. He gave a false name and an address in Italy, also false. His next stop was a major department store where he bought a serviceable laptop. He took the computer and one of the phones back to the hotel but activated the other phone and pocketed it. Then he went to Kings Cross by tube and bought a train ticket to Manchester for the following day, Tuesday.

In her office at NCIS HQ Mel Dunn was on the phone to Cheltenham. The computers that had been seized had been unlocked easily enough. It was clear to the techies that there was military-grade encryption software installed, and having two machines with the same kit was a godsend. The only thing they needed was a password for each. The techies feared that too many attempts to log in would cause the machines to shut down forever and permanently eradicate their own hard drives. Any ideas?

Mel called Jake, who was out and in meetings most of the day. She told Raj it was urgent. Jake called back, a bit rushed and breathless, ten minutes later. Mel told her about the password problem. Jake said she had already mentioned it to Hugh Cavendish but she would get on to it and give him a nudge.

A further ten minutes passed and Mel's office phone rang. It was Cavendish. He suggested a quick coffee in ten minutes at the Madeira café. She almost ran to get there.

Hugh arrived looking relaxed and affable. It was a trick he had developed to disguise his razor-sharp mind and a savage need to win.

"Jake said you'd called, but she's up to her ears in hysterical policemen. I said I could have a chat with you, if it would help."

"Thanks Hugh. Cheltenham have the two computers that were recovered on Friday. They've unlocked them, but they need passwords to access the special encrypted sections. They're concerned that the machines will wipe themselves if too many incorrect attempts are made. Since they, and we, know practically nothing about whoever used the laptops they can't even hazard a guess. I was wondering if you or Justin might have any ideas. Jake said she had mentioned it."

"First of all, Mel, our source in Kiev, the one who's really sick, has identified the dead man from the photograph that Jake sent me. He is, was, an FSU Alpha operative, as we already knew. His name isn't relevant, but what is relevant is that he was definitely on Kuznetsov's team. Kuznetsov gave them all pseudonyms which they must use, even between each other. Kuznetsov is a big Tarantino fan - I don't care for his films myself - and of course the team all have colour pseudonyms à la Reservoir Dogs, in Russian obviously. The dead man was known as *Gospodin Zilionyi* – Mr Green. Kuznetsov calls himself *Gospodin Zalatoi*, Mr Gold. I would hazard a guess that Mr Green's laptop password with be something like 'Mr Green' or *Gospodin Zilionyi*, either in Cyrillic or Roman script. The other one will have belonged to someone of similar status within the group. They like watching snooker apparently, so I would hazard another guess at snooker ball values indicating ranking in the team.

The other machine might belong to Mr Yellow, *Gospodin Zholtyi*, or Mr Brown, which is a bit of a mouthful in Russian. It's *Gospodin Kareechnivyi*."

Mel was scribbling all this down. She thanked Hugh Cavendish and rushed back to the office. She made a call to Cheltenham and passed on the spy's thoughts. A few minutes later they called back – bingo. Mr Green in Cyrillic worked on one of the laptops. They were trying Mr Yellow and Mr Brown on the other. If it was right, they would be into the Ukrainians' communications. Mel sent a short text to Jake saying simply that the west country folk had made progress. Then she sent an equally brief email on the secure network to Hugh Cavendish confirming success and thanking him.

The second laptop did indeed belong to Mr Brown. He had been out buying cigarettes when the house was raided. He saw the commotion as he rounded the corner to go back, so he just kept walking in the opposite direction. He had nothing but the clothes he stood up in and the cash in his wallet. His phone, computer and weapons were all in the house. He had no way of contacting Mr Gold. He also had no identity papers, could speak very little English, and was a long way from home. Mr Gold's team had been severely reduced. Mr Brown kept walking. He knew of a Russian / Georgian bar in Lancaster Gate, not far from the Russian Embassy, but he had no real idea of where that was or how to get there. He figured that if he could meet some like-minded Russians or even Ukrainians he might get some help to get home. He assumed Mr Green had been taken and that he, Mr

Brown, was now unemployed. He arrived at the South Circular Road, turned right and kept walking, just following the unfamiliar road signs. He and Mr Green had worked as a team. Mr Green was better at English and did the navigating and talking while Mr Brown did the driving and hurting people. They hadn't used the BMW, there was the other car, not as smart as the BMW, but Mr Gold had assigned it to another team member for a task.

Artur Kuznetsov, aka Mr Gold, was worried. He had seen the news reports and recognised the images of the idiot Mr Green's blue BMW behind the police cordon in South London. He hadn't heard a word from Mr Brown, and he assumed that the fatality reported was Mr Green. That left just him and the four others to implement Phase 2. Luckily, he had planned for this too, but he needed to discuss it with his employer, known as Mr White, *Gospodin Belyi*, the white ball being the one needed to play the game. He was in the company building so he made his way to the Chairman's office and asked to see him. He was told to wait.

On this busy Monday Julia Kelso had just emerged from a long and fretful meeting in the main conference room at Scotland Yard. Several police chiefs from around the country had joined by video, lengthening the meeting by at least an hour while the inevitable IT failures were resolved. The outcome was an agreement among all the major forces affected by the overdose epidemic to launch a major offensive and round up all known and suspected cocaine dealers. The operation, wittily entitled 'Snowstorm', would commence that

173

afternoon and continue with maximum ferocity until the lethal cocaine had been removed from the market. All the remaining dealer phones linked with the overdoses were placed on intercept and a central unit at the Yard was deputed as the point of contact and coordination for any intelligence arising from them. Julia had appointed a planning team as well as an operational one. She was in overall charge as Gold Commander, with deputies dubbed Silver and Bronze to lead the logistics, planning and tactics, and operational implementation respectively. Let the Snowstorm begin.

In his hotel Thomas composed a brief draft email for Mel to read. He gave her his new mobile numbers, just to keep a look out for, and said he would be in the North West for a couple of days. He was assuming that proactive policing would be geared up, which suited his plan just fine. He would be in touch.

All over the UK as neighbourhood drug dealers were about to depart on their evening rounds doors were being kicked in and people were being taken away. Space had been made at the major charging centres normally kept for mass public order arrests, complete with on-site drug testing facilities and Crown Prosecution Service lawyers ready to prepare charges. The idea was to charge anyone who could be proved to be in possession of cocaine with intent to supply immediately, get them to court and remand them in custody, all on the same day. It would cause mayhem.

The next morning's early editions had picked up the story and were applauding the police's long overdue response to the endless cocaine problem. On his train to Manchester Thomas Donohue read the articles with interest. It all helped.

Chapter 24

Instead of going all the way to Manchester Piccadilly Thomas got off at Stockport and took a cab to Manchester Airport to find a hire car. Once he was sorted he set out to the west to find the nasty little club. He was smartly dressed and had on his best Belfast accent.

Although it was barely noon the club was already open. When Thomas walked in all conversation among the few drinkers present stopped. He looked around at the faces, hoping he would recognise someone. Luckily the bar manager was the same one who had been in situ while Thomas was using the place a few years earlier.

"Tony," said Thomas, "how're you doing. It's been a while. You remember me? Tommy Donohue."

Tony looked at him and a light went on in his head. "Tommy! Good to see you! Welcome back. You here for long?"

The other drinkers relaxed and resumed their muttered conversations. Thomas took a seat on a bar stool and spoke quietly to Tony. "Business isn't going too well, Tony. It's all this overdose stuff going on, there's cops everywhere booting in doors and lifting people. It's very bad for business. Reason I'm here is I want to have a wee chat with Ricky and Bob, the squaddies. Are they about, or are they away?"

"They've been away somewhere, but they're back now. They'll be in in a while, or I could give them a call if you like. What do you want with them?"

Tony wasn't being nosy. He just needed to ensure that he wasn't about to drop two of his clients, who had nasty tempers, in deep shit.

"I've heard that there's a team of foreign mercenaries been hired to stir up the coke market. Possibly getting ready for some kind of takeover. No one wants that, do they? I was wondering if they might have heard something, being as how they're in that line of business, so to speak. Plus I need them to get something for me. It'll be worth their while," Thomas slipped a thin wad of £20s across the bar towards Tony, "and yours too, of course."

A long half-hour later Ricky and Bob appeared. They looked rough, clearly not too used to being up and about in daylight. As their eyes became accustomed to the gloom they scanned the room. The first of the barmaids had come on shift and was with Tony behind the bar. They nodded at her.

Their eyes landed on Thomas. He could see them struggling to recognise him, and he was relieved to see that they had done so.

"Tommy," said Ricky, "it's been a while. You look different. Like you're doing OK."

"How're you doing yourself, Ricky? Bob? How long is it. Three years?" Thomas knew it was much longer than that, but a bit of suggestion was always useful.

"About that," agreed Ricky.

"I hear you've been keeping busy. Tony said you'd been working away."

"Did he now? Yeah, we have. A bit of work came up in Lebanon and Syria. It's good there, better than Iraq or Afghan."

Thomas bought them all drinks.

"What do you want, Tommy?" asked Bob, the quiet one.

"You've heard of the cocaine overdose thing that's going on? It's killing business, not just for me but for everyone. The cops are going crazy and the shit is really flying. We need to stop it."

"Who's we?" asked Ricky.

"Us businessmen. I'm here for me and my associates, but others are hurting too. So, I've heard through the grapevine that there's a team of mercenaries, Russian or Ukrainian or something, that's been hired to fuck up the coke trade. You're both in the military world. I was wondering if you'd heard anything, or if you knew how and where anyone would hire people like that."

"Russians and Ukrainians? Russians tend to stick to their own language. There's enough to keep them all busy what with Chechnya and Dagestan and everything, but some of them were in the Balkans, Serbia and that. Ukrainians are right crazy fuckers. You see them all over, but mostly fliers. Aeroplanes and choppers. They don't seem to care how dodgy an aircraft is, they'd take off in a plane with only half a wing on and expect it to fly. It's like they've never heard of gravity and have forgotten what pain's like." Ricky paused. "But fighters? Not so much. Not internationally. One thing, though. You wouldn't find Ukrainians in the usual places you'd find people to do your fighting for you. You're Belfast, right? You know where to find folks for hire on your own turf. In the military world if you don't want to go through one of the more legit private security outfits you head for Marseille or Brussels, or maybe Prague. There are bars and clubs there where you can find people. With Ukrainians you'd need to go to Ukraine, or maybe Russia. I wouldn't know where to start.

"Funnily enough I did hear some talk about foreigners being involved. A group of local lads in Manchester tried to take on a stranger making deliveries to punters in their territory, well-paying punters. They didn't like it. They're tasty lads, so three of them ambushed the guy. Only one of them survived, and then only just. One lad was killed on the spot, classic special forces neck-snap, another died in intensive care with massive internal injuries. The survivor just got out last week. He told a mate of mine that the foreign bastard was a squat little fucker but built like he was made of bricks. And quick too. He floored all three of them in about three moves, no noise. He did have a shooter, the guy saw it, but he didn't draw it. Just wiped the floor, unarmed combat. Definitely SF."

Thomas sat quietly, waiting to hear if there was any more. There wasn't.

"Thanks Ricky. If you do hear anything let me know." He wrote down his mobile number. "One more thing. I'm just off a plane and I'm in England for a few days. I need some hardware. Can you help me out?"

"What sort of hardware?" asked Bob.

"The usual. Nine mil, good order. I'll buy, not rent. Ideally, it'll be new. I don't want to be done for ancient matters if things go wrong on me."

"It'll cost you a grand. Ammo included. New and still wrapped."

"When?" asked Thomas.

"When do you want it?"

"Soon as."

Ricky and Bob nodded to each other. "You wait here with Ricky. I'll be a few minutes. You got the cash on you?"

Thomas nodded. If these two were going to do the dirty it would be when Bob came back. If they were being straight Bob would come back on his own with the package. If not, he would come back mob-handed and take what he could from Thomas. Thomas ordered more drinks, although he hadn't touched his first one yet. Without raising his voice or changing his tone he quietly withdrew a ten-inch carving knife from where he had been keeping it up his sleeve. He let Ricky see it.

Ricky understood. He didn't say anything, there was no point. In truth he did remember Thomas and thought he was OK. Bob had gone to the old guy's flat, a place not five minutes from where they were. It was where they stored hardware which they sold or rented out. They paid the old guy a few quid and brought him tobacco. He was no trouble and no one would suspect him.

Bob came back in. He was alone and carrying a plastic bag. He put it on the table, looking at the knife but not commenting. It was only sensible to be prepared.

"There you go," said Bob, "have a look. No one will see."

Thomas peered into the bag. There was a bundle of cloth which contained a cardboard box. It was weighty. It was a compact Makarov 9mm semi-automatic pistol, still in its manufacturers' box. The Makarov was standard issue to police and military throughout the former Soviet Union, as well as in China, Latin America and Africa. It was a reliable, low-maintenance sidearm, produced in its millions. Although in use since the 1950s it remained as popular now as it ever had been. There was another bundle with two magazines and a box of cartridges. He repacked it all. He pulled a wad of noted from an inside pocket and counted out fifty £20 notes, then he added a further ten notes.

"There's a wee drink there for you as well. Good to see you again. I'll be back before you know it. Don't forget to give me a call if you hear anything. My friends and I will be grateful." Thomas didn't disabuse criminals who assumed he had links with paramilitaries. It made people a bit more wary of him if they thought the boys would come to his aid or to avenge him.

Thomas went to his hire car and sat for a good twenty minutes. Ricky and Bob didn't come out of the club, and there was no sign of unwanted attention, from the police or other criminals. Thomas made a call to the car hire company and said he had a change of plan. He would leave the car at Heathrow that evening, if that was OK. No problem, they said.

Before joining the M6 Thomas pulled over and got a briefcase out of the boot of the car. He stowed the carrier bag in the briefcase and locked it, placing it on the front seat beside him. He drove south past Birmingham and onto the M40. At Heathrow he followed the hire car return signs and left the car with them. Then he took the shuttle bus to the terminal. He didn't go into the building but went directly to the taxi rank and took a cab back to the Millennium in Grosvenor Square.

Chapter 25

The police operation to track down the dealers and his conversation with the two squaddies caused Thomas to revise his thinking on getting closer to whoever was behind the overdose crisis. He hadn't had much of a plan anyway, but now he started to think a bit more about how a 'British Capitalist', the term Jake Kelso had reported being used by her MI6 contact, would get to know a killer like Artur Kuznetsov.

Since the collapse of communism and the Soviet Union, Russia and Ukraine as well as the other former Soviet states had attracted ruthless exploitation by western businessmen. They were fighting back now, but the only people they had who really understood free-market economics were criminals. Vladimir Putin, in power since 1999, had adopted a strategy of snatching state assets and giving them to his friends, most of whom were fellow KGB officers or reformed, maybe not so reformed, criminals. The understanding was that what Putin could give he could also take away, and every now and then he did so, just to keep the others in line. Putin's friends were becoming known as oligarchs, a misnomer if ever there was one. The oligarchs shared neither power nor government, they were merely tools of the President.

The oligarchs spent a lot of time getting cash and assets out of Russia and its satellites, the extensive network of former Soviet Socialist Republics, and for this they needed some help. In the early days of the new Russia foreigners were eager to snap up Russia's assets at fire-sale prices. Many people became amazingly wealthy as a result, but few of them were Russian. That had changed. Russians, in the guise of the said oligarchs, were now the nominal owners. The foreigners were needed to invest the proceeds and syphoned-off profit in places that they didn't have access to, and where hopefully even Mr Putin couldn't get his hands on all of it. So foreign investment bankers, venture capitalists, hedge funds, asset managers and the like moved into Russia like locusts.

Thomas started up his computer and inserted the dongle. He started researching British financiers with Russian connections. There were a lot of them. He discarded the well-known multinationals. He thought it unlikely that big firms would want or need to kill off middle-class cocaine users, or to hire Ukrainian mercenaries for that matter. By late afternoon he had a list of around a dozen smaller firms, many family-run, that had publicised, or had had reported, their activities in Russia or the former Soviet Union in the past year or two. He checked the Companies House website for names of directors, and where the firms had their own websites he examined these too for names of senior staff, office addresses, and annual reports.

He typed up a list of company names and names of individuals associated with them. This he copied into a draft email for Mel to access. He wanted her to run all the names through her databases, and have Jake do the same, just to see what fell out of it.

He stretched, his eyes weary from the computer screen. Thomas changed into shorts and a tee-shirt and went down to the hotel gym where he sweated for an hour. He showered in his room and went out looking for a place to eat and think.

******

In his plush office high above the City Sir Charles Murston was seething. What the hell did the police think they were up to? In his time he had been a Minister of State at the Home Office and it was partly his knowledge of how disjointed the UK police services were that gave him the confidence to embark on this current operation. Now that Plod seemed to have started doing joined-up thinking the operation could no longer proceed as planned. Concerted efforts by the police to take out drug dealers up and down the country screwed everything up. His plan required disruption of the demand side of the market - only the demand side. Screwing up the supply side effectively cancelled out his advantage and would serve to keep the price of cocaine stable. That would not do. It would not do at all. He summoned Artur.

When Kuznetsov arrived Sir Charles turned on the TV in his office and they watched a recording of the press briefing given earlier by the jumped-up Scottish policewoman. Sir Charles froze the screen on a clear shot of Commander Kelso's face.

"Find out who she is, Artur, where she lives. Husband, kids, everything, anything. She's ruining the operation and she must be stopped. Also, we need to change Phase 2 immediately. Forget what Charlie has told you to do, we go with the plan you and I discussed. Do you have the material?"

"Yes. It arrived a few days ago. It is safe, with the rest of the commodity. I will activate Phase 2B as we discussed. What is the timing you want?"

Sir Charles had become accustomed to Kuznetsov's refusal to show him any deference, but it still irritated him enormously. He was a Knight of the Realm, a Member of the British Parliament, a former Government minister, and a bloody multi-millionaire to boot. The odd 'Sir' from Kuznetsov would not go amiss.

"We're coming up to the half-year bonus awards in the City. The first announcements come out next Thursday or Friday, and lots more the following week, so there'll be celebrations everywhere. My sources say that profits this half-year are excellent and bonuses will be huge. So Artur, you basically have a week to get Phase 2B ready and all the components in place. We need to be ready to start implementing in 8 to 10 days. Can you do it?"

"Yes. I can do it. But everything else must stop. My team is short of two men. I must bring the others in to get Phase 2B ready. I have made plans for this."

"Excellent. But can you still find out about that bloody policewoman, Commander bloody Kelso?"

"I will do that myself when the team is working on 2B. What do you want to happen to her?"

"I don't know yet. I just need her stopped. Find a pressure point that will stop her. If you can't, you will have to eliminate her as you did the other irritants. You may go."

Kuznetsov stood firm.

"Killing a senior British police officer in the UK was not in the contract. It will cost you more. It is a big risk for me. I will do what you say, but it will cost another one million sterling, half when I have the information on her, the other half before she is killed."

"That's a bit bloody steep, Artur. A million pounds?"

"That is what it will cost if you want me to do it. If you don't that's fine, you can find somebody else to do it, and for Phase 2B also."

Murston stared at the Ukrainian. If he walked out on him now the whole thing was dead. The hundreds of thousands already spent would be wasted, and the audit that could be his nemesis was looming.

"Very well, Artur. Just get the information on Kelso for me, I'll consider what to do about her later. I will pay 250K for the information I want, but that's all. You find it for me, and carry on with Phase 2B."

Kuznetsov nodded, turned on his heel and left the room.

He had been allocated his own small office in the company's rented suite. He sat down having locked the door and drawn the window blind. He extracted a laptop from a drawer and started it up. He went through the log-on procedure for the encrypted channel and opened the email programme. He composed a short email to his remaining comrades, Black, Pink, and Blue. They were to stop all operations and make their way to London separately. Yellow was already here, with Kuznetsov. They were to destroy all telephones before starting the journey back. They were each to buy a cheap cell phone and send Gold a secure email with their new number. They would be contacted by text on the new phones and informed of a rendezvous place and time. They were to be in London by Thursday at the latest, the day after tomorrow. He sent it and closed down his computer.

The faithful Kolya, not his real name of course, also known as Mr Yellow, was waiting with Murston's Rolls Royce in the basement. Kuznetsov called him on the car phone and told him to bring one of the other cars to the front of the building immediately. He needed to go out.

A few moments later Kuznetsov slid into the passenger seat of a dark blue Audi. He directed Kolya to Westminster. Kuznetsov surveyed the area around New Scotland Yard looking for opportunities to find Commander Kelso. He settled on the small park opposite the shorter of the two towers, a place popular with derelicts and lunching office workers. He spoke to Mr Yellow in rapid Russian and gave him a still photograph of Commander Kelso taken from the video recording. It was grainy but good enough. Leaving Mr Yellow in the car Kuznetsov strolled through the street market in Strutton Ground where he bought a cheap workman's donkey jacket and some boots in Mr Yellow's size. Within the hour Mr Yellow was installed on a bench in the park with a sandwich and a newspaper, which he could not make any sense of. He sat and watched, waiting for the pretty blonde policewoman who seemed to have upset his boss so much.

Kuznetsov drove back to the City and resigned himself to two days of chauffeuring the arrogant

Capitalist Pig. He comforted himself by planning Sir Charles Murston's fate once all this was over and the millions were safely in the bank in Mariupol.

******

Julia Kelso emerged from Scotland Yard shortly after 6pm. Mr Yellow almost missed her, but his eye was drawn to her as she answered a call on her mobile. She was engrossed in conversation as she waited to cross Victoria Street on foot. Mr Yellow stirred himself and followed the distinctive blonde head from a safe distance. Kelso walked quickly and by the time she had finished her call she was already crossing Vauxhall Bridge Road. Mr Yellow could not believe his luck. He watched as Kelso went into a large square building, the name of which was Dolphin Square if his reading of the Roman script was correct. Mr Yellow found a place to wait, but quickly realised there were just too many entrances and exits to cover. He called the number Mr Gold had given him and reported in. Mr Gold told him to go home and resume first thing in the morning. Mr Yellow detected that Mr Gold was pleased with his progress.

Chapter 26

At 6am on Wednesday morning Julia Kelso went for a run. She was familiar with the area around Dolphin Square, and with the regular inhabitants who were out and about at such an hour. The squat, fit-looking man in a baggy donkey jacket was not someone she had seen before. He didn't seem to be doing much, just sitting on a bench studiously reading yesterday's Evening Standard. She didn't take much further notice but when she saw he was still in the same place when she returned from her run alarm bells were starting to ring in her head. Julia took the lift to one of the upper floors from where she could look down on the bench the man still occupied. With her phone camera she was able to take a few fairly decent shots of the man. She decided not to walk to the office but called for a car and driver, asking that she be collected from the riverside entrance to Dolphin Square. She called Mel and arranged to meet for a quick coffee in Vauxhall, then she called Hugh Cavendish and asked if he could bring Justin Evans, the SAS Major, to meet them.

The pool car dropped Julia outside one of the many cafés on Albert Embankment and waited in a side street. Mel and the two SIS men arrived at almost the same time. Julia quickly told them all about the possible watcher she had spotted. She described him accurately and showed them all the pictures on her phone, tiny as they were on the little screen. Justin studied them carefully, looking serious.

"It could be one of Kuznetsov's men, but I'll need to check. Did you see him before this morning?" he asked.

"I don't know," Julia replied, "I may have seen him last night on my way home from the office, but I can't be sure."

"Can you get these pictures to me, Julia?" Justin asked.

"Not sure," she replied.

Mel, silent until now, interrupted. "I can do it. Can I have your phone Jake?" She fiddled for a few seconds.

"Right. I've transferred them to my phone and can download them when I get to the office. You'll have them by 9 Justin."

Julia looked at her. "How did you do that?" she said.

Hugh Cavendish was looking pensive.

"I don't like this, Julia. If Kuznetsov has you in his sights you could be in big trouble. Give me a few minutes, then get your car to drop you back at Dolphin Square. When I call you, leave the building and walk to the Yard as you normally would. I know you have your own resources, but mine are nearer, and they've been trained by Justin's lot."

"Just this once, Hugh, to get me to work and confirm whether or not there is a threat. If I used the Met's resources to do this I'd be filling in forms for a year. Tell your team that I'll be coming out of the front entrance behind Pimlico School."

Cavendish made a phone call, speaking quickly and quietly. When he had finished he said simply "All set."

Julia said her goodbyes and called for her car. Alone with Mel for a few seconds she squeezed her hand and told her not to worry, all would be well. Mel nodded, but didn't believe a word.

Back at Dolphin Square Julia's phone rang. It was Cavendish. If possible, Julia should leave by the exit she had identified at exactly 9.15. She would not be aware of her protection but it was very much there. She thanked him.

At 9.15 Julia Kelso strode out of Dolphin Square in her usual purposeful manner. She passed within a few feet of Donkey Jacket, still studying yesterday's paper. He didn't seem to notice her, but as she glanced over her shoulder while crossing Lupus Street she noticed that his bench was now vacant. She continued towards the Yard as usual, catching the odd glimpse of Donkey Jacket as she crossed roads. Her phone rang as she got to her office.

"Jake, it's Hugh. Justin has received the pictures from Mel, and he confirms our suspicions. It is one of Kuznetsov's team, known as Mr Yellow – *Gospodin Zholty*. I hope you don't mind but Mr Yellow is now enjoying SIS hospitality, or he will be when he wakes up. Justin thought it best to get him out of the way, and I agree. I had our team lift him. You'll be pleased to know it was quick and discreet, but Mr Yellow will probably be asleep for a few hours yet."

"I don't mind at all Hugh. One less for us to worry about. Thank you for your help."

"Anything for you Jake. Oh, by the way, Mr Yellow had a phone on him. I take it you would like it? I'll have it sent over." He hung up.

Chapter 27

Mel had reported back that none of the companies on Thomas's list were 'of interest' to NCIS or the agencies, but one or two had sensitive flags on them. This meant that some individuals connected to a few of the firms were high-profile media figures, politicians, or otherwise capable of causing embarrassment to the Government. Mel ran through these briefly in her draft email to Thomas. Mel wanted to speak to Thomas. Could he call her?

He did, and Mel told him about the tail on Jake, how it had been linked to Kuznetsov, and how it was now neutralised. She told him that Cheltenham was making slow progress decrypting the steganography but they were hopeful that they would have it cracked soonish. Jake, now thankfully tucked up in her office, was up to her ears and Mel was worried about her safety. Kuznetsov would realise sooner or later that his man had been taken. Hopefully that would make him abort his mission, but there was a chance that he could send more people after Julia. There was nothing significant emerging from her telephone analysis as yet, but a new phone had been retrieved by SIS from Kuznetsov's man and she was expecting to get details any minute. It might give a pointer towards Kuznetsov.

Thomas listened.

"Probably spurious advice, but you should tell Jake she needs armed protection for the time being. I'm going to do some leg work on the finance angle, but let me know if anything comes from your sources." He hung up, worried.

Thomas made his way to Wimbledon and retrieved the motorcycle. He spent the rest of the afternoon and early evening checking out the list of finance houses with Ukrainian or Russian links, more in hope than expectation, but he felt he had to be doing something. He arrived back at his hotel late in the evening and went directly to his room. He was up before 6 the following day and he set off again to visit the next firms on his list.

******

Mr Gold – Artur Kuznetsov – was behind the wheel of Sir Charles Murston's Rolls Royce Silver Spur, painted a deep luxurious grey with a slightly lighter grey interior. It was a fine motor car, but of no interest to Kuznetsov. He was worried that he had not heard from Mr Yellow since he had reported in before 6 yesterday morning. Mr Yellow was loyal and reliable. The silence could only mean that he had been taken or had an accident. He was running short of men. Green was dead, Brown was missing, and now Yellow seemed to have been taken, or had at least disappeared. That only left Black, Pink and Blue. And himself of course. Not enough!

Murston was in the back seat reading the financial sections of the major newspapers. They had left home a bit later than usual, and it was now peak rush-hour, 9 am. As he pulled up at the office Kuznetsov was still distracted, so although he noticed the motorcycle courier standing next to his bike opposite the main entrance he didn't see him as a threat. Kuznetsov was always looking out for hostile surveillance teams, but just one person on his or her own standing in full view was not how professional surveillance worked. The lone courier was talking into his phone.

The courier looked up and looked straight at the face of Artur Kuznetsov. The courier pulled on his helmet and mounted his bike, an old-ish Honda. He rode away as Artur opened the door for Murston to disembark. Murston always liked to get out of the car by the main entrance to the office, rather than in the basement as Kuznetsov had advised. He liked people to see him and to see that he was rich and powerful. The fool, Kuznetsov thought.

Thomas could not believe his luck. The previous evening he had scouted the addresses of the first two financial firms on his list, not really knowing what he was looking for. He just wanted to get that essential 'feel' for each of them. This morning he was outside the third one around 6am before moving on to number four, Murston Asset Management, where he had been since around 8.15. He had nursed a cardboard cup of coffee as he watched the comings and goings of the building. He knew that Murston Asset Management had the three top floors of the tall tower block. He saw the sleek grey Rolls Royce arrive around 9. He was looking directly at the driver, unmistakeably the same man as he had seen in that grainy picture shown to him by Jake Kelso. He had been looking straight at Artur Kuznetsov, the former Ukrainian special forces officer and current mercenary, and seemingly now chauffeur to Sir Charles Murston if Thomas was not mistaken.

Game on, he thought. A plan started to form in his mind. He hurried back to his hotel and spent the morning researching Murston as much as he could.

Sir Charles Murston, career financier and a Member of Parliament for the last ten years, was married with one adult son, also called Charles, or Charlie. Charles senior had done a bit in the military – a short service commission – before taking over the family investment house from his aging, and seemingly decent, father. The firm had done alright, but it was not a spectacular success. That changed with the collapse of Communism. Murston had seen opportunities in the former Soviet Union and his firm had made a killing for quite a few people, including Murston himself. For a few years Murston had kept a flat in Moscow and spent the working week there, picking up some very basic and, according to some reports, badly pronounced Russian. It seemed he had always been dependent on hired locals for advice and support. He paid well. He let his son Charlie take over the reins in Moscow while he returned to the UK. A large donation assured his nomination as candidate in the forthcoming elections and he was duly returned as MP for a safe seat in the Shires. Another very hefty donation smoothed the way to a knighthood and an early ministerial appointment, only in Agriculture at first but it led to another in the Home Office. The newly knighted Sir Charles wasn't particularly public spirited or even interested in politics, but it looked good on the letterhead and it gave him access to some very useful information.

Thomas was reading between some of the lines he was seeing, and he wasn't forming a very good opinion of Sir Charles Murston, MP. He couldn't work out why someone like Murston would have a hired killer driving him about, a hired killer linked to a spate of cocaine overdose deaths across the length and breadth of Britain, not to mention the murder of a Security Service officer, a civil servant and several security staff.

Thomas moved on to look at the Murston family. Lady Murston, Lucy, lived a quiet life at the family estate in Hampshire. She was seen from time to time at society dos in London or was wheeled out for constituency dinners. Charlie, the son and heir, had a slightly more colourful internet profile. He had had a few run-ins with regulators and the fraud squad, but nothing had stuck. The gossip columns suggested he was financially irresponsible. The financial pages were carefully scathing about his business acumen. He was a regular on the exclusive London nightclub circuit, and he still travelled throughout the former Soviet Union. Although married with two children he spent little time at home, which, some commentators suggested, suited his wife Serena well.

Thomas collated what he could find about Charlie Murston and he spent several minutes studying various media images of him. He wanted to meet Charlie. Charlie would be Thomas's route into whatever his father was up to. Thomas made a list of

Charlie's regular hangouts and found his London address easily enough.

Around 4.30pm he made his way back to the city in his courier gear again. His luck was holding, and within ten minutes he saw the grey Rolls Royce pull up outside the entrance to the building where Murston had his offices. Kuznetsov was at the wheel, looking at his watch. Sir Charles emerged, slim and neat, with greying hair just a little too long. Beside him was a quite plump, quite pink, younger version of himself: Charlie. Charlie was talking too loudly and laughing at his own jokes. Kuznetsov jumped out and opened the rear door for Sir Charles. He let Charlie open his own door.

The Rolls Royce pulled out into the City traffic. Thomas kept well back but was able to keep tabs on the distinctive car from a distance. Father and son were deposited at an address in Chelsea. Kuznetsov drove the car away but returned a few minutes later on foot. There must be a garage nearby. Thomas cruised around the block slowly before finding a space for the bike between two parked cars. He pulled in and waited. At around 7pm Charlie emerged from the house. He had removed his tie but otherwise was dressed as he had been earlier. He hailed a cab, which Thomas followed easily to Browns Hotel in Mayfair. Charlie went in. From his viewpoint on the street Thomas saw that he had bypassed the reception desk and headed straight for the bar.

Under his waxed cotton jacket Thomas was wearing a silk and linen mix jacket and an expensive open-necked shirt. His trousers, although casual, could also pass as smart. He changed his biker boots for the loafers he had in the top-box, tidied his hair, and strolled into the bar at Browns Hotel. He found a seat and ordered a gin and tonic.

The bar was not yet busy. Charlie was alone at the bar, talking loudly into a phone. A bottle of champagne stood in an ice bucket at his elbow. Charlie's talk was about a deal involving Russian aluminium. Thomas finished his drink and went to the bar. He took a seat a few stools down from Charlie, who had just ended his call. He ordered another gin and tonic. Charlie looked around the bar. It wasn't clear if he was waiting for anyone in particular or just on the lookout for a diversion.

Thomas caught his eye. He raised his glass. "Cheers," he said.

Charlie responded. *"Na Zdrovie!"*

"Russian?" asked Thomas.

"Indeed it is, but I'm not! Do you speak it?" Charlie responded.

"Can't say as I do. I'm no linguist, and I've never been there. Do you speak Russian fluently?"

"No, not really. Just a few words, enough to get by when I'm there. I do a lot of business in Russia and the Former Soviet Union. Everyone speaks Russian still, despite the new-found freedom of the allegedly Independent States," Charlie paused for a slurp. "It's a great place if you have an appetite for an opportunity, if you get my drift. Not too much red tape; a willingness to get things done. Are you in business yourself?"

"In a way, yes. Some commodity dealing, a bit of currency, anything to turn a profit."

"Can I get you a drink? I'm Charlie Murston."

"Thomas Donohue." They shook hands.

"Irish?"

"Originally. World citizen these days, following the trends."

They talked on for a couple of hours and several more drinks. Once the champagne was finished Charlie went on to brandy, to which he was clearly very accustomed. Nevertheless, he was slurring slightly as Thomas stood up to leave.

"Got to go, Charlie. I have a call with the west coast and an early start tomorrow."

"Fair enough, Thomas, I need to get some nosh anyway. But before you go, would you be interested in an investment opportunity?"

"Always. What sort of investment?"

"Not here," Charlie tapped the side of his nose, "too many ears. Why don't you come to my office tomorrow and I'll talk it through for you. Say 11? If all goes well we can have lunch." Charlie handed Thomas a card with his name, office address and mobile number printed on it.

"11 it is. See you then Charlie. Sleep well."

Thomas left the bike where it was and walked back to Grosvenor Square.

Chapter 28

Alone in his room Thomas was weighing up his options. To alert Jake Kelso to the fact that Sir Charles Murston, MP, was employing Artur Kuznetsov would undoubtedly prompt some swift decisive action. It would also mess up any chance of finding out what the whole thing was about, and it would also probably allow Murston to escape any kind of sanction, if indeed he was behind the cocaine deaths. Kuznetsov would probably end up dead, and there were still other cannons loose on the ground. The prospect of Kuznetsov dying didn't bother Thomas; the man undoubtedly deserved it. Murston getting off any kind of hook did bother him a lot. His mind made up, Thomas decided to keep the news to himself for now and go ahead with the meeting with Charlie boy the following day.

Early the next morning Thomas's mobile rang. It was Mel. She was tense and business like.

"Morning Thomas. We have a development. Cheltenham have broken into the steganography and decoded an email sent on Tuesday from a Mr Gold to Messrs Black, Pink and Blue. It was copied to Mr Brown, who we think is Green's partner and has gone missing. That's how we got the message. That's the good news. The bad news is that they were instructed to return to London and regroup, to get new phones and email the numbers to Gold. They were to await instructions to meet up for new orders. The deadline to get back to London was yesterday, and we don't have the new numbers.

"The phone recovered from the guy following Jake had only been used to contact one other number, which I've cell-sited to somewhere in the City. I can't be any more precise. A warrant application for it to go on cover is with the Home Office, and in the meantime I'm collecting call data, but there will be a 24 hour lag due to a computer issue at the service provider.

"Jake has all this, but I thought I should let you know what's happening. What have you been up to?"

"Just following hunches. Can you do me a favour and start doing some digging on Murston Asset Management, it was on the list I sent you. I'd like to know what anyone has on them, and on the firm's chairman, Sir Charles Murston. He's an MP, by the way, and a former Home Office Minister."

"Bugger," said Mel, "MPs are off-limits anyway, and a former minister is double off-limits. If anything is held on him it will be locked away so tightly that it would probably need the PM's say so to look at it. With the best will in the world Thomas, even your best hunch wouldn't swing it. I'll ask Vauxhall Cross about the company though." She ended the call.

Mel's comments about Murston senior being off-limits reinforced his decision to go it alone. He dressed carefully, smart and understated, but not too formal. He decided against a tie and wore a light roll-neck sweater instead of a shirt, a grey woollen sports jacket and charcoal flannels. Satisfied, he left the hotel and hailed a taxi.

He arrived at the Murston offices shortly before 11am and he rode the lift to the 21st floor. As he emerged from the lift he came face to face with Artur

Kuznetsov, who was waiting to descend. Thomas hoped that he hadn't shown any sign of recognition. Kuznetsov hadn't seemed to have taken any notice of him. Close up he looked intimidating. Not much taller than Thomas, Kuznetsov had a tension about him, and it was clear that he was extremely fit. He had a cruel harshness to his face, and icy cold blue eyes. His hair was close cropped and greying. There was a hint of some sort of pungent aftershave in his wake.

Thomas announced himself to the receptionist and took a seat in a large leather armchair. Charlie emerged, slightly breathless, just after 11.

"Sorry to keep you, Thomas, long call." Charlie shook his hand. Thomas caught a whiff of stale alcohol on his breath.

"No bother, Charlie. I was admiring the view." Thomas nodded at the floor to ceiling windows that gave onto the City skyline and on towards the river. "Good spot for an office."

Charlie led the way to his own office and summoned coffee.

"So, Thomas, what sort of business are you in again?" he asked.

"I invest in things, for decent profits. I work with some people and handle some investments for them; they trust me to make good decisions. I'll say no more than that for now. You said you had an 'opportunity'?"

"I need to know a bit more about you first, I'm afraid. It is very sensitive, good returns are likely but only for the right type of investor."

"What type would that be, Charlie?"

"One with imagination, not too hidebound by convention. Don't get me wrong, this is all legitimate, above board."

"I hadn't thought it could be anything else, Charlie. But don't worry, my associates and I are sophisticated investors, but we're also very protective about our privacy. I'm the only person you will, or can, know about or meet. If you want to check my credentials you can check with my lawyers in Dublin. They'll confirm that I am what I say I am, and also that I have significant funds at my disposal, with authority to make investment decisions. But I'll need to know more about you and this firm too. My associates and I are prepared to lose money but would rather not. If I made a commitment without doing proper due diligence they would be severely unhappy, as would I. So you can check my credentials, and I will check yours. OK?" Thomas was letting his Belfast accent become subtly more pronounced. Charlie was watching him intently. Thomas wrote down the name of Eugene Flynn's law firm, with Eugene's name alongside it.

"Here you go, Charlie. I'm sure your secretary can find a Dublin number."

Charlie excused himself and left the room for a little over five minutes.

"Sorry about that, Thomas, all is in order, as I was sure it would be. Mr Flynn wouldn't be pushed on the level of funding you have available, but he did indicate that it was enough for any conceivable investment purpose. Could you give me a steer on a figure?"

Thomas smiled. "No," he said. "Your turn now, Charlie. Why should I invest with you?"

Charlie's face had become flushed. He took a sip of water.

"Fair enough. My grandfather established Murston Asset Management as an investment banker over 40 years ago. There was a lot of loose money around in the 1960s and the British Labour government was very keen to get hold of as much of it as possible. 95 per cent income tax for high-earners, currency controls and all that. So Grandpa, who had been in merchant and investment banking for years, found lawful ways to invest offshore. He did very well, not only keeping the taxman's hands off clients' money but also creating wealth, the wealth that was later needed to grow the British economy once political sanity returned. My father took over when Grandpa retired, and he grew the business substantially. The collapse of the Communist system in the late 1980s and early 1990s threw up all kinds of opportunities. We invested heavily and bought well in Russia. We have a select client base, small but loyal. At present we have almost a billion sterling under management and are returning an average of 14 per cent based on the last three years. Some funds do a lot better, but carry more risk as I'm sure you'll appreciate. Our best performing fund has an average return of 24 per cent over the same period."

"We normally look for a better return than that, Charlie, especially these days. 14 to 24 per cent is pretty pedestrian. What's the opportunity you want to tempt me with?"

Charlie took a deep breath. He was out of his depth with this savvy Irishman who clearly knew as much about murky investments as he did, not that he knew much anyway. That was his father's domain.

"I can give you an outline, and if you're interested I'll introduce you to my father who can give you more detail. Essentially, we have clients who are keen to get a substantial slice of equity in the Russian energy sector. For complicated reasons they don't want to buy on the open market. Once it's known that they are interested the price of stock in the company they want to buy into will escalate sharply. We have an agreed sale price with the clients for certain stocks, and now we need to acquire them. At current market prices we will make 40 per cent on the deal, but we need a wider range of intermediaries than we normally use to do the transactions. The total value of the project, purchase price, is 100 million Euro, and if we can buy at today's price, which is the same as it has been for the last month, we will clear 140 million. The big sweetener is the time scale. The clients want it all done extremely quickly, and I mean extremely. Within a few days. We still have some space for further investors. If you want a return of 40 per cent in a matter of a few days the opportunity is there, but only for the next couple of hours at most. Are you interested?"

"How much do you have committed already, how many investors?"

"Confidential, I'm afraid. What I can say is that we are inviting a few of our investors to put in 10 million Euro each, no more, no less, and we plan to start the ball rolling as soon as the Moscow market opens on

Monday morning. Moscow is two hours ahead so we will have done the buying by 8am London time. Our clients will buy from us the same day, as soon as it can be done. The Moscow market has a 48 hour settlement, so profits will be paid out on Wednesday morning. I'm flying out to Moscow this afternoon to manage the deal personally."

"Four million Euro in five days isn't too shabby. OK, I'm interested. Let's go meet your dad." Thomas stood up. Charlie was turning out to be a pushover.

Charlie knocked on his father's office door and entered.

"Morning Pa," he started, "I'd like you to meet Thomas Donohue. He's interested in the Moscow project. I've done the necessary and all is good."

Sir Charles stood and extended a hand to Thomas. It was dry and cold. "So, Mr Donohue, how do you know my son?"

"Just met him in a bar and got chatting." Thomas deliberately didn't use any name or title when talking to Murston senior.

"Typical Charlie," Sir Charles said, "he'll pick up anyone. Tell me a bit about yourself."

"Charlie's already called my lawyer in Dublin. I represent a group of investors, myself included, and we have funds available immediately for the right sort of opportunities. He says you're looking for tranches of 10 million Euro with a guaranteed return in a few days of 40 per cent. I can do that. You can have the money by lunchtime if we sign a contract before then. I don't want or need to know any further details, not about the stock being bought or the clients you're going to sell it on to. My associates and I will give you the benefit of the doubt, and if this works out we'll be interested in working together again. What do you say?"

Sir Charles looked at the Irishman, sizing him up. "Have you done much in Russia before, Mr Donohue?"

"It's Thomas, if you like. No, not Russia. We've tended to do more in Latin America, the Caribbean and West Africa. We like big returns and are prepared to take a risk where necessary. To be honest a 10 million Euro investment is a bit small-time for us, but with the short time scale I'm happy to do it as a trial."

Sir Charles nodded. He sat down, inviting Thomas to do the same.

"I'll have the contract drawn up. What is the name of the other party?"

"Just me, Thomas Donohue. My address will be that of the law firm I gave Charlie. I move around a lot. Once we've signed I'll give my lawyer a call and get the money moved to your account. You can get the account details to pay the profits into from my lawyers as well. I don't know where I'll be next week, I've other deals going on that need me to be more hands on."

Sir Charles spoke quietly into his desk phone. They chatted casually over more coffee until a young man appeared with a sheaf of papers. Thomas scanned the contract, initialling where necessary and signing at the bottom. The young man witnessed his signature. Sir Charles Murston signed it too and had his secretary witness it. The two men shook hands.

Thomas pulled out his mobile and called a Dublin number. He issued instructions to the person on the other end to transfer 10 million Euro immediately to Murston Asset Management's Euro account, the details of which he gave.

"Now, Charlie mentioned lunch," Thomas said.

Chapter 29

While Thomas Donohue was dressing up for his morning in the City, Julia Kelso was dressing down for her morning at Lippitts Hill in Epping Forest. After her encounter with one of Kuznetsov's men Julia had spoken to her Assistant Commissioner about her own security. He had agreed that she should be armed for the duration, but insisted that she have some additional training and accept an official car with an armed driver. She agreed. She arrived at the Met Police firearms training centre in the back of a black Jaguar wearing jeans and a sweatshirt, with a change of clothes and a wash bag in a backpack. In Scotland she had been a top-flight firearms officer, so the concept of a day of running around, shooting and fighting was not new to her. By early afternoon the instructors were happy that she was more than up to standard and they issued her with her own Glock pistol and enough ammunition to deal with most eventualities.

While the instructors were satisfied Julia was not. From the car she called Justin Evans at Vauxhall Cross. Any chance of a weekend workout, just a refresher, with the boys in Hereford? He agreed immediately and said she should divert to Northolt where a helicopter would be departing for Stirling Lines at 5pm. He would be on it too. Julia told her driver, a grumpy-looking police constable with a large bulge under his left armpit, to go to RAF Northolt, leave her there and go home. She would call him with a pickup time, either Sunday evening or Monday morning. He grumbled something about overtime, which Julia ignored.

They touched down in Hereford just after 6pm. Julia was allocated senior officer's guest quarters and invited to dinner in the Mess. It was a civilised and unusually abstemious affair as the unit at the base was the on-call team and they had to be ready to deploy at a moment's notice. Julia turned in early and slept well until she was woken at 6.30 by a steward with a tray of coffee and a light breakfast. "CO's compliments, ma'am. Could you be ready for training to start at 07.30?"

And start it did. As with most SAS training it was live firing, no blanks or wax bullets, apart from the simulated attacks in which Julia would need to shoot back at the SAS troopers, and it was tough. Julia didn't stop all day. She impressed the SAS instructors with her fitness, stamina, judgement and skill, both with weapons and in unarmed combat. They did the same again on Sunday, and by the time she collapsed exhausted onto the bed in her quarters on Sunday afternoon Julia felt much more confident about her chances if she came across another of Kuznetsov's apes, or even the man himself.

She and Justin flew back to Northolt on Sunday evening. He declined a lift, kissed her on the cheek and said she had done well. The grumpy constable dropped her back at Dolphin Square, and Julia spent the rest of the evening relaxing. She phoned Mel while she wallowed in a warm bath.

"What have you been up to Kelso?" Mel demanded. "I've been calling you all weekend. And Thomas too. I thought you'd run away together."

"I've been having fun with the army," Jake said.

"What, all of it? My god, I've created a monster!"

"Cow! No, just the SAS. They've been giving me some additional training in case I meet another Ukrainian. I'm now a super-trained killer, so mind what you say." Julia raised a leg out of the water and looked at the many grey marks on her pale skin.

"They do play rough, though; I'm one massive bruise. I'll be in trousers all week. What have you been up to?"

"Since I had no one to play with I have been at work all weekend, crunching phone data and Sigint reports. It looks like Kuznetsov's remaining team – there are only three left besides him now – made it to London. The phone which we think is Kuznetsov's was in touch with three others in quick succession, but we didn't get what was said as the warrant got stuck somewhere. We may be able to get something from Cheltenham, though. Anyway, the new numbers are now all dead, as is Kuznetsov's phone, so it's back to square one. Kuznetsov's phone was located in the City when it contacted the others, but that's no help to us. The others were dotted about all over London, seemingly at or near train stations. I'll let Raj have the details, such as they are, first thing tomorrow if you want to go after CCTV.

"Nothing new on the laptops. Cheltenham have been doing well and have recovered quite a few deleted emails. They show that Kuznetsov's team was

212

distributing the cocaine as we thought, but not why. They also show that Kuznetsov and his boys were targeting specific dealers, some of whom have been 'eliminated'. It seems that someone was providing the names and numbers of the ones to go after. I doubt that the team members would have known why they were doing it. Just following orders."

Julia chipped in "Justin told me that Mr Yellow, as everyone is calling him, is doing the name, rank and serial number thing. They gave him a few pills to loosen him up, but he just kept saying the same things over and over. Justin thinks he doesn't know anything significant, but apparently he mumbled something about a beautiful rose, whatever that means. They're going to keep working on him while they decide what to do with him. Where's Thomas?"

"I have absolutely no idea. I spoke to him on Thursday. He has a suspicion that whoever is behind this whole thing might have financial connections with Russia or Ukraine. He came up with a list of possibles, but nothing looks compelling for now. He does seem to be focussing on Murston Asset Management. It's a fairly small outfit, family run. The current chairman is a sitting MP and a former Home Office minister, so completely out of bounds. I asked Hugh's lot if they knew anything, but they just went quiet on me. You might want to chat him up tomorrow. I'll keep digging.

"For now, it seems that the cocaine distribution has come to a stop. If Kuznetsov has recalled his remaining troops it could be that it is all over, which would be a relief."

Julia thought for a moment.

"I doubt it somehow. I think I'll keep up the pressure on other dealers. Until we know why this is being done I want things to remain unsettled, I want the cocaine trade to stay broken. Let's try to catch up during the week, even if it is just by phone. And let me know what Thomas is up to when you get hold of him. Sleep well." She hung up.

As Julia hung up the phone Mel wondered why she hadn't mentioned that she had spent Saturday night with Sven. She supposed she would tell Jake and Thomas sooner or later, it wasn't supposed to be a secret. Being with the two of them was a joy, but their lack of experience in bed did show through. Mel wanted a night as a pupil again, rather than a teacher. Sven had done the job very nicely, and she was still tingling.

Meanwhile, Thomas was in another bath at his hotel. Lunch with the Murstons on Friday had been interesting. After signing the contract Murston senior was clearly delighted to get a call saying that 10 million Euro had arrived in the firm's account from a bank in Ireland. Sir Charles told his secretary to have Artur bring the car to the front of the building, and then to book a table for three at his club. Sir Charles, Charlie and Thomas rode down in the lift to the lobby. The Rolls Royce was waiting, Kuznetsov standing by the open rear passenger door. Sir Charles told Charlie to get in the front next to Artur so he could talk to Thomas in the back. The car purred off through the lunchtime traffic towards St James's.

Sir Charles was chatting to Thomas, some probing gentle background questions that he was able to answer easily without giving anything away that he didn't want to. In the front Charlie asked Artur where the other driver, Kolya, was.

"He is sick," growled Artur, "I will get another one to drive on Monday."

The club was not to Thomas's taste. It was brash, loud and full of braying money-men. They were shown to a reasonably quiet table. Thomas and Sir Charles had a glass of champagne each, while Charlie started on the gin and tonics. The food was quite good, potted shrimps, sole meunière, fruit salad, all washed down with a decent Sancerre.

"I'm sorry to dash, Thomas, but I have constituency business to see to, then a dinner tonight. It's always amused me that a Member of Parliament or a Minister can spend all week dealing with great matters of state, and then have to feign interest in Mrs Miggins' dog shit problem on a Friday afternoon. I shall be quite glad to give it all up! I'll be going to Hampshire tomorrow for the rest of the weekend, such as it is. Why don't you come too, if you're not too busy. Artur is off this weekend, we could motor down together in the morning."

"Thank you, Charles, I'd like that. I 'm at a bit of a loose end until Monday."

"Excellent. Come to the house in Chelsea around 10.30." Sir Charles gave him the address, which Thomas already knew.

"Grand. See you then. Have a good trip Charlie. See you next week."

Sir Charles went off in the Rolls Royce with Kuznetsov. Charlie, having extracted his weekend case from the boot, hailed a cab for the airport. Thomas strolled thoughtfully up St James towards Piccadilly, pleased with his day's work.

The following morning he took a cab to Chelsea and rang Sir Charles Murston's doorbell at 10.30 sharp. The man himself opened it. He looked fresh and rested.

"Most punctual, Thomas. A quick coffee before we go?"

Once they were settled with their coffee in the drawing room Sir Charles said " I hope you don't mind me asking, but would you mind driving? We're taking the Rolls, of course. These days I find I get a headache when I drive for too long. It may be that I need better glasses, but in all honesty I'm just as happy being driven."

"I'd be delighted. It's a fine motor car."

"Aficionados call them 'proper motor cars', and rightly so. That is until the bloody Germans bought Rolls Royce and Bentley. Mine is one of the last real Rolls Royce cars, hand built by British craftsmen, with British made engines. The current models are just jumped up Volkswagens and BMWs."

"I'm afraid the Britishness of them isn't a winning point where I come from, if you forgive me saying so. In Ireland the cars have a great following, but that's for their quality, and the fact that they made bloody good armoured cars to use against the British occupying us." Thomas was seeing how far he could push Murston.

216

Sir Charles threw his head back and roared with laughter.

"Just my luck! A rich Fenian. I look forward to some serious, booze-fuelled debate on the Irish question with you this evening. Let's go!"

In the car Thomas asked about Sir Charles's career in politics, his time in government, his interest in Russia. To his surprise he was almost warming to the Patrician who made his living collecting crumbs dropped from other people's money.

"Tell me, Thomas, you mentioned that you had business interests in Latin America, the Caribbean, and West Africa, was it?"

"Not interests so much, but we do business in those places. There's good money to be made."

"Which parts of Latin America, specifically?"

"The northern part of South America mostly, Venezuela, Colombia, places like that."

"Aren't those areas very risky? Dangerous for foreigners?"

"You should know the answer to that, Charles. Where there's a profit there's risk. The more risk, the more profit. We're not boy scouts, you know. We can do the staring each other out in smoke filled rooms bit with the best of them. And anything else that's needed. Are you thinking of doing anything down that way yourself?"

"Possibly. Possibly quite soon. If I did, would you be available?"

"For what? How do you mean available? I'm not a person for hire, if that's what you mean."

"Good grief, no. Sorry. I didn't mean to offend. If something does materialise I would imagine a partnership. Equals at the very least."

"Let's not get ahead of ourselves, Charles. Of course, I'll listen to any proposal and decide if I, or rather we, are interested. But only after this trial run has played out. If your boy Charlie comes back with four million profit for me on Wednesday, we can talk about doing something else. Maybe."

Sir Charles sat back and pondered. He wasn't used to the robust approach that Thomas Donohue was adopting. But he did have to admit that the man had a certain presence and charm, as well as a likely mean streak. He could be just what was needed for Phase 3, especially if he had connections in Colombia and the Caribbean, as he implied.

They arrived at the Murston estate and spent a very enjoyable afternoon and evening in the company of Lady Murston. Thomas borrowed a willing Labrador and took a long walk around the estate, making a lot of mental notes.

On Sunday afternoon Thomas drove Sir Charles back to London in the Rolls. Instead of going to the house in Chelsea Sir Charles directed Thomas to a nearby mews and told him to stop outside a small house with a garage underneath.

"Artur will put the car away later. I'll just stroll back to the house." Sir Charles took the keys from Thomas. "Come to the office tomorrow afternoon. I'll tell you how the Moscow deal went, and maybe we can talk further. Say 2pm?"

Thomas agreed. He said goodbye and walked through the quiet Sunday streets of Chelsea back to Grosvenor Square. He had a few beers and took the rest of the day off.

Chapter 30

Early on Monday morning Thomas called Mel. She was still at home finishing breakfast.

"What have you been up to, then?" she asked him.

"I was enjoying a weekend in the country. You?"

"Pig! I was slaving away. Kelso went off to play at being a soldier, you buggered off, so I went to work."

"Why was Kelso playing soldiers?"

"She was bothered by that guy that Kuznetsov sent after her. She went for some extra training at Hereford in case he sends another one. The one she saw is a guest of SIS now but saying nothing at all. Kuznetsov has recalled his remaining team to London, there are just three of them plus him now. We're getting some patchy comms from them, but always a couple of days behind. I located the phone that Kuznetsov used to talk to the guy he sent after Kelso somewhere in the City but can't narrow it down further than the Liverpool Street area. It's been dumped now anyway.

"It looks like the cocaine distribution has been halted for now. No more obvious overdoses over the weekend. Mind you, Jake's just about wiped out cocaine use across the UK anyway. What are you thinking?"

"I'm not sure. I might be onto something, but I can't say just yet. Did you get anything on Murston?"

"No. The firm's boss is off-limits, as you know. The company doesn't have much of a reputation, good or bad. It's minor league in the international finance world. It does quite a lot in Russia, although, some of it is pretty close to the wind, but then the financial press say that just about anything in Russia is like that."

"Can you do me a favour, Mel? Ask Cheltenham to report anything at all they hear about Murston to you, the company or anything to do with the name."

"I will if you tell me why."

"They're doing something dodgy with the Moscow stock market, doing it today. Don't ask how I know. It would be handy to know what it is and what the reaction is. I need another favour, too."

"Of course you do."

"Do you have anyone you trust who knows Colombia?"

"I do. NCIS is full of them."

"I need to talk to one of them. Can you fix it? It would be good if it was this evening. I can find a place where we can talk."

"Why am I getting nervous about this, Alf, Thomas, whoever? What are you up to?"

"I'll tell you as soon as I can. Promise. Send me a text if this evening's on." He hung up.

Thomas went out to Selfridges and bought himself a reasonably smart waterproof jacket with large patch pockets. Back in the hotel he opened the room safe and took the Makarov pistol out of its packaging. He tested the mechanism and loaded the two magazines, inserting one in the pistol. He racked it and put the safety catch on. The small handgun fitted neatly and unobtrusively in the side pocket of his new jacket. He put the spare magazine in the other pocket. He felt he needed some protection if he was in the vicinity of Artur Kuznetsov. Now his face was known it was unlikely that Kuznetsov would be overly suspicious of him, but who knew?

His next stop was Scott's, the famous fish restaurant in Mount Street. It was early and there were no customers in yet. He booked a private dining room for that evening, leaving a hefty deposit. Then he took a stroll back towards the mews in Chelsea where he had left the Rolls Royce the day before. There was a small café opposite one end of the mews with a couple of tables on the pavement. He sat at one of them and ordered coffee and croissants. He had a clear view of the mews, and it was a nice morning. He picked up a discarded newspaper and pretended to read it while keeping an eye on the mews house where, he assumed, the Rolls Royce was garaged. He had been there almost an hour and was on his second coffee when he saw one of the Ukrainians. He had the same stocky, muscular physique as Kuznetsov. He had a grim unhappy expression. He was wearing nondescript dark clothing and was carrying a supermarket carrier bag. Thomas didn't know it, but he was looking at Mr Blue, *Gospodin Seenii*, and he was in a bad mood because he had been sent out to do the shopping for the other two, Pink and Black (*Rosavyi and Chornyi*), like he was an errand boy. Mr Blue unlocked the small door beside the garage and went in. The three mercenaries were now based in the mews house, unbeknown to either of the Murstons. Their task for the next few days was a tedious one. While one of them kept watch from a window, the other two would carefully be weighing and mixing two types of white powder. The powder in the plastic box on the

222

left was to be mixed with the powder in the plastic box on the right one measure to two. The mixing was done on a sheet of clear glass laid on a table using a sharp blade to make sure the powder was smooth, fine and well mixed. The powder on the left was strychnine, a tasteless and odourless poison used in pest control. The powder on the right was 97per cent pure cocaine. There was a kilo of strychnine and two of cocaine. It had to be weighed and measured out in 10 gram portions, each to be sealed in a small plastic envelope. The work was fiddly and time-consuming, and the two packing at any one time had to wear eye protectors, facemasks and latex gloves. Hot and sweaty work, but they were getting well paid, weren't they?

Thomas finished his coffee and left. He was sure he was onto the hideout being used by Kuznetsov's team. He would let Jake know as soon as the time was right. He made his way to the City, adopting some neat anti-surveillance moves, just in case. He didn't see any sign of a tail. He took the tube from Sloane Square to Westminster, and from there he boarded a river bus to Tower Pier. He lost himself among the tourists for a while before cutting through the back streets towards Fenchurch Street. He arrived at Murston's offices at 2pm precisely. He went up in the lift and announced himself. There was no sign of Kuznetsov.

Sir Charles came to greet Thomas, a wide grin on his face. He took Thomas into his office, where a bottle of champagne was chilling in an ice bucket.

"I take it things have gone well, Charles," Thomas said.

"Things have gone excellently. The boy Charlie did something right for a change. He managed to acquire the stock at a really good price, partly because of the Euro / Rouble exchange rate but also by using a wide range of brokers rather than just the usual one. Charlie means well, but he can be a bit lazy, sadly. The broker he normally uses is watched like a hawk. As soon as he starts to trade the whole market joins in and the prices shoot up. Our usual trader is quite pissed off that we've used others this time, but he'll get over it. So, we've actually acquired 15 per cent more stock than we were bargaining for. The buying client is delighted and has taken it all at the agreed price. That means that your 4 million profit is now 4.6 million, a 46 per cent return in the space of a weekend. Not bad at all! It will be in your account in Dublin on Wednesday morning." Sir Charles popped open the champagne. Thomas accepted a glass with a broad smile.

"Well done, Charles. I briefed my associates and they're watching with interest. They'll be pleased." The two men each had another glass, and Sir Charles looked at his watch.

"Charlie will be back tomorrow afternoon. I have some other things to attend to this afternoon, so why don't we regroup later? If not tomorrow, then Wednesday? Actually, Wednesday will be better. Here at 3pm? We can check that everything's gone through smoothly and then make an evening of it."

Thomas agreed. "If everything goes through smoothly, the evening will be on me. See you on Wednesday."

Thomas was grateful for the extra time. He would need it to bone up on Latin America, where he had never been in his life.

He sent Mel a text. She responded immediately, saying she had found a willing victim.

He replied 'Scott's Mount Street 7.30 dinner. Ask for Mr Donohue's private room.'

He got a reply. 'flash git!' it said.

Chapter 31

As Thomas Donohue made his way back to Grosvenor Square, the missing Mr Brown, *Gospodin Kareechnivyi*, was having a very bad day. He had had nothing but bad days since his partner had been killed. His footsore quest for a friendly face and a language he could understand had gone quite well, at least initially. It had taken many hours to find the huge park in the middle of the city, to the north of which was the area he sought, Lancaster Gate.

His heart was lifted as he saw the red, white and blue flag of Russia flying proudly above the mansion next to the park. A fitting place for it, he thought. He tried to approach the Embassy but was stopped by heavily armed police officers. They were asking if he had an appointment, and of course he hadn't. He made off before they started asking for his papers. He tried to find a place to sit and watch, just in case he saw anyone he knew from the FSB or one of the other services. He didn't know it, but his efforts were being watched by others, the British, Americans, Chinese, anyone who kept a close eye on the Russian Embassy and its personnel. His image would be sent later that day or that week to the various headquarters, and sooner or later one or other of them would identify him for what he was – a fugitive war criminal. But Mr Brown knew nothing of this.

He found a bar nearby. He heard the familiar sound of Russian being spoken. He relaxed. He ordered vodka. Although he was disappointed by the minuscule measure, at least it was ice-cold. He ordered more and handed over some of his British bank notes. Before long a pretty Russian girl joined him. He bought her champagne. She chatted to him and stroked his thigh. He drank more vodka. The pretty Russian girl, who had rightly clocked the man getting rapidly drunk as Ukrainian and therefore a member of the lower orders, invited him back to her place for 'a real drink'. Mr Brown readily accepted. It was a short walk to her apartment block. She showed him in, and poured him a proper glass of vodka, followed by another, one which had a special flavour, she said.

Mr Brown woke up the next day lying in a street, he didn't know where. He had no jacket, no wallet, and not even his shoes – shoes in which he had stashed some of his money. His head ached. He had no idea where he was. He tried to stand but fell over.

He was hauled to his feet by two men in dark blue uniforms. They put handcuffs on him and put him in the back of a white van. At the police station he was searched and put in a cell. His Special Forces training, such as it was, kicked in and he refused to speak or say anything. Being considered a simple drunk the police didn't take his fingerprints or DNA, and when they became bored with him they gave him a pair of someone else's ill-fitting trainers and threw him back out into the street.

Mr Brown was perplexed, and then slightly pleased, by the fact that every time he sat down in a doorway to rest his painful feet someone threw some money at him. Not much, but enough to get a hot drink or a sandwich to eat. He survived like this for the next few days, but then realised he would need to devise a strategy to get home. He wandered the streets looking for anything that could be a Ukrainian Embassy. He had given up on the Russian one. He wandered, but based himself in the area of Holland Park, it being a place where people seemed charitable, if not overly friendly. Once or twice people approached him, hostile people, but most saw that he had nothing left to steal so they left him alone. One young man pushed him too far and was startled to find that this scruffy looking tramp could actually look after himself.

Then, that Monday Mr Brown found himself in a small park near a busy road. He dozed on a bench, footsore and utterly exhausted. He was getting sick, coughing, dizzy, sweating. He looked up across the road. He couldn't believe his eyes. There on the front of a grand building across the road was the blue and yellow flag of Ukraine! Mr Brown picked himself up off the bench and trotted towards the magical flag. It was the last thing he saw. As he stepped out to cross the road he looked to his left, the wrong way. The delivery truck hit him at 30 miles an hour and killed him instantly. It would be several months before his identity became known, by which time his body would have been placed in an unmarked grave in a remote untended corner of Kensal Green cemetery, thousands of miles from his home.

Chapter 32

On Monday evening Artur Kuznetsov returned the Rolls Royce to the mews garage. He went upstairs to check on progress. The team had wound up for the day and were demolishing a microwaved supper. They had a brief conversation. Mr White was still keen that the pretty policewoman be eliminated. Artur had told him that he couldn't risk any more of his team, already at half-strength, and it would have to wait until all the preparations for Phase 2B were complete. In short, the policewoman or the operation, his choice.

Sir Charles had reluctantly agreed with Kuznetsov. She would have to wait. He would need to rely on Phase 2B to have the price impact needed for the operation to succeed. The street price of cocaine had to crash, and crash big. Sir Charles and Artur eventually agreed to deal with the policewoman once Phase 2B was all set to go, and they also agreed a fee of £500,000 sterling. It was a huge amount of money for a single hit, even on a senior police officer, but clearly Mr White had no idea what the going rate was.

Kuznetsov briefed the remnants of his team. They had three more days to weigh and pack all the 300 bags needed for Phase 2B. Mr White had said that Charlie would be responsible for placing the bags with users, with the help of Kuznetsov and one team member. Mr Black had been nominated. The remaining two, Mr Blue and Mr Pink, would have one more task to do before they stood down, and that was to eliminate the policewoman. She was Commander Kelso of Scotland Yard. She lived in a place called

Dolphin Square, near the river. Kuznetsov had a photograph taken from a TV news broadcast. It showed an attractive young blonde woman in the uniform of a police Commander looking serious and determined as she described the threat posed by contaminated cocaine which, she had said, was being deliberately planted to take lives. Mr Pink asked Kuznetsov why she was important, not that it mattered, just curious. Kuznetsov told him that Mr White knew that this woman was coordinating police activity all over the country that was jeopardising the success of the operation. If she continued the operation would fail – they would fail. So she had to go, at the end of next week - once Phase 2B was ready to go but not yet initiated. Mr Pink and Mr Blue nodded. It was just a job, even if she was very pretty. They asked if they could have some time alone with her, maybe kidnap her for a while and have some fun, before killing her? The boss said no, too risky. Just kill her.

******

Thomas arrived early at Scott's and sat alone and tranquil in the private room he had reserved. The table was set for three. He ordered a malt whisky and waited. At 7.30 exactly Mel entered, accompanied by another woman of a similar age. The companion was shorter than Mel, quite a lot shorter. She had jet black hair and olive skin and was really quite plump. Mel kissed Thomas on the cheek.

"Thomas, this is Cristina. Cristina, Thomas." They shook hands.

"Hiya Thomas."

He had been expecting a Spanish or South American accent, but he got Liverpool.

"Cristina's mum is Colombian, her dad isn't. He's a customs officer, as is Cristina. She's worked in Bogota and Caracas, as well as Jamaica and in Spain. She's on the NCIS cocaine team, and she's a mate. Are you going to get us a drink?" Mel sat down.

Thomas ordered drinks, gin and tonic for Mel, rum and coke for Cristina and another single malt for himself. Both women's drinks were downed quickly so he ordered two more.

"Mel said you wanted to talk about Colombia, but wouldn't say why. Just said to trust you, and make sure that you spent an awful lot on a posh dinner and loads of booze," Cristina grinned. "So what are you then? Some sort of trainee spy or a reporter or something?"

Thomas had given a few moments thought to this line of questioning. "I'm writing a book about drug trafficking," he said.

"Jesus, not another one!" Cristina groaned. "Please try to make it a good one for a change."

"I'll do my best, I promise," Thomas said. Mel was smiling quietly.

"So, what do you want to know? You can tell me while I look for something outrageously expensive on the menu." Cristina opened the menu and whistled quietly when she saw the prices.

"Two things, really," Thomas said, "firstly a picture of regular life in Bogota and a couple of other cities in Colombia, maybe Medellin, Cartagena or Barranquilla.

Then something about how cocaine prices are worked out, what happens if the market changes?"

"Not much, then. I'm going to start with scallops, then grilled plaice, off the bone, with a beurre blanc sauce. And a decent white, none of your Italian rubbish. And another rum and coke. Mel?"

"Sounds good. I'll have the same. I think a Montrachet would work. And another gin and tonic."

Thomas glared at her. He pressed the bell for a waiter and placed the order, getting another malt for himself too. The place was pricey, but what the heck? He had already made about four million quid that day.

Cristina started. "Everyone thinks that Colombia is nothing but drugs. In fact drugs are a minor part of Colombian life. It's a cultured commercial and industrial country, or it will be once the politics get sorted out. Most Colombians are more bothered by politics than narcotics, even the so-called narco-terrorists. The Americans invented the term. They, the Americans, spend billions trashing Colombia and hunting down 'narco-terrorists' when they would be better off persuading their own people to stop snorting up tons of coke. US allies, including the UK and most European countries, are now doing the same as the Americans, going after the problem 'upstream'. It's easier politically to shift the blame somewhere else rather than accept that the domestic demand drives the upstream supply, not the other way round.

"So, Bogota is a high-altitude city. It makes for a nice climate mostly, but it can get awfully hot in the summer. It has great galleries and museums, a very Europeanised café culture, good food and bars. It's a great place to live, especially as a foreigner. It's very safe, too, apart from the kidnap risk. Sadly kidnapping is almost a national sport; it affects all aspects of Colombian society from the richest to the poorest. There's always someone poorer than the next guy, and kidnapping or stealing from someone even slightly less poor than you is seen as OK. If a rich person is kidnapped they have a very slim chance of being returned to their family alive. The lower down the wealth chain you go the better the chances of survival and a safe return. There are reasons for this, but let's not go there for now.

"Medellin is north of Bogota and lower down. It is a bit more tropical, but it also has quite a nice climate. Never too hot and never ever cold, and it's very gradually turning into a nice city. You've probably heard of the Medellin cartel and yes, it does exist and yes, it is a powerful force in the area. Less powerful than it was when Pablo Escobar was alive, and still more powerful than the government, but that's changing slowly as corruption gets rooted out of the police and the military, and the government of course. Medellin is still not a place to hang out if you're not from round there. With Escobar running the show Medellin was the most dangerous place in the world. Since he was killed, what is it, nine or ten years ago, life's a lot more peaceful. Everyone's still a bit edgy, though. But these days there is a normal day-to-day life for the *Medellinense*, that's what they're called. There is a lot of industry – textiles mostly – and engineering. There's a good metro system and a lot of money is going into social investment projects. It's a rich buzzing place but I'd give it a few more years before putting it on your holiday wish-list.

"The coastal area. Cartagena is very scenic and very touristy. Historic too. It's been inhabited for about 6,000 years and archaeologists love it. It's been popular with the upper classes forever, and when life up-country gets a bit crazy people flock to Cartagena. It's safe. It has an old walled colonial city at its heart. Good hotels and night-life too. It has a massive port, one of the biggest in Latin America, so commerce is important. But the city isn't too big, around a million people, and only growing slowly. Being on the Caribbean coast it's a popular destination, tropical climate, good beaches and amenities. It's also quite handy if you're shipping coke too. It's a short and easy hop up to Jamaica and the other islands, and on into the US. A lot of speedboats, known as go-fasts, take loads of coke north from the Cartagena and Barranquilla areas.

"Barranquilla is a much bigger place. It's also a major port and important for internal river transport inside Colombia. It's a bit like Marseille, I suppose. It was a rough place once, really rough, and dangerous too. Now it's on the up, like most of Colombia. It's more tropical than Cartagena, hotter and steamier.

"I don't know why I'm bothering to tell you all this. It's all in this book." Cristina delved into a capacious bag and pulled out a travel guide to Colombia. She also pulled out a slim folder.

"This is the liaison officer manual for Colombia. It sets out a lot of the dos and don'ts, stuff about traffic, emergency services, hospitals, shops, currency, you name it. Fill your boots, but don't tell anyone I gave it to you."

Cristina paused as the first course was served. The scallops vanished, along with the first bottle of Montrachet.

"Yummy," she said, "now, what was the second bit? Coke pricing, wasn't it."

"Yes. How fixed is the price of a shipment? If there's a major market upheaval, what happens to stuff that's already on the way to Europe, for example."

"Interesting," said Cristina, "essentially all coke is dealt on a cash on delivery basis, at every stage. Nobody pays up front until they have control of the stuff. That puts a bit of a stabiliser on the upstream supply price. The closer the stuff gets to the market the more susceptible it is to price fluctuation. This can be managed within normal price ranges by adjusting quality. The lower the price the weaker the gear. There's only a certain market range for consumer prices so dealers need to be quite good at mental arithmetic to work out what strength they can get away with and still turn a profit.

"A lot of shippers buy for a specific market, normally where they have the infrastructure to distribute the stuff to end-users. The major cartels have more flexibility as to where they can place their gear. Smaller players are more restricted; they usually have to sell in their home territory, so they'd be affected by localised price variations more than the big boys.

"The overdoses in recent weeks in the UK were starting to have quite a strong downward influence on price as demand dropped, but it was local, only in the UK. The blitz on dealers stopped that dead by practically eliminating downstream supply, but it has served to keep the upstream price stable. Had the blitz not happened I think we would have seen the bottom fall out of a big chunk of the domestic coke market, and that would have hit the upstream price.

"So, what would happen to stuff already paid for that was in transit or just hitting the market? I think that the middlemen would want to get whatever they could for their cargos as far upstream as they could. The closer to the end user you get the higher the risk of total losses. It would have to be a big price shift though, there's a big enough margin in the midstream for the middlemen to take a reasonable hit and average it out over time, or to divert the cargo to a different market. If there was a fifty or even forty percent drop in market prices I think there would be some panicking. Cargos would be offloaded to other middlemen at rock bottom prices, but they, the buyers, would have to be prepared to take the risk. Not many of the major players would take up the slack in a falling market. Cocaine has a relatively short shelf-life and its value deteriorates anyway. Nobody wants to be left with a whole load of worthless but very costly dust."

"Are there other middlemen along the route who would pick up cargos en route? If so, where are they?" Thomas asked, once the main course and more wine arrived.

"He's quite nosy, isn't he, Mel? Well, it all depends on the routing and the price. The price holds up best on the lower risk routings, the routes where there might be a higher chance of losing your gear but the monetary value is relatively small. So that's your stuffers and swallowers from Jamaica, your greedy tourists willing to risk everything by bringing a few kilos ashore in their luggage, airport baggage handlers getting bags onto passenger planes - it's called ripping-on - but it's small stuff. The major lower-risk routes, meaning high value but with a lower risk of detection and seizure, into Europe, traditionally, would be big shipments. By big I mean over a tonne, in containers or on small boats crossing the Atlantic into the Iberian peninsula, the Galician coast or Portugal these days, or to a major port in Holland or the UK. To get to the UK from mainland Europe the stuff is put on trucks, with or without the knowledge of hauliers and drivers, and it comes across on a ferry or through the tunnel. Other up and coming European routes are through Albania, southern Italy or even Greece. Coke destined for the UK is coming on all these routes. The organisations involved in these shipments are well-established and well-funded, often by the upstream cartels. They could absorb a hefty price fluctuation, for a while.

"If you wanted to find cheap cargos, or people to buy them, you'd have to look at what I call the entrepreneurial routes, those being used by chancers trying to get in on the market. Cargos on these routes tend to be smaller, one or two hundred kilos, sometimes up to half a tonne. These get across the Atlantic on the shortest, fastest, and riskiest routes. If you look at a map the shortest route across is from

237

somewhere in Brazil to the Gulf of Guinea, but we've seen some traffickers shipping their cargos on small, very fast ex-naval boats from the Caribbean to Cape Verde or São Tomé. These boats can do 40 or 50 knots all the way, and they are not comfortable. But they are quite cheap. Even with the extra fuel needed you can still get half a tonne on board, and there are loads of places to hide in West Africa once you get to Cape Verde. There are always Nigerians coming up from the Niger Delta on coasters who are willing to pick up spare, damaged or abandoned cargos. There's a small but growing consumer market for cocaine in West Africa, and also well-established trade and transport routes up to Europe. The Nigerians know them all inside out."

"So," said Thomas, "if you want to get your hands on cast-off cocaine West Africa would be the place to do it?"

"Yes," Cristina replied, "but you make it sound easy. It isn't. The chances of an outsider getting ripped-off and killed are massive. Law-enforcement is weak, to say the least, and you'd be on your own. Loads of people will offer to sell you protection in West Africa, and it'll be very good right up until the moment you need it. Then it will vanish."

They finished eating. Thomas was thoughtful. He thanked Cristina profusely, offered and ordered nightcaps for them all, and paid the eyewatering bill. Afterwards he hailed a cab for them all. They dropped Cristina first at Charing Cross. Alone in the cab Thomas kissed Mel warmly.

238

"Raynes Park, please driver," Mel told the cabbie, kissing Thomas back.

Chapter 33

When they got to Mel's flat Thomas tried to kiss her again. She pushed him away, gently.

"Drink first," she said.

Mel went to the kitchen and poured herself a glass of white, him a large scotch. She handed him the glass.

"Are you going to tell me what's going on, what you're up to? You keep asking disconcerting questions; you were asking Cristina all kinds of weird stuff. What are you doing? Are you going into coke trafficking or something?" Mel took a long slug of wine. "Fuck it, I need gin! I blame it on Kelso," she said.

When she came back Thomas was looking pensive.

"The thing is, Mel, I don't really know what I'm doing. I've an idea about what's going on, but I just don't know for sure. I just really don't know. If I tell you and Jake what I've found out to date she'll have to do something, it's her job. And if I don't tell you and Jake I could fuck it all up."

"Alf, Thomas, whoever. This is me you're talking to, Mel Dunn! I'm an intelligence analyst. I talk and listen to crap all day long for a living. Just fucking tell me what you think is going on! Then I can help you decide what, if and when to tell Jake."

"OK," he paused for a few seconds, "what I think is going on is this: Sir Charles Murston, MP, former minister of state for something or other, is into dodgy financial dealings. I know he's doing border-line, if not totally, illegal, money stuff in Russia. I think he's hired the team of Ukrainian mercenaries to help him and his

240

idiotic son manipulate the UK cocaine market with a view to crashing the street value of coke to next to nothing. His aim is to then buy up cocaine shipments in transit at really low prices and release them onto the UK streets as soon as the demand recovers. His strategy, partially successful so far, has been to obtain high-grade cocaine and release it onto the market. To do this he needed to take out established dealer networks. I don't know exactly how he identified them, but I'd imagine the boy Charlie might have had something to do with it. He moves in those sort of circles. Murston replaced selected dealers with his own people, i.e. the Ukrainians. They pushed virtually pure cocaine to casual users, causing the large number of deaths and serious injuries. His aim was to slash demand for cocaine in the most profitable sector of the market. What he plans to do next I can only guess at."

"And what you've just said isn't a guess?" Mel asked.

"Not entirely. I do know some things."

"Such as?"

"Artur Kuznetsov is acting as Sir Charles Murston's chauffeur. Kuznetsov's goons are, as of this morning, holed up in a Chelsea mews house where the Murston Rolls Royce is garaged. I've just made over 4 million pounds in a dodgy Russian deal engineered by Sir Charles Murston, MP. That is what I know. The rest I am guessing."

"Fucking hell, Ferdinand!" Mel grasped her forehead, "what now?"

"I don't know. I just answered your question. I've a way into the Murston operation. I've got to know Sir

Charles and his son, Charlie. Charlie's been in Moscow doing the deal I bought into, he's due back tomorrow. I'm supposed to meet them on Wednesday to celebrate. I put a few million Euro into the deal – proceeds from the Carlton family business. It seemed appropriate to use it for this. Sir Charles has been gently pumping me about Latin America. I'm planning to let it run and see what happens. That's why Jake can't know what I know for now. She'd have to crash the mews garage right away. I think, actually I'm pretty sure, the immediate risk from the pure cocaine has passed. The next phase will be worse, and I need to know what it is and when it will happen, and what the end game is. I plan to stop it, and to destroy the Murstons, both of them and their little financial operation."

"Can't argue with you, Thomas," Mel said, "I'm just not happy leaving Jake out."

"Think about it, Mel. If I or we told Jake it would put her in an impossible position and the Murstons would probably be able to just walk away, unscathed."

"I suppose you're right. Have another drink while I get ready for bed. Then you can tell me what you want me to do."

She stood and went into the bathroom. The sound of running water followed; Thomas fetched another scotch. When Mel came out she hadn't bothered with a towel. She stood in front of a mirror and dried her wet hair. Thomas sipped his whisky and watched Mel Dunn's naked back and bottom as she moved the hair dryer. When she was done she went back to the bathroom to get one of her long tee-shirts. Now

242

clothed, she sat in a chair opposite him. He reached for her, but she ignored him.

"Do you know what you're doing, Alf?" she asked, using his name from a previous life.

"Honestly? I'm not sure, but it hasn't stopped me before."

"Are we going to bed?" she asked.

"I hope so."

He showered and joined Mel in her bed. She opened her arms to him, and for once she let him take the lead.

"I love you, Mel," Thomas said as he climaxed, and he hugged her tightly.

Mel heard the words but said nothing. She lay beneath Thomas, breathing hard. After a few minutes she tapped his shoulder.

"Suffocating!" she gasped.

He rolled off but kept her close. Their breathing became more even. Mel pushed him away.

"You said it," she stated.

"What?" he asked.

"Cast your mind back to the first time we fucked. I sucked you dry, you licked me beautifully, I fucked you until you thought you were going to die. In the night I fucked you again, and then for afters I blew you senseless. Do you remember all that?"

"How could I forget?"

"And then what? What did I say to you?"

"You said I would never own you, you would never be owned by me. You said that I could never assume any rights over you."

"And?"

243

"You said I could never say I love you."

"And you just said?"

"I love you."

"Why?"

"Because I do, I think."

"What does it mean, Alf, Thomas, whoever? I don't even know your bloody name."

"It's just a word, Mel."

"No, it isn't. Love is a very powerful and misunderstood word. It messes with people's heads, makes them crazy. It's not *just* a word. What do you mean by it?"

"I mean that I love, or I really like, being with you. I mean that I want to make love to, sorry, to have sex with, you whenever you want me to; that I never want anything bad to happen to you; that I care about you; that I want you to be happy. It doesn't mean I want to own you, I promise. I'm even happy that you have sex with Kelso, and anyone else you want, I think, even it does feel a bit weird."

"So, you like me having sex with Kelso?"

"Yes."

"Do you like having sex with Kelso?"

"Yes."

"So you like having sex with us both?"

"Yes."

"Do you like fucking her more than you like fucking me?"

"Stop it."

"OK, Thomas, whoever. How you say you love me is OK, but just don't say it again - ever. It's how I feel about you and Kelso, and about my group, but I really can't be doing with possession or ownership or exclusivity and any of that emotional shit. I fucked Sven on Saturday night. Does that bother you? He fucked me too, a lot."

"It's not just about the sex, Mel. Sex with you is amazing, mind blowing. I'm slowly getting my head around how you do your life. It's you that I love, as you are and doing what you do. I just want to stay close to you. Is that pathetic?"

Mel smiled at him. "Not pathetic, no. I've been thinking about it, about me and you and Jake, and about me and the group. I think we do all 'love' each other, but in the way you said. But no possession. Ever! Agreed?"

"Yes, please."

"OK. Now, do you want more sex or a cup of cocoa?"

"I'll take the cocoa," he grinned.

"You rude unappreciative bastard!" She threw a pillow at him.

Chapter 34

On Tuesday morning Charlie Murston was in his first-class seat on the BA flight from Moscow to Heathrow. For once he wasn't drinking, but instead was holding an ice pack to the side of his head. His right eye was closed by swelling. His abdomen throbbed from the kicks that had been landed, he still felt nauseous with the pain from his battered testicles. The people who had done this to him made it clear that the deal he had just done was not appreciated by, or in the best interests of, the Russian state. Murston Asset Management would pay dearly for their impertinence as tools of enemies of Russia. If he, Charlie Murston, ever showed his face anywhere in the Russian Federation again he would never leave it alive. The same went for his father. Then they beat and kicked him some more before dumping him like a dead dog on the wet sidewalk at Domodedovo airport. Charlie was in no doubt that they meant every word. Nevertheless, the deal had been done and his father had confirmed that the payment from the buying clients was going through. He just hoped it had been worth it. The flight attendant was concerned about him and asked if he needed a doctor when they landed at Heathrow. Charlie declined politely.

The night before he had celebrated, mostly alone, in his plush hotel in Moscow. After a few drinks in the bar he had a word with the concierge and parted with a large denomination dollar bill. A short while later Irina arrived. He knew her well. She often 'visited' him when he was in Moscow. She liked him, not because of his charisma or his personality, but because he was easy work. He always called for her when he had already had too much to drink, and after she had had a couple of glasses of champagne he would take her to his room. She would undress, administer a very quick blowjob or maybe even just fiddle with him for a while and he would fall asleep snoring. She could then plunder the minibar and order a decent room service dinner, watch TV, take a nice bath and sleep in a comfortable bed until the fat Englishman woke up. Then she would say how wonderful he had been, get dressed and depart a thousand dollars richer. Easy.

So Charlie was feeling pretty good when he checked out and took the hotel courtesy car to the airport. Domodedovo is about 40km south of Moscow city centre, a long haul through the dreary sprawl of Moscow's endless estates of tower blocks and the bleak forests beyond. Charlie dozed in the car. After leaving the city limits the road becomes quieter. Charlie was awoken by the car bumping over rough ground. He started to protest to the driver when his door was pulled open and he was hauled out. Two young men in jeans and leather jackets set to work on him while the hotel chauffeur sat quietly in the car smoking a cigarette. When Charlie was a bloody and muddied wreck and they had delivered their warning he was thrown back into the car and the journey to the airport continued. On arrival the same two men, who had been following in their own vehicle, hauled Charlie out of the car, gave him a final kicking and a slap and threw him to the ground in an oily puddle. His compact suitcase landed beside him, along with his cashmere overcoat. Two airport policemen watched impassively but did not intervene. The two attackers got back in their car, a black VW with Moscow plates, and drove off. A passing American businessman helped Charlie to his feet and into the terminal building, after which he was on his own. At the BA check-in the counter clerk looked at him with distaste, probably assuming he had been out on the town all night - especially as he still smelt strongly of alcohol. He tried to clean himself up as best he could in the first-class lounge toilets but he was still covered in mud and dried blood when the time came to board the flight.

At Heathrow the immigration people looked at him with suspicion. It wasn't that often that they saw a first-class passenger who looked like he had survived a boozy fist-fight followed by a car crash. Charlie made it as far as the taxi rank before his knees buckled and he fell to the floor, vomiting blood. When he eventually came round he was in the Intensive Care Unit at Ashford Hospital.

Sir Charles took a call from the ICU nurse who suggested he might want to get to the hospital a soon as he possibly could. His son had suffered significant internal injuries and would be undergoing complex surgery to assess and repair the damage. He was very ill. For some reason he chose not to use the Rolls but called a taxi. When he got to the hospital Charlie was still in theatre.

******

On Wednesday morning at 11am Thomas turned up at the Murston offices. He was shown into Sir Charles's rooms. Thomas was shocked. The man looked wrecked, his eyes were bloodshot, his tie askew. He hadn't shaved and his hair was greasy.

"Something wrong, Charles?" Thomas asked.

"It's Charlie. He had an accident in Moscow, a car crash I think. He made it back to Heathrow but he collapsed there. I've been with him all night at Ashford Hospital. They operated; he has internal injuries. They say he has a good chance of pulling through, but for now he is in a critical condition."

"Jesus, I'm sorry to hear that, Charles. Should I leave you in peace?"

"No, Thomas. Life and business must go on. Lucy is coming up to town later, but I plan to go back to the hospital before then. Could you come with me? We can talk in the car. No, I think we'll take a taxi. The driver is less likely to be curious than Artur or one of his boys."

"Sure, I can come with you."

They hailed a taxi in the street and set off.

"Who is Artur, Charles, and who are his boys? Tell me to mind my own business if you want, but he doesn't seem your type."

"He's only temporary. He's done some security work for me in Russia over the past few years, and I hired him and his team to help me with a current project. It will soon be over, hopefully, and I won't be sorry to see the back of him. But let's talk about the Moscow deal."

"Yes, let's. I've been following the Moscow press, and stories in the FT about the Russian market. I think you've pulled off a bit of a stunt, Charles."

"Just an inspired move, Thomas. The good news is that the deal was settled in full this morning – the RTS – the Russian Trading System – has a two-day settlement rule like NASDAQ. I was slightly concerned that the payments might be withheld this morning, but it has all gone through. We traded all the stock we bought instantly, the moment we had it, with our buying client, also through the RTS, so payments each way happened early this morning. Your money is winging its way to Dublin as we speak."

"What was the stock, Charles?" Thomas didn't expect a direct answer, which he knew anyway.

"Just some stock in a small oil and gas venture. Our buying clients are shrewd analysts and they think it's going to take off."

"A small oil and gas venture? Like Stavroneft? The small oil and gas venture that published a claim of a major oil and gas discovery in the North Caucasus yesterday? Its stock price doubled immediately and is still climbing this morning. A company like that?"

"You know?"

"I worked it out. Don't worry Charles, one man's insider trading is another man's astute interpretation of market data, wouldn't you agree? The only thing that puzzles me slightly is why the buying client would use a foreign entity like Murston Asset Management to start the deal. I assume they used another to buy from you. It seems like a waste of profit, unless there was a massive risk to them in doing the deal more directly."

"Sometimes, Thomas, it pays not to ask too many questions and just take the commission and run. It is Moscow, after all. Anyway, I don't think the London regulator is going to be too concerned over a fairly small deal on the RTS."

"How small, Charles?"

"We had 40 million in play. Your 10, I put in 10 as well, and two other investors. That's all."

"Charlie told me it was 100 million."

"Did he now?"

"Nice work if you can get it, Charles. Did Charlie's 'accident' have anything to do with this?"

"It's at the back of my mind. I hope not, but we will see."

Sir Charles's mobile rang. It was the hospital. Charlie was awake and doing well. Sir Charles breathed a sigh of relief.

"Thank God!" he said.

"We may get to celebrate after all, Charles. I might have something for you, one good turn deserves another and all that. But first, you said you wanted to talk to me about another venture you're lining up."

"Yes Thomas. It's delicate, though, and risky. The returns could be spectacular, but for it to work I need someone to play an active part. Someone with your sort of connections in Latin America."

"You'll need to be a bit more specific, Charles."

"It was Charlie's idea. He had a notion that you could manipulate the price of a certain commodity, a perishable one. His idea was to bring about a temporary price crash, buy up supplies of the commodity that were already in the supply chain and which would be losing value by the hour – buy it up really cheaply. Then revive the market in time to make a massive profit."

"That is risky, Charles. Lots of moving parts and variables. Plus shorting a commodity market has been done before. The regulators know what to look for and have mechanisms for stopping it."

"Not if the commodity is illegal. Not if the market isn't recognised, let alone regulated."

Thomas stared at him.

"You wily old bugger!" he said. "You're talking about cocaine, aren't you? Is that what Artur and his goons are doing for you?"

Sir Charles stared back at him, saying nothing. After a pause he spoke.

"It was going well. Events happened that applied downward pressure on a strategic section of the market. It was working. Then some bloody interfering woman stuck her oar in and messed it all up, screwed up the supply and demand imbalance and evened it up again. We've had to change tack. Charlie being out of action will slow things up, but it should be back on track in a week or so."

"So what do you want from me, Charles?"

"I know almost nothing about you, Thomas, but I like the cut of your jib. You're a bandit in smart clothes, a bit like me. You stumped up a fair amount of ready cash for a dodgy deal, and happily took the profits. Are you up for another investment? And some active participation?"

"I think you know the answer to that, Charles," Thomas said.

"I want you to buy me as much cocaine as you can at a knock down price when I give you the nod."

"How much cocaine?"

"Twenty-five million pounds worth, plus anything you want to put in yourself. At the going rate that's about a quarter of a ton, but by the time we've finished you should be able to get a ton or more for that price. When we pump the price back up again that could mean a 400 per cent profit. What do you say?"

"I'd say you don't seem to know how the international cocaine market works. Getting hold of a ton of cheap, reasonable quality coke isn't like buying listed stock on the Moscow exchange. It's cash up front, for a start, and going out looking for cocaine with 25 million quid or more in your pocket isn't too smart. There are some very greedy people involved, ruthless greedy people. It would take some organising."

"So, you can't do it?"

"I didn't say that, Charles. I just said it would take some organising. It's very risky. I'd want a fee up front, win or lose, to compensate me for the personal risks I'd need to take. It would need to be separate from any profit I might make from an equity investment. I'll do it for five million sterling. Cash. Up front. I'll get your cocaine, good quality, at the right price at the right time. I can turn your 25 million into 100 million for that fee." Thomas extended his hand. Sir Charles Murston took it and shook.

"We have a deal," he said.

Thomas smiled. Inwardly he was planning the downfall of the killer sitting next to him in the back of a London taxi. He was going to enjoy it.

Chapter 35

Thomas left Sir Charles Murston to visit his son alone. He was troubled, more than troubled, by his conversation with Murston in the taxi. The man had all but confessed to being behind the overdose murders, for that is what they were, and admitted that he was planning to manipulate a crash in the street price of cocaine in the UK. Firstly to bring the price crashing down, which must entail more deaths among users, maybe in greater numbers or of higher profile, but how was Murston going to bring the price back up again in time to cash in on his investment? As he thought about this, it dawned on Thomas what the real purpose of the Ukrainian mercenaries was. They were there to take the blame for the bad cocaine. Once they were visibly blamed and then publicly eliminated the users would feel reassured and go back to the drug. And the whole thing could be blamed, at least by insinuation, on 'a foreign power'. Clever. Very clever, but utterly evil.

Thomas was also very concerned about Sir Charles's reference to 'some bloody interfering woman'. That mention gave a context for Kuznetsov's man stalking Julia Kelso. Her actions against drug dealers had negated the impact of the mass poisoning. The poisoning was meant to eliminate demand, thus reducing the price. Her assault on the supply side had wiped out the drop. Murston must have instructed Kuznetsov to get rid of her. She was in real danger as long as Kuznetsov and his team were on the loose.

Thomas found a taxi near the hospital and told the driver to drop him in Piccadilly. He made a call to Eugene Flynn in Dublin, who confirmed that 14.6 million Euro had been transferred that morning to his account. Eugene didn't ask any questions. Thomas told him that he would be over to see him in a few days, once some current matters were resolved. He would explain all then.

"As you wish, Thomas. As you know I am always curious but never nosy. It will be good to see you."

"By the way, Eugene. I expect there to be another significant deposit, possibly two, in the next few days. Could you send me a message when the money hits the account? I'll text you the message 'Thomas is unwell' and when you get it could you close the account and move anything in it to my other one?"

Eugene said of course, and hung up.

In Piccadilly Thomas paid off the cab and went in search of his motorbike. He changed his jacket for the waxed cotton one in the top box and donned his helmet. He made his way to the mews in Chelsea where he believed the Ukrainians were hiding out. All was quiet. He rode past the Murston house and saw a tearful Lucy Murston getting out of a taxi. She went into the house. Thomas found a café from which to watch the house, and he waited. After half an hour Sir

255

Charles arrived in another taxi, and shortly after that Kuznetsov arrived in the Rolls Royce, which was being driven by another of the Ukrainians.

Thomas went back to his hotel. He made a call to Sir Charles Murston.

"How is Charlie doing, Charles?" he asked, "are you still at the hospital?"

"I'm back in Chelsea. He's making a good recovery, thank God. He's being moved out of intensive care later this evening. Once he's well enough I'll have him moved to a private hospital in town. Good news is he should be out in a few days. He'll need some time to recuperate but he could be back in harness in a fortnight."

"That's excellent news, Charles. I could see how worried you were."

"Blood is blood, Thomas. He's the only son I have, for better or worse. Look, why don't we get together to continue our conversation? I've put everything on hold vis-à-vis the project I mentioned. Artur's boys are putting the finishing touches to a few things and I've told them to take a few days off. Things will get busy from next Thursday onward and they are back on duty on Wednesday. Let's you and I meet over the weekend? I'll give you a call when Charlie's position is clearer."

"Sounds good, Charles. Just give me a call." He hung up.

At about 6pm he left the hotel and took the Honda back to Raynes Park. He sent Mel a text when he got there, he needed to talk to her.

He watched from the pub until he saw here walk past. Draining his pint he went to her street door and pressed the button on the entry-phone. The lock buzzed immediately.

In her flat they kissed briefly. Both of them knew he wasn't staying.

"What is it Thomas? What have you been up to now?"

"Well, now I do actually know what's going on, and I have an idea of the timescale. It's a crazy plan, something that the idiot boy Charlie Murston dreamt up, and he's managed to talk his dad into doing it. The old man must have lost his marbles or something, or there's some hidden reason. In a nutshell, Murston father and son are behind the cocaine poisoning that kicked all this off. What they want is to drive the price of cocaine down by scaring off well-heeled users. They've worked out that cocaine in transit is vulnerable to price fluctuation, and they want to snap up a chunk of it at a very low price and release it onto the UK market once the price bounces back. Murston senior, wants to put in 25 million quid and he's expecting to quadruple his money."

"Have you gone mad, Thomas? How do you know this?"

"Probably, gone mad, that is. I know it because Sir Charles told me."

"Why would he want to do that?" Mel asked.

"Because Kelso has pissed all over his strawberries and he needs some help to see this thing through. He's hired me to get hold of his cocaine for him. I expect he'll want me to help with the implementation of the next price crash as well."

"How has Kelso 'pissed all over his strawberries' as you put it?"

"By coordinating the rounding up of every coke dealer that can be found she's stymied the supply side of the coke price equation. Only the demand side was supposed to be hit to bring the price down. Murston is furious. He's now cooking up an alternative price crasher, along with Kuznetsov and his boys. I think it's going to happen next weekend, in eight or nine days."

"This doesn't make much sense. How is he going to make such an enormous amount of money by killing off the cocaine trade? I don't get it." Mel frowned.

"He plans to bring the market back to life in short order. Kuznetsov doesn't know this, but he and his boys will be exposed as the people behind the poisoning on behalf of 'a foreign power', meaning the Russians. They'll get the blame for both the first lot of poisonings and the next lot, which will be worse or of a much higher profile. Once Kuznetsov and his team are exposed and very publicly taken out – I'm pretty sure they're not meant to survive to tell tales - the threat will be taken to have vanished and everything will return to normal quickly."

"And what are you proposing to do about this? Are you still keeping Kelso in the dark?"

"Kelso is in danger. Real danger. I'm going to try to remove the danger - I think she is reasonably safe until a week today, but I can't be completely sure. She needs to be kept on her toes. Ideally she needs to be somewhere else for a few days. Can you fix that?"

"You know Jake, she's not easily fixed. I can suggest a long weekend at a spa or something. There's a nice one near Guildford. How are you going to 'remove' the danger to her?"

"I'm going to try to take out a couple of Kuznetsov's team before they have a chance to get to her. Kuznetsov and at least one other will have to remain in play until everything is ready, but the other two need to be got rid of."

"Do you mean what I think you mean?"

"They're hired killers, Mel. They're very dangerous people who mean to kill Jake. So yes, I do mean what you think I mean."

"Jesus, Thomas! Why can't we just tell Jake now and let the police handle this?"

"Mainly because Murston could simply walk away unscathed. Too many people have suffered or died already because of that man, and he's utterly contemptuous of them. I want to make sure he pays a heavy price, and for him that means humiliation. I want to break him, Mel. I can't do that if the police move in now. I can stop the next phase of poisoning. I can stop Murston making money from buying and selling cocaine. I can expose him publicly as a cheat and a swindler, and then I can bankrupt him. Then the police can have him. They'll have plenty of evidence, I'll make sure of that too."

"Thomas, what are you like when you get *really* cross with someone?" Mel asked. "How are you going to do all that?"

"Alone."

"You have it all worked out?"

"Mostly. I need a few bits and pieces though. Firstly, there was a trade on the Moscow stock exchange, it's called the RTS, on Monday. The trade involved stock in a company called Stavroneft, it's a small oil and gas company operating in the Stavropol area of southern Russia, in the North Caucasus region. Murston arranged to buy the stock for someone else, probably someone at or close to the heart of the Russian establishment, meaning inside the Kremlin. Charlie Murston was in Moscow to handle it, and he got very badly beaten up on his way back to the airport. He's in hospital near Heathrow, by the way, he nearly died. I'd like to know anything that can be found or hoovered up on the trade, on the attack on Charlie Murston, and on who might be behind the deal. I know there's insider trading going on, but there needs to be more to it than that.

"Secondly, you remember the two sisters who died early on, Mercy and Chantelle? There was a little boy, Mercy's kid. Can you find out what's happening to him, and get an address for wherever he is being looked after?"

"I can try. Why do you want to know about the boy?"

"Nothing bad, I promise, but I can't tell you yet."

"You are a very strange man, Thomas Donohue." Mel kissed him lightly and pushed him out of the door.

Chapter 36

Thomas went out early on Thursday and waited at the usual café from where he could keep watch on the mews house. He wanted to keep an eye on the Ukrainians until Julia Kelso was safely at work. At 10.30 he saw two of the Ukrainians, ones he hadn't seen before. They were laughing and each had a soft travel bag. They hailed a taxi at the other end of the mews. Thomas was able to follow the taxi easily to the Park Lane Hilton. He saw the two men go to the check in desk. They were taking the weekend off and planning to party. By chance Thomas saw Kuznetsov entering the hotel as well, and a few minutes later the fourth team member joined him. It dawned on him that Sir Charles had let them loose on purpose to give the world a photo opportunity in retrospect – hotel video images of the 'Russian' poisoning drug killers at play. Nevertheless London was a safer place, at least for the weekend.

He left the hotel, pulling over after a few minutes to send a text to Mel. "Jake safe for now"

His phone buzzed. "good but I was looking forward to a nice weekend"

He replied "have one anyway"

Thomas returned to his hotel, hung the 'do not disturb' sign on the door and opened up his computer. His first task was to book a flight to Dublin on Monday. His second was to start piecing together a tempting scam that would look irresistible to Sir Charles Murston and seal his fate.

Later that afternoon, stiff and weary from being still for too long he went to the gym. When he got back there was a message from Mel asking him to meet her. There was no indication of time or place, but he went to her flat anyway at 8pm.

She opened the door and gave him a brief hug.

"What a hornet's nest! Whatever gormless Murston was up to in Moscow he's really upset a lot of people. Have you seen any financial news today?"

Thomas hadn't.

"Stavroneft stock plummeted sharply this afternoon. Last night it was four times what it was on Monday, and it opened well today. It started to fall back during the morning, the financial press thought it was just some profit taking. By midday the oil ministry in Moscow issued a statement saying that the report published by Stavroneft about the oil deposits was fake; there was no discovery at all and the whole thing had been a fraud. The Director General of Stavroneft was arrested in his office at the same time, and the share price went into free fall. It's completely worthless now.

"One of the financial wizards at NCIS says it looks like an insider's double cross. Someone knew how the whole story would pan out before the Monday deal took place, and presumably a good while before then if they had time to put the deal together using Murston for the first part."

"He was lining this up at least a week ago, maybe longer," Thomas commented.

"It's likely, according to my wizard, that someone very high up the food chain cooked all this up. He says

262

that knowing about the discovery report, which may well actually be genuine, and about the plan to discredit it on Thursday, they – whoever they are - would have put an electronic buy order on Stavroneft stock to start buying once it hit a specific price, presumably just a bit below where the price was when Charlie boy jumped the gun. They, the people behind it, would just need to sit and wait with an electronic sell order in place to kick in once the stock rose to a predetermined level, knowing that the price would crash on Thursday afternoon. Apparently this sort of thing goes on all the time. Charlie interfering on behalf of A.N. Other kyboshed the whole thing. The people who planned it never got a chance to buy up and cash in. They made nothing at all instead of the many millions they were expecting. Murston would have made a few quid, as would the people who handled the sell-off, and the people who hired them both will have made a few tens of millions. The real losers have been the investors – individuals, employees, pension funds and so on - who believed the discovery report and sank funds into the company. The real insiders will have lost, or rather failed to make, their hundreds of millions. According to Six at Vauxhall the Kremlin is spitting bullets. Murston father and son are barred from Russia and both have been 'referred for special measures', meaning put on a list for further punishment at a later date. The same treatment will be meted out to the finance house which arranged the stock sale this morning. The team that gave Charlie a kicking - they were FSB - got bollocked for not kicking him hard enough. The powers that be wanted him dead, but not until he got to London. There's a hunt on for the double crossers. Six are watching the obituary columns for likely names to appear in the next few weeks.

"What's clear, though, is that Murston was only an extra on the stage, not a main player. My wizard and Six both think that there could be a faction inside the Kremlin who are not at all happy about the level of corrupt control of the Russian economy and are sabotaging plots by the high-ups to enrich themselves with schemes like this. Scamming the scammers. Don't you think that's a ridiculous idea, Mr. Thomas or whatever your name is?" Mel had a slight smile on her face.

"As for young Etienne, that's Mercy's son's name, his grandma has taken him in. He's living with her in her council flat, modest but decent. I can get you her name and the address. Now, how do you know Jake's safe for now?"

"I saw the Ukrainian team at the Park Lane Hilton, in party mood. Murston told me he had sent them off to take a long weekend break. It looks like they've all gone to the Hilton to play. Now, are you and Jake going away for a break?"

"I suggested it. She's not sure she can get away. Why?"

"Just curious. I think it'll do you both good. It's been a stressful time."

"What about you? Stress, I mean?"

"I'll have plenty of time to get over it when this is done. For now I've got things to do. I'll be meeting up with Murston over the weekend, and I need to go to

Dublin early next week. I'll be back by Wednesday at the latest."

Mel hadn't offered him a drink or anything. He didn't mind. He had to keep moving.

Chapter 37

The call from Murston came late on Saturday morning. He and his wife had just been with Charlie, who was recovering well in his private hospital room, and now Lucy had gone shopping. Did Thomas fancy a bite of lunch? Thomas said yes, and Sir Charles said his club did lunch at weekends. They met there a little before 1pm.

In the club bar Thomas asked about Charlie.

"He's badly bruised and still feeling fragile. He was lucky not to suffer permanent damage, although his spleen is still touch and go. His liver too is badly bruised and swollen – I don't suppose the alcohol will have helped with that, but there we are."

"That doesn't sound too much like an car accident, Charles. What really happened?"

Sir Charles sighed. "I don't know. Charlie is being vague about it, just keep saying he had an accident on the road to the airport, which is always possible. That road is a nightmare. Whenever Charlie's been in Moscow with me he's behaved himself, but I imagine he plays hard when I'm not there. I'd like to believe him about the accident, but if it wasn't one I think he may have been roughed up over a woman – a prostitute or something."

"You don't think it might have something to do with the Stavroneft deal?"

"It had crossed my mind, but the deal was no great shakes. I mean the Russians let the purchase and sale deals reach settlement, they let the money change hands. If someone was so hacked off about it the Russians could have blocked the settlement process."

"I can't agree with you, Charles. I do think that what happened to Charlie was a message, a message to you as much as to him. You spoiled a much bigger deal, I think, a top-level insider deal intended to make some high-ups a huge amount of money. But they need people, investors, to trust the RTS so they let the settlements take place. If I were you I'd steer well clear of Russia, and keep yourself safe here as well."

"Why do you say that, Thomas? How do you know?"

"I don't know, as such, but I've seen this sort of thing before - not in Russia but in enough other places that are similar. People like the Russians, the Bulgarians, and loads of others, don't like being taken for mugs by foreigners. They don't like it nearly as much as they don't like being taken for mugs by their own side. They seek revenge, and often get it too. But let's leave this. I'm going away on Monday for a couple of days to start laying the groundwork for the deal we spoke about in the taxi. I'm going to need my fee this week, and the stake money for the purchase. I'm going to match what you put in, so we'll be partners. You OK with that?"

Sir Charles nodded. "You need it all this week? All 30 million? Why do you need it now?"

"Well, firstly there's my fee. If I don't get paid up front I'm not going to do it for you. Then there's the cash to buy the stuff. I need to be able to access it at short notice, which takes some setting up, especially where I plan to go shopping. That's why I need the funds up front. If the deal goes tits-up before I've paid for the gear you'll get the stake money back, but my fee is non-refundable. So yes, Charles, I need 30 million sterling from you by the end of the week, cleared and in an account that I will give you when I get back to London."

"30 million will be a stretch, in cash I mean."

"I'm sure you'll figure it out, Charles, a man of your stature and standing. Now, you did me a good turn with the Moscow deal – I like quick dirty deals like that. So I'm going to do you a favour in return, if you're interested in making a great deal of money. Not as much as the coke business, but certainly a 100 per cent return within four to six weeks. Are you interested?"

"Is the Pope a Catholic, Thomas?"

"OK. Are you familiar with Cabinda?"

"No idea, what is it?" Sir Charles asked.

"It's a place in West Africa, a bit south of the equator. It's part of Angola, but is actually separate from it and bordered on three sides by one or other of the Congos. The Atlantic Ocean is on the fourth side. To the east and south it's the Democratic Republic of Congo, the DRC, to the north is the Republic of Congo, known as Congo B as its capital is Brazzaville. The DRC capital is Kinshasa, which is why the DRC is sometimes called Congo K. Angola grabbed Cabinda, or rather the Portuguese did, in 1885 when they were the colonial power. Congo B was the French Congo,

267

the DRC was the Belgian Congo; what is now Angola was the Portuguese Congo. The DRC is huge and unstable, but it has loads of mineral wealth. Congo B hasn't got so much by way of minerals but has oil, and it's more stable – even if it is a virtual dictatorship. Angola has been engaged in a civil war since 1975, on and off, but it looks like it is calming down now. The leader of the western-backed faction was killed back in March and his lot have lost the will to fight. The side currently winning, and which almost certainly will be the outright winner, is theoretically Marxist, the MPLA. It's been the government all the way through the war. Angola's main source of income throughout the civil war has been oil, and most of Angola's oil is in Cabinda or rather just offshore. Bizarrely the Americans have kept the oilfields working all the way through, thereby supporting the Marxist government even though the US government policy was to bankroll the west-leaning rebels in the FNLA.

"Anyway, that's enough history. The DRC is rich in minerals, the sort of minerals that are needed for the booming electronic and tech sectors, things like cobalt and copper and manganese. To date, the biggest deposits have been found in the central southern part of the country, Katanga province, and there is big money being made. The Angolans have been eyeing the market for cobalt and the other minerals with envy, as has Congo B. There are deposits in Congo B, and some in Angola too. The Angolans have been thinking about these, and they got the idea that it might be worth having a good look at the geology in Cabinda. They've been doing it on the quiet for a couple of years, and now that the civil war is winding down they've been able to get some top-class geological surveys done. Guess what? They've found something, a dual deposit of copper and cobalt in major commercial quantities. The trouble is, only a bit of it is under Cabinda. The deposit extends northwards into the Pointe Noir region of Congo B.

"The French are on to this, according to my information, which comes from a very good source. The French are all over Congo B, as they are in most of their former colonies. There's a small French-Congolese mining operation already working in the area. It's been there for years and it makes a decent but modest profit for its shareholders. It's on the French alternative stock exchange, trading well below one Euro per share.

"My very good information is that one of the French mining majors has had sight of a purloined copy of the Angolan survey report and they know what it says. They've looked at the location of the mining operation, which is very close to the Cabinda border, and they reckon that it can get into the cobalt deposit long before the Angolans will be able to start extracting. The French major will be launching a hostile takeover of the smaller mining company in the next few weeks. At present they could get it for a song, but my associates and I have been quietly buying up stock in the small mining company since we found out about this. We currently have around 15 per cent of the shares, and we need to get up to the 25 per cent mark so we can apply pressure on the big outfit that wants to buy us out and get a much better price than the one they have in mind. The major wants to pay less than one Euro 40 cents per share, but we know for a fact that they have budgeted to go up to two Euro a share, and they are prepared to go that high to secure the takeover. They think the deposits are big enough to challenge the DRC's market dominance. They want to do a cash offer rather than equity to keep full control. The market cap. of the small company is modest at the current share price, around 200 million Euro. We've already put in 30 million, very quietly like I said, and we need to do another 20 before the big feller makes his move. Which will be in two to three weeks tops. We can do it all, and planned to, but I'm offering you a chance if you want to take it. I'm offering you an opportunity to invest 15 million Euro, safe in the knowledge that you will walk away with double that by the end of next month. What are friends for, Charles?"

"Bloody hell, Thomas. How do you know this?"

"You can't expect me to tell you that now, can you Charles? Let's just say that my associates and I have a long reach and friends in many low places. Are you up for this? It doesn't matter to me if you are or you aren't, but I trust you not to breathe a word of this to anyone. Are you interested?"

Sir Charles paused, and summoned the steward for more drinks. When they arrived he looked at Thomas. "If what you say is right, then yes I am interested. I believe you, but I'd like some evidence. Do you have any?"

"Well, it's not being bandied about and any business intelligence outfits sniffing about will alert the French major and the whole thing will fall down. You have to bear in mind that there is a lot of skulduggery going on here. Most of my information has been passed verbally by people I've known and trusted for years, people who wouldn't dare lead me or my friends up a garden path. Like I said, we can do it all ourselves. I'm just offering you this chance in return for the favour you did me on the Moscow deal. It's up to you."

"I do like you, Thomas. Yes, I'm interested. I'm in!" They shook hands.

"So, that's another 15 million, Euro this time. I make that more or less 10 million sterling at today's exchange rate. Can you do that this week as well? 40 million in total."

"In the circumstances, yes. But it will need a bit of juggling. I'll have it sorted by the time you get back, which will be…..?"

"Wednesday at the latest."

"This is turning out to be a costly lunch, Thomas. Shall we order?"

"It will be the making of you, Charles. I'm buying lunch, if you like."

"Sadly, Thomas, not allowed. Club rules. I'll be stuck with lunch as well!"

The two men laughed.

Chapter 38

Once more Thomas spent most of Sunday on his computer. He was researching articles in the financial media about Murston, either his company or his family. He was not disappointed, and what he found was very interesting. Sir Charles Murston certainly had his detractors as well as a few sycophantic supporters. Thomas saw that Murston Asset Management was heading down the league tables for investment performance. Some commentators put this down to the ineptitude of Charlie Murston, others to the rather pedestrian attitudes of the company itself. Estimates of the company's current funds under management were lower than the one billion that Charlie Murston had boasted of to Thomas - the consensus was that the fund was now a lot less than one billion - some said less than 500 million. There were hints that the regulator might be showing an interest in Murston Asset Management, and not before time.

Sir Charles Murston himself seemed to have been haemorrhaging money in recent years, partly through poor investment decisions but also through a very expensive lifestyle. It was said that his impending departure from political life had been planned to allow him to try to rebuild his fortunes. Others said that he wanted to leave Parliament voluntarily before he was pushed out through bankruptcy or some other financial scandal. His most vocal critics said that his personal net worth was barely positive, a bit of money in the bank and a few properties at best, but all set against growing debts. So where was he going to get all the cash, Thomas wondered? As if he couldn't guess.

Thomas identified one financial journalist who seemed to be very interested in Murston but who also kept the tone of his criticism reasonable and measured. He worked for a reputable paper. Thomas felt that a damaging piece from this particular reporter would be far more effective than the same piece from one of Sir Charles's more virulent critics. Thomas noted the reporter's email address and started writing.

"I have evidence that Sir Charles Murston is involved in insider trading. If you want to know more get in touch." Thomas wrote. He pressed send. Even though it was Sunday he got a reply within minutes.

"What evidence?"

He responded "I have a signed contract between SCM and an investor involved in the Stavropol trade in Moscow. I can give you the details and context."

"Why?" came the reply.

"Murston is corrupt. I don't like corrupt people."

"Fair enough. Can we meet?"

"Tuesday evening, London. I will send you the time and place."

"OK."

The plan was proceeding nicely.

Thomas turned his machine off and had an early night.

On Monday morning Thomas took a cab to Heathrow. He was in Dublin just after 10 and he went to Wynn's, his favourite hotel in the city. From there he made a call before walking across the river to the

Shelbourne Hotel on St Stephen's Green. He announced himself to the head waiter and was shown to his table. He waited patiently for Eugene Flynn.

Eugene arrived at 1pm precisely. He smiled at Thomas and waved across the room. Thomas stood to greet him.

"You're looking well, Eugene. It's good to see you."

"You too, Thomas. Are you here for long?"

"Just the day. Back to England tomorrow to conclude a matter."

"Would that be the matter you involved me in a couple of weeks back?"

"It would, Eugene, and I need to talk to you about it. But first a drink and we'll order."

"It's beef on the trolley on Mondays," Eugene said, "I'll be having that. And a decent Margaux. I think a sherry to be starting with."

"You can't keep a good socialist down, can you Eugene?" Thomas smiled. Eugene Flynn was, or had been, an old Sinn Feiner with hard-left tendencies before becoming a very successful lawyer.

"Privation is for the young and angry, Thomas. I'm no longer either. The beef is always excellent – melts in your mouth. It would be a crime and an insult to the poor beast not to honour it with a proper wine."

Thomas ordered. He also opted for the roast beef.

They chatted as they ate, keeping business for later. As always the men found each other's company relaxing and enjoyable.

When they were done Eugene sat back. He looked at Thomas in an enquiring manner, but said nothing.

Thomas took the cue. "You've never asked questions of me Eugene, nor I of you. I think we trust each other, but there's something I need to tell you. You may not like it."

Eugene said nothing. Thomas continued. "I've only ever told you one lie, Eugene. That lie is my name. I am not Thomas Donohue. There is no Thomas Donohue. My real name is Alan Ferdinand, or at least it was, and Alan Ferdinand was a British policeman. Thomas Donohue was a name he used when he was an undercover officer working against Loyalist criminals. It was what he was doing when he met you, that day when the INLA were trying to kill you."

Eugene looked at him. "A British spy? Against the Loyalists. Who killed an INLA murderer and saved my life? And why the third person?"

"I did save your life. It was the right thing to do. I use the third person because I am not Thomas Donohue and I am not Alan Ferdinand. I'm between names, I suppose. Alan Ferdinand was being framed by some corrupt criminal cops in England. He managed to turn the tables on them, with your help, and some of them died. The others are in jail for a very long time. The money you helped me move about and are still looking after is money I took from them. I wanted to bring down their whole organised crime racket, not just a few individuals, and it worked.

"Alan Ferdinand faked his own death and he's now officially dead. The money is all in the name of Declan Walsh, which is the name I'll be using for a while. As Declan Walsh I've been working with two good friends in England to fight more corruption we've come across, which is what I'm doing now. A corrupt British politician is responsible for the deaths of hundreds of people whose only crime was a liking for casual cocaine use. Not to everyone's taste, I know, but not a capital crime. The deaths were a test, no more than that, to see if he could manipulate the cocaine market to make a massive profit. I've found out who he is. I pretended to let him talk me into investing in an insider trading deal. That's where last week's 14.6 million Euro came from. Now he trusts me and he's confided his plans for the cocaine market. I've spun him a yarn and he thinks I can buy him a ton of cheap cocaine. He'll be putting a lot of money in my account, probably on Thursday. I've also persuaded him to invest in another insider trading deal, which doesn't actually exist, and to pay me a fee to buy the cocaine for him. The equivalent of 40 million sterling will be deposited in the account that has the 14.6 million Euro in it. I'm pretty sure he'll need to steal the money from his investment company and when it comes out it will bankrupt him at the very least. Once I have his money I'll ensure that he's arrested and he will go to jail. He's the sort of man who would say he prefers death to dishonour, so his disgrace will be the worst and most fitting punishment for what he's done."

Eugene studied Thomas intently. A smile slowly spread across his face. "You cunning fucker. I said last time that I didn't want to know what you were up to, just that the cause was honourable. It seems to me it was, and this one is too. I'll overlook the deception and forget that I ever entertained a British police spy in my home. You've always been Thomas Donohue as far as

276

I'm concerned, and always will be. Now, what do you need me to do?"

Thomas was relieved. He had half expected Eugene to erupt. He told him what he would need.

After the meal Thomas walked Eugene to the door and watched him board the magnificent Bentley, chauffeured by the loyal Kevin. Kevin nodded at him, Thomas raised a hand in greeting. The car purred away. Thomas settled the not insignificant bill, not that he begrudged a cent of it, and strolled back to Wynn's. That evening he spent a couple of hours unwinding in one of the many music pubs before turning in. It would all come to a head this week, of that he was certain. And then what?

Chapter 39

Thomas arrived back in London on Tuesday afternoon. He emailed the journalist and arranged to meet at a pub on the South Bank, not far from the recently opened Tate Modern art gallery. Thomas arrived early, more alert now that he was meeting a stranger. He recognised the journalist from his photo in the paper. He arrived and looked around. Thomas waited a few moments to ensure that the man was alone, and it seemed he was. Thomas approached him.

"Luis?"

The journalist, Luis, turned. "Yes. And you are?"

"Just call me Eddie for now," said Thomas, "let's go somewhere quieter."

He turned and walked out of the pub onto the riverside footpath. Luis followed. They sat on a bench. Luis lit a cigarette, not offering one to Thomas.

"You said you have something on Murston," Luis said without preamble.

"Yes. A copy of a contract I signed with him. I have the original here, and I'll show it to you. I also have a redacted copy that you can keep. I don't want my name involved. Murston persuaded me to invest 10 million Euro in a scheme he had cooked up to buy stock on the RTS in Moscow. He didn't tell me what the stock was, but it was Stavroneft. The contract is dated the Friday before the Stavroneft trade. Murston was doing the trade on behalf of someone else, someone who knew about the plan to publish the report about an oil discovery and then trash it a couple of days later. Someone with inside information.

Murston put up 10 million Euro himself, although I doubt it was his own money, and there were two other investors. I don't know who they are. The promised return by Wednesday morning was 40 per cent, a profit of four million Euro each. Charlie Murston went to Moscow to handle the trade through a number of different brokers, and it went smoothly. He bought at a better price than predicted, and the actual return was 46 per cent. The insiders went on to sell the stock at its peak price just before the discovery report was branded a fake and the boss of Stavroneft was arrested."

"It was Murston who was behind it?" Luis asked.

"No. He was just a bit part player. I don't know who was behind it, other than it must be someone with inside knowledge at the highest level in Russia. Charlie Murston was attacked and badly beaten up as he was leaving Moscow. He could have been killed, but the Russians didn't want a dead Englishman on their streets. I understand that Murston, both Murstons, are on a Russian hit-list and will be banned from visiting Russia ever again.

"Furthermore, Murston is involved in some very underhand criminality. I can't say more right now, but it will become clear in a few days."

Thomas paused. He took two folded documents from his inside pocket. He passed them to Luis. He read the contract and the redacted copy, which he put in his own pocket. He handed the other one back to Thomas.

"You've seen my name, Luis, but I don't want it used if you run with this. Will you be taking up the story?"

"The Stavroneft deal intrigued me. This makes it clearer. Your view is that the whole thing was a set-up, to boost the price then crash it, to make money for someone 'at the highest lever', by which you mean the Kremlin."

"Yes. The intervention by insiders not only made them some money, it also disrupted the Kremlin scheme. It seems that the plan was to make a huge amount of money, not just the few tens of millions that the insiders made. I've heard a theory that there may be a clique inside the Kremlin who are not happy with all the greed and corruption and they're doing their best to disrupt schemes like this. A high-risk occupation I would imagine."

"So, what's your angle, 'Eddie'?" Luis asked.

"As I told you. I don't like corruption. Murston is corrupt in the worst possible way, as will become apparent. I want to destroy him, financially and reputationally. I want the story about him being connected to Russian insider trading to come out, ideally on Friday. It should wipe out Murston Asset Management."

"How do I know you're being straight with me?" Luis asked.

"You don't. That's why I am talking to you now, to give you a chance to speak to your sources, check out what I'm saying. If you don't want this I can go to someone else. But whoever does take this will get something else. They'll get the whole story about

Murston's criminal activity too, but not yet, not until Murston has sprung a trap. I came to you first because I like the way you write. Your writing is reasoned and rational; others might take this and just rant, which would devalue it in my opinion. I want the story to be believed by people who have money invested in Murston's funds."

"How will I get the rest of the story?"

"You'll get it all in an email by Friday afternoon at the latest, but probably before then."

"Are you involved in the criminal activity? Sorry, I have to ask. It's the paper's policy."

"The person you're talking to is not involved."

"That's a strange answer, 'Eddie'."

"It's the only answer you'll get."

"OK. I'll do some digging. If it's bollocks I'll run a different story about a crazy man called Thomas Donohue running con tricks. If it's genuine I'll ask my editor to run it on Friday and I'll wait for your email. Is that it?"

"Yes. It's all I'm asking. I don't want anything else from you. If you decide it's not bollocks and you run my name you will regret it. Don't think I'm threatening you, because I'm not. It's just that you'll attract yourself a lot of very unwelcome attention from some nasty people who will be trying to find me."

"That sounds fair. If I have any questions how can I get hold of you?"

"You have an email address, that's all. It will operate until I see your piece on Murston in the paper on Friday morning. You can use it until then, but I suggest you talk to your other sources first."

Thomas stood and walked away. Luis watched his retreating back and reflected. There was something intense and quite disturbing about 'Eddie' – Thomas Donohue. Luis had calls to make and people to speak to. He was already composing his article in his head. He would love to see Sir Charles Murston go down in flames.

Chapter 40

On Wednesday morning a tetchy Julia Kelso called Mel from her flat.

"Where the bloody hell is he, Mel?"

"I have no idea. I haven't seen or heard from him in days. Why?"

"I get nervous when I don't know where he is or what he's up to. Give me a call if you hear from him will you? Do you fancy a drink tonight?"

"I get nervous too. Yes, and yes. See you at the usual place. Bye." Mel hung up.

At that moment he, Thomas, was outside Julia Kelso's apartment block. He had risen early and gone to the mews in Chelsea and taken up a position at the café he had taken to using. With his coffee and pastries he sat reading a newspaper, like several other people in the place. He had a good view down the mews. Just after 7am a dark blue Audi pulled up outside the mews house. The driver remained in the car, clearly waiting for someone else. He didn't have long to wait. By the time a second Ukrainian got into the car Thomas was out of the café and on his motorbike. The Audi came towards him and he was able to fall in a couple of cars behind it. The follow was not as easy this time. The Audi driver was clearly alert and looking for a tail, which could only mean they were on business. Following an instinctive hunch Thomas turned off into a side street letting the Audi go. He rode as fast as he could to Dolphin Square where Kelso lived. He arrived in a few minutes, hoping that the Ukrainians' local knowledge wasn't as good as his. He was right, and after about five minutes he saw the Audi pull up by the main entrance. Nobody got out, instead the car did a slow circuit of the building. Thomas followed, but in the opposite direction. He came across the Audi parked in one of the service roads that surrounded Dolphin Square. Its two occupants stayed in the car. Between Thomas and the Audi was a black Jaguar, parked with its engine running. The driver was a large man who looked bad tempered. Thomas rode past the Jaguar and the Audi before doing a U-turn. The Audi was now between him and the Jag. He saw the blonde head of Julia Kelso emerge from a side entrance and duck into the Jaguar, which accelerated away. The Audi didn't move. After a few moments it pulled away but turned the opposite way to the Jaguar. It was just a dry run. Thomas relaxed, for now.

Thomas returned to his hotel and spent a couple of hours composing two long emails. One was for Julia Kelso, the other for Luis. When he was satisfied he saved both as drafts and closed his computer. He phoned Sir Charles.

"Charles, it's Thomas. I'm back in town. Can we meet up? I've some positive news for you."

"Good to hear from you, Thomas. My good news is that Charlie is being discharged today. He'll be at home with me this afternoon. Why don't you come to the house at 3? I'm sure he'd like to see you. We have much to talk about."

Thomas agreed and went to the gym for an hour.

Julia Kelso arrived at Scotland Yard. She thanked the driver, Howard, as she always did. He didn't respond, as he always didn't. She smiled sweetly at him, promising herself that when all this was over Howard would have the worst posting she could arrange, and have his transfer requests blocked forever. In her office Raj gave her the overnight messages. The cocaine situation had calmed down, no further reports of overdoses anywhere. The dealers who weren't already convicted or in jail were starting to get released on bail, but it would take them a while to get up and running again, especially as just about anyone on any of their phones had received a visit from the police. The dealers' phones had all been seized as evidence, as had any cash, notebooks, anything really. The dealers would have to start all over again from scratch.

She worked through her messages and meetings, and before she knew it, it was early evening. She packed up and called grumpy Howard. She was meeting a friend at the St Ermin's hotel. He could escort her on foot and bring the car round in an hour. Howard grunted. Mel was already in the bar and halfway down a large gin and tonic. The two friends brushed cheeks.

"I never used to touch this stuff, Jake. Now you've made me a gin addict."

"You're getting me addicted too, you know, but not to gin," Julia smiled and ordered two more gin and tonics.

"How are you doing, Mel?"

"I'm OK. It just feels like we're a bit in limbo at the moment. The lull between two storms maybe. I could do with another break. It'll be autumn soon, but the weather's still good and warm. If I book a villa I went to a while back will you come with me? Just for a week, maybe ten days. It's just a bit south of Bordeaux, where the wine comes from. It's not posh or fancy, but very comfortable and with a lovely pool. We could just rest and read books and eat far too much French food."

"I *have* heard of Bordeaux. That sounds wonderful, Miss Dunn. When?"

"Week after next? I've checked and it's available. Cheap too, being end of season."

"Let's do it!" Jake said.

Mel smiled and squeezed Jake's hand.

"Shall we take Thomas?" they asked, simultaneously.

The friends laughed.

"It would be handy to have someone to carry the luggage and do the washing up." Mel said.

"And a few other things too!"

"You worry me sometimes, Kelso. Another drink?"

They chatted on for another 40 minutes when Jake said she had to leave. They kissed again.

"I can't wait for the holiday, Jake. It's going to be wonderful." Mel watched as Jake left. She didn't notice the dark blue Audi following Jake's car. Nor did Jake.

Chapter 41

Thomas was sitting in a large leather armchair in the Murstons' drawing room in the Chelsea house. Charlie was resting on the sofa. He looked pale but after a week of enforced rest and no booze he actually looked better than he usually did. Sir Charles was in another armchair.

"You're looking good, Charlie. I was worried when your dad told me about your accident in Moscow. You're lucky you made it back to Heathrow. You don't hear many good things about Russian hospitals."

"And hopefully I'll never get to find out if they're true, Thomas. I won't be going near Russia any time soon. What have you two been cooking up?"

"This and that, Charlie," Sir Charles replied, "we'll fill you in all in good time. It's good to have you home."

"We still have Phase 2 to kick-off. We were supposed to do it last week, this weekend is really our last chance if we are to have any success. I take it you've told Thomas about Phase 2, Pa?"

Sir Charles groaned. "Actually, I hadn't. But now it seems you're about to. Thomas will be working with us on Phase 3, as a full partner."

"How did that happen?" Charlie was clearly not happy. "You never asked me."

"Have you forgotten you were unconscious for several days? I couldn't just sit around waiting for you to surface. The operation needs to keep moving." Sir Chares was not happy having this discussion with his son in front of Thomas.

287

"Don't mind me, Charles. You should hear what goes on in my family. Since you've started, Charlie, what about Phase 2?"

With hardly a glance at his father Charlie started. "Phase 2 is the catalyst to bring the street price crashing down. That bloody policewoman stymied the original Phase 2, which was going to be a much wider distribution of the really pure cocaine. We were getting a good 50 overdoses per kilo, that's what Phase 1 told us, and with the amount we have available we thought we could cause sufficient panic to drive the price right down. Rounding up street dealers has kept the price up, and we've had a few losses on Artur's team, so we're short-handed and short of time. Phase 2B, as we're calling it, involves fewer people but will be just as effective, probably more so. Artur's boys have been busy mixing an interesting cocktail which is now neatly packed up in 10 gram party bags. It's bonus time in the City, and everyone is celebrating like mad. We're going to leave the bags lying about at various party venues and wait for the headlines on Monday. But being a bit crocked still, I was wondering if you might be able to give me a hand? I get invited to just about every party going, and I've made a list. I don't want to collapse, though, so would you come along with me? I can say you're looking after me after the Moscow business. No one will be surprised."

"You're asking me to babysit you, Charlie?"

"Don't take offence, Thomas. Not babysit, not as such. But there is no one else to do it. Artur and his boys can't. They can't just stroll into ritzy venues and schmooze the punters, can they? They'll be driving us

288

and giving us a bit of protection. Unless this works, there won't be a Phase 3."

"OK then. Charles, if I'm to do this we need to sort out the financials pretty quickly. Like right now."

"OK, old boy. I'll make a call, but it's too late to complete a transfer today. Do you have the account details?"

Thomas passed a card to Sir Charles. It had Thomas Donohue's account details written on it. Sir Charles made a call to his finance director at Murston Asset Management and ordered an immediate transfer of 40 million sterling to the account details he gave. Sir Charles hung up. Seconds later his land line rang.

"Standard verification procedure, Thomas, just making sure I'm not being coerced." He answered the phone and went through a scripted series of questions and answers.

"All done Thomas. The transfer will be initiated immediately, and your bank will be notified within a few minutes. The funds can't be cleared until tomorrow though."

"I'll call Dublin in a wee while. I'm sure everything's fine. Now, Charlie, talk me through Phase 2B again."

Thomas listened as Charlie set out the details, and expanded on the nature of the 'cocktail' in the party bags. Inwardly he was horrified but he kept his expression and tone of voice neutral.

"That should do it, Charlie. Pick me up tomorrow in Grosvenor Square at 6pm and I'll help you with your errands."

Thomas called Eugene, who confirmed that the transfer of 40 million sterling, just shy of 62 million Euro, had been initiated and could not be recalled.

"OK, gents. I'll leave you in peace. Charlie, I'll see you tomorrow evening. Charles, I'll call you tomorrow and see you on Friday. I have a sound plan for Phase 3. I've heard there are a couple of decent sized shipments about to leave, destined for the UK. I should be able to get my hands on them by the end of next week, but I'll need to get down to Africa."

"Africa? I thought they made the stuff in South America."

"Indeed they do, but West Africa is a convenient shipping route for the smaller players aiming for the British market, and that's where I'll be able to buy up as much cheap cocaine as we need. Cape Verde or the São Tomé and Principe islands are favourites. Nice too at this time of year. I'm booked on a flight on Monday."

With that Thomas departed, his mind racing. Father and son were both clearly stark raving mad. Powerful cocaine laced with strychnine would almost certainly kill anyone taking more than a couple of hits, and who only did a couple of hits of free cocaine? The strychnine could take a while, anything up to an hour, to take effect, by which time it would be too late.

From the street he called Mel, there was no answer. He tried Julia Kelso. It went straight to voicemail. He hailed a taxi. "Grosvenor Square, please."

Chapter 42

Thomas spent an anxious night and was up before daybreak. He didn't dare risk loitering near the mews in Chelsea again so went straight to Dolphin Square on his motorbike. Luckily for him, Dolphin Square was a busy place, even at that time of the morning, and motorcycle couriers came, went and waited there all the time.

He bought a takeaway coffee from the cab shelter and waited. Shortly after 7.30 the dark blue Audi appeared, the same two Ukrainians inside. It cruised round the block a few times before pulling in at the top of one of the service roads beside the apartment block. Thomas mounted the Honda and did a circuit to pull up behind the Audi but a few yards away from it. He sat on the bike and consulted his phone as if checking the address of a pick-up. The Ukrainians were sitting in the car smoking, the front windows open. Both were staring down the service road and totally ignoring the motorcycle a few yards from them. The front passenger door opened. Thomas got off the bike and propped it on its side stand. He gripped the Makarov in his right-hand pocket – he had checked the weapon and reloaded the magazines before he left his hotel. He released the safety catch.

The Ukrainian in the passenger seat got out. His right hand was in his jacket pocket. The driver was watching his passenger, oblivious to anything else. Thomas walked towards the Audi. Glancing down the service road he saw the black Jaguar, Julia's car. Her driver was standing beside it. He ground out his cigarette and got behind the wheel, starting the engine. Thomas caught sight of a flash of blonde hair and a dark blue suit, Julia was coming out of the building and moving towards the car. The Ukrainian on foot started moving quickly towards her. Thomas was too far away to intercept him, and the Makarov was no good at more than a few metres. Yelling would do no good. Thomas strode up to the Audi with the Makarov in his hand. The driver looked up and started to raise his hand, which also held a pistol. Thomas fired four times through the open window, each shot hitting the Ukrainian driver in the head.

Julia's blonde head jerked up at the sound of Thomas's first shot. The Ukrainian on foot looked over his shoulder but kept going towards Julia. He raised his pistol and fired twice at the Jaguar. The Jaguar driver had opened his door and was getting out, his own weapon drawn. The Ukrainian's shots hit him in the chest and he fell to the floor. Thomas saw Julia fall to the ground. He started to run towards her. Then he saw her emerge from behind the Jaguar, her Glock pistol now in her hand. She rose to a crouching position as the Ukrainian moved in front of the car, which was now between him and Julia. She rose further, drawing a bead on the Ukrainian as he came into view. The moment she saw him in her sights she fired two pairs of shots, the first pair hit the Ukrainian in the head, the second his chest. He fell, pulling the trigger of his pistol as he did so. Julia ran towards him, her Glock still pointing unwaveringly at the fallen killer. He was clearly dead, his face slack, his eyes open, two neat holes in his forehead. Her eyes turned to the Audi. She ran towards it, seeing the back of a man in a waxed cotton motorbike jacket as he mounted an old Honda and sped off. She made a mental note of the number plate. The Audi driver was also clearly dead.

She ran back to the Jaguar. Howard was on the floor, he was unconscious but breathing. She reached into the car for the radio handset.

She spoke into the radio, giving her Metpol call sign.

"Dolphin Square, shots fired, officer down. I need an ambulance and urgent armed assistance. Two confirmed fatalities."

She heard sirens almost as soon as she put the radio handset back in its cradle. She turned to Howard. She removed her jacket and rolled it so she could prop his head on it. She could see he was badly hurt. She took his pulse, which was becoming weak and febrile. As she prepared to start CPR an ambulance pulled up in the road, its way blocked by the Audi. She stood and waved her arms at the paramedics.

"Casualty is here. He's been shot twice in the chest, he's alive but unconscious, his pulse is weakening."

A paramedic approached at a trot, his colleague following on with a portable defibrillator.

"OK, miss, we've got this. Are you injured?"

"No, I'm fine." As Julia said this her knees buckled and she leant on the car.

"Best sit down, miss. Another ambulance is on the way. They'll look after you."

As Julia stood, shaking, the first police car arrived. Two officers got out, weapons drawn. She waved them over.

"Commander Kelso, SCD," she identified herself, "there's been an attempt on my life. One of the attackers is there on the floor. I shot him. The other is in the blue Audi. He's been shot too, but I've no idea who did it. They're both dead. I have reason to believe that they are hired killers, probably Ukrainian. Can you secure the scene and send the first senior officer who gets here to see me? I need to go to my apartment and get changed. I'll preserve my clothing, obviously."

The officer nodded. Julia cleared her weapon and handed it to him, and gave him a card with her official mobile number.

"The senior officer can call me on that number."

"Yes, ma'am," he said, "good work. You did well."

She gave him a wan smile and went back into the building. A crowd was forming. Other police officers arrived to control them and push them back from the scene.

In her apartment Julia stripped off her clothing and changed into casual jeans and a sweatshirt. She couldn't shower until cleared to do so by whoever the senior investigating officer was. She started making coffee and called Mel.

"I'm OK, Mel, but someone tried to kill me just now. You'll hear about it on the news, no doubt. I've a feeling Thomas was somewhere nearby. He might have saved my life, but I'm still furious with him. Do you know where he is?"

"Someone tried to kill you?"

"Yes. I shot him first."

"Fucking hell, Jake!"

"Well put. Now where's Thomas?"

"I have no idea. Honestly, if I knew I'd tell you."

"Got to go, lots to do," Julia hung up.

While she was waiting Julia made a quick call to Raj. She cut him off as he started to question her – rumours were already flying around the Yard about the attack.

"Just tell everyone that everything is under control. I'll be with the SIO for a while, but give the Commissioner my compliments and say that I'd appreciate a few moments of his time when I'm through."

The SIO had arrived. He called her, she invited him up to her apartment. He arrived a few minutes later with a female Detective Sergeant in tow. She knew him as a Superintendent on the homicide squad. He was good. He had arranged to secure the scene downstairs, screens had arrived to block the view of both cars. Howard had been taken to St Thomas's hospital. He was in a serious condition but had a good chance of pulling through. Julia pointed at her discarded clothing on the floor.

"I'll take care of that, ma'am," the female officer said. She placed each item in a paper evidence bag. "I'll need to swab your hands as well, then you can clean yourself up."

Julia nodded. She was familiar with the procedure, but it still felt strange to be subjected to it. The female officer was gentle and efficient. When she was done Julia poured them all coffee and recounted the story of the Ukrainian team distributing toxic cocaine. She explained how one of them had followed her home, presumably having seen her on TV. She had been leading the investigation and had done several televised press conferences. The SIO wrote everything down diligently and asked her questions for an hour or more.

When he was done they all shook hands. The female officer asked if Julia wanted her to stay, which Julia politely declined.

"I'm fine. I need to get showered, then get to the office. I'd appreciate a lift in about half an hour."

"I'll be downstairs, ma'am," she said.

Julia showered and changed into a fresh business suit. Raj had texted her saying the Commissioner would be available as soon as she got to the office. She went downstairs and found the female officer, whose name was Sophie. They drove to the Yard.

Chapter 43

Thomas disappeared into the back streets of Pimlico as he heard the first sirens. He stopped the bike once to vomit into a drain, his hands shaking. Within a few minutes he rode the bike into an underground car park beneath a modern block of flats near the railway lines. He parked the bike in a distant dark corner.

He took a black bin liner from the top box and placed his waxed cotton jacket in it, together with his crash helmet, motorcycle gloves and boots. He also placed the latex gloves he was wearing in the bag. He changed into the spare clothing he was carrying in the top box. His other jacket, a pair of slacks and some slip-on shoes. The Makarov went into the right-hand pocket of his fresh jacket. He took a few deep breaths and climbed the stairs to a street door. The street was deserted. He strolled casually over the railway bridge, turning left toward Chelsea Bridge and the barracks. As usual, there was a queue of dustbin lorries waiting to discharge their smelly loads into one of the barges in the refuse dock, from where Westminster's detritus would be exported to Essex. He crossed the road behind one of the trucks, casually lobbing his black bin bag into the back of it as he passed.

He walked toward Sloane Square. He paused at a café for a strong black coffee, hoping his hands would stop shaking soon. He thought about how close Julia had come to death, something he could barely acknowledge. He felt he should have done more to protect her, but then again it seemed she was quite

297

capable of protecting herself. He took out one of his phones. He used one to speak to Mel, the other one to speak to Murston and anyone else. He called her.

"Where the fuck are you, Thomas?" Mel started. "Jake's furious with you. I think I am too. Did you know someone was going to try to kill her this morning?"

"She's OK, though?" Thomas asked.

"Yes. She's fine. What's going on?"

"It's all coming to a head. It'll be over very soon. The cocaine threat will go away, along with the Ukrainians and the Murstons. Is there any new intelligence?"

"Not a peep. No calls, no emails, nothing."

"Can you get hold of Jake? If she can swing it with the Met can they put out a statement saying that a senior officer has been seriously injured in a shooting, or even that a senior officer has been killed? It will buy me a few more hours."

"What do you mean, buy you a few more hours?"

"Just that. As soon as I can I'm going to send you an email, one you can give to Jake. It explains absolutely everything, including who's done what and who needs to be rounded up and locked away. If you don't get it, it will mean that I'm dead, in which case you need to call Eugene Flynn in Dublin, he'll know what to do. Do you understand?"

"I'm getting fed up with people dying and getting shot at, and with all this mysterious stuff. Why migh you be dead?"

"There are still two Ukrainians in play. If they piece together what's been happening I'm a dead man, unless I get them first."

"Fucking hell, Thomas!" she hung up.

Thomas's other phone beeped. A text from Eugene saying 'mother has come home'.

'Thomas is unwell' was Thomas's reply. The funds had been cleared in Dublin, now Eugene would immediately empty the account and close it. The money, around 76 million Euro in all, would be whizzing around the world before landing in one of the Declan Walsh accounts on Monday. No one would ever find it.

******

In his office in the City Sir Charles Murston was cheered by the news of a shooting incident in Westminster. A statement just released by the police saying that a senior officer was critically injured and on life support cheered him even more.

His mobile rang. It was Thomas.

"Good news, Charles. All's well in Dublin. Tell Charlie everything is on. I'll see him as planned."

"Splendid, Thomas. The day is getting better and better! We must celebrate soon. Come down to Hampshire at the weekend. We can watch the news and play some tennis." Sir Charles hung up, laughing.

Tennis, my arse, thought Thomas.

He started walking back to his hotel, suddenly weary. He stopped for some lunch. Looking at his watch he realised that it would all be over in less than five hours, one way or another.

Back in his hotel he cleaned and reloaded the Makarov. He unloaded and reloaded each magazine to make sure the springs were in good order, he tested and retested the mechanism. Satisfied, he put the weapon back in his jacket pocket and tried to relax.

The TV news was all about that morning's shooting in an affluent area of Westminster. TV crews were all over the place, beaming pictures of the scene to the world. The Met Police issued a further statement saying that a senior officer had been the victim of an assassination attempt. An officer, who was not being named, was on life support in a London hospital.

The truth was that the officer being referred to was Howard, the driver, who was still in a serious condition. The Met's press people didn't want to tell outright lies to the media, which would be tantamount to declaring war, but smudging a few facts early on would be OK. There was no mention of the dead Ukrainians.

In his room below Sir Charles Murston's elaborate office Artur Kuznetsov was following the news carefully. He was pleased that Mr Pink and Mr Blue had carried out their mission, but he was concerned that they had not made contact with him. Maybe they were just being cautious. Either way, the assassination was the last of their obligations to him. They were now discharged and would be paid off in full, along with himself and Mr Black, the following morning.

Artur made himself a coffee. He didn't offer one to Mr Black, who was dozing in an armchair across the room.

Chapter 44

Julia Kelso was not happy. She was not happy about being shot at, and she was not happy about the call she had received from Mel Dunn. She reluctantly complied with the request about the media statement, although it took nearly all of her considerable charm to persuade the head of media relations to do it. It's not lying as such, she told him. There's just been a major incident and facts can and do get confused in the first few hours. We can put it right later, she had told him. He grumbled but went along with it.

When they had spoken Julia demanded that Mel come to her office. It was not a request. Raj had just shown her in.

"Sit!" Julia commanded.

Mel was about to respond, but thought better of it.

"Tell me exactly what he told you, every word." Julia demanded.

Mel told her, word for word, as best she could recall.

"He told you the cocaine threat and the Ukrainians and the Murstons would go away? Who or what the fuck are Murstons? He needed a few more hours? What for?"

"I can tell you about the Murstons, but not why he needs more time, because I don't know. The Murstons are Sir Charles Murston, MP, his son and his company, Murston Asset Management. We've mentioned them before, remember?"

"Yes, vaguely. Why are they important?"

"Sir Charles Murston is behind this whole thing, or so Thomas says. He hasn't given me the ins and outs, but he has said he's close to Murston now. He says he's going to put it all in an email and send it to me so that I can give it to you as soon as I get it. He says that if the email doesn't arrive it will mean he's dead. Thomas, that is."

Julia buzzed for Raj.

"Could you get me anything we have, anything at all, on Sir Charles Murston, his son, also a Charles I believe, and his company Murston Asset Management. Ask Special Branch as well as Registry. Invoke my name and say it is very urgent."

Raj said yes boss.

"I'm pretty sure he was at Dolphin Square this morning," said Julia, "I think he dealt with the Audi driver and gave me a head start on the other one. I suppose I should be grateful, but as of now I want to rip his nuts off."

"Very ladylike, I'm sure," said Mel.

For the first time Julia allowed herself a little smile.

"I don't like being kept in the dark, especially by people I trust and am close to. Do you understand that, Mel?"

"I do, Jake. I'm sure he has his reasons. Let him explain it to you in his own good time. If you stop and think about it he's got you over a barrel. He's officially dead, but you know he isn't. If he wasn't dead he'd be wanted for murder, quite a few of them, and god knows what else. And you, Commander Julia Kelso of New Scotland Yard, not only know all about it you also go to bed with him from time to time! Explain that to the Commissioner, or worse still to the Daily Mail."

"Fuck it, you're right," Jake sighed, "but I still want him to explain himself."

"I'll fix it, if he comes through this. Trust me, Jake."

Mel and Jake stood up as Mel was about to leave. They started to embrace but pulled apart rapidly as the office door opened. Raj looked at them both suspiciously.

"Not much in Registry. I called SB and they went all secret on me. Said their Commander would be in touch with you soon."

"Thanks, Raj," Julia said.

As he closed the door the two women collapsed in giggles.

"That would be a better story than getting shot at. Commander Kelso snogging another woman in her office!" Jake laughed.

They kissed, but briefly. A knock on the door.

"Commander Edwards to see you, ma'am." Raj announced.

"Thanks Raj. Could you show Miss Dunn out."

Tim Edwards, an old family friend of the Kelso's and the Commander of Special Branch, entered. Julia hugged him.

"Tim, you're looking well. Come on in. I'll make coffee."

"Bit of a rush, Jake. How are you? After this morning's business? It sounds awful."

"I'm here, Tim, safe and sound. My driver isn't doing too well. I'll be going to see him as soon as he's awake, fingers crossed. Have you come to see me about my Murston questions?"

"I have, Jake. Why are you interested?"

"I have some information, untried and untested, suggesting that Sir Charles might be involved in some very serious criminality that I'm investigating."

"You do know he's a Member of Parliament, a former minister, and that he sits on the Home Affairs select committee? As such he's out of bounds."

"You didn't come all the way down here to tell me that, did you Tim?"

"Murston is up to something. You may be on the right track, I don't know. You know we have a working-level Europe-wide liaison unit. We speak to our counterparts throughout Europe on an informal basis. Great for rapid communication and getting things done. Well, someone we know in the BKA, the German federal police, was asking about Sir Charles and his son Charlie just a couple of days ago. Seems that one of their informants is a sex worker who got picked up by some Russian in Berlin. Pillow talk implicated the Murstons in some scam on the Russian stock exchange, insider trading. Apparently, the Kremlin is hopping mad and has contracts out on them both. The BKA think that Charlie, the Murston boy, got a proper kicking from the FSB before he left Moscow.

"Trouble is we can't do anything with it. The BKA have very tight rules about informants and privacy and all that, so they can't report private conversations if conducted in an intimate setting."

"Like when the speaker's getting shagged by the informant, you mean?"

"I can always rely on you, dear Jake, to call a spade a bloody shovel, but yes. So the Germans can't tell us something about someone we can't report on. Is it relevant?"

"It's not what I was expecting, but it could be. Do you have any details on the scam?"

"No, but it shouldn't be too hard to identify. I've got our financial team doing some digging and I'll let you know."

"Thanks, Tim."

"Jake, you need to be careful. It's not often that the bad guys have a go at us personally. They have to be crazy to go after you like they did this morning. I would hate to have to pay a visit to your dad with bad news." He hugged her. He had known her since she was a child.

"Off you go, Tim. I'll be fine," Jake hugged him back.

Later that day Julia received a call from the hospital. Howard was making good progress and was out of intensive care. She could visit if she wanted to. She went immediately and sat with the very groggy Howard for half an hour.

"I'm sorry you got tangled up in this, Howard," she said.

"Not your fault, ma'am. You didn't ask to get shot at, you were just doing your job."

"The medics say you're doing well. I spoke to your wife outside, she'll come in to see you in a minute."

"She's a good one, my missus. Been through a lot with me. I guess I'll think about jacking it in now, I've got my time in and we'll need a good long holiday when I get out of here."

"Whatever you want, Howard. I'll get you an injury award and a medical pension if that's what you want. I appreciate what you did, so does the job."

"Thank you ma'am."

"Julia, please," she smiled at him.

Chapter 45

In his hotel room Thomas dressed for the evening. He had packed his few possessions and would be checking out the next morning, if all went well. He wore smart casual trousers and an open-necked shirt. He put a latex glove on his right hand. The evening was pleasantly mild, but he needed to wear the coat with patch pockets. At 5 he went down to the bar, feeling the weight of the Makarov in his pocket.

He ordered a large scotch and watched a news channel on a TV in the bar. The sound was off, but the subtitles rolled on and on. It was all about the shooting. The subtitles were saying that the officer who had been shot was still in a critical condition with life-threatening injuries. He knew they must be talking about the driver, but he still had a lump in his throat thinking that they could be talking about Julia Kelso.

One more scotch, then he made his way out into the square. He strolled along away from the US embassy. At 6pm exactly the sleek grey Rolls Royce rounded the corner and slowed. Artur Kuznetsov was in the front passenger seat, another Ukrainian behind the wheel. It was Mr Black, but Thomas didn't know that. Charlie Murston was in the back, behind Kuznetsov. He didn't look well.

"How're you doing, Charlie?" Thomas asked as he slid in behind the driver. The door closed with a solid clunk. "You don't look so good."

"Just feeling a bit under the weather. Getting ready for the evening took it out of me somewhat. I suppose it'll take a while for me to get up a full head of steam again. Did you hear about what happened this morning?"

"I've seen the news. What specifically?"

"That shooting. The police officer. Dad's cock-a-hoop. He says the copper who got shot was the one that scuppered Phase 2 for us. So Phase 2B will serve her right, it'll be her fault, if she survives, that is."

"She?"

"Yes. Kelso, whatever her name is. Do you remember a few weeks ago there was another shooting. South London somewhere. The guy who was killed was working with us on Phase 1. One of Artur's boys."

Thomas watched Kuznetsov's shoulders tense up. Charlie was pushing it.

"I think maybe we should talk about something else, Charlie. Where are we going first?"

The evening traffic was heavy and they were making slow progress. Thomas couldn't make his move with so many people about.

"Some old chums are having a party at the City of London Club, Old Broad Street. We're going there first, then on to a restaurant near Liverpool Street. I've got eight or nine places on my list. Each one with a bonus party in full swing! God, I wish I was match fit, there'll be fun to be had. I'll be dropping a handful of party bags at each of them - I have 60 with me."

Thomas didn't respond. The repugnant creature next to him was talking about killing probably hundreds of his own kind. City flyers, plus all the clerks and secretaries and trainees. Ordinary people just to make some speculative gain.

The early evening news was on the car radio.

"Do you mind turning that off please, Artur," Thomas asked.

He saw Kuznetsov bristle when Thomas made the request, but he complied. The car fell silent.

"Tell you what, Charlie, let's stop for a drink. I had a quick one before I came out and I've got the taste. There's a great little private bar I know off Wigmore Street, in Manchester Square."

"Good idea! Artur, do you know Wigmore Street?"

Kuznetsov grunted.

"I'll give directions," Thomas offered.

He guided the Rolls Royce through the back streets of Mayfair onto Park Lane. Then around Marble Arch and into Oxford Street. They turned left towards Portman Square. The light was starting to fade now. Thomas directed the Rolls left off Wigmore Street into Manchester Square. The square was quiet, practically deserted. Thomas had chosen it because there were few security cameras, few streetlights, and even fewer people.

"Just here, on the left." He pointed to a building in one corner of the square that had a light burning above the door.

"Doesn't look much like a bar to me, Thomas."

"You'll be surprised, Charlie, very surprised."

As the car slowed Kuznetsov was studying the buildings closely. Thomas quickly but smoothly pulled the Makarov from his pocket with his gloved right hand.

Swiftly, he levelled the pistol at Kuznetsov's head and without a word fired twice. Kuznetsov's head rebounded off the window and he fell back. The driver let out an oath in Russian and went for his own weapon. He had no chance. Thomas's Makarov fired twice more into the back of the driver's head. Charlie's mouth hung open. He started to speak. Thomas turned towards him, placed the pistol against Charlie's right knee and fired again. Charlie screamed. Thomas placed the pistol on the seat and punched Charlie in the face, very hard. Charlie howled and passed out. Thomas placed the pistol in Charlie's right hand, making sure that he wrapped his fingers round the stock. With his own hand gloved, he raised the pistol and squeezed Charlie's finger on the trigger. Kuznetsov's dead body jerked as the round entered him. The car's light grey headlining was smeared with blood and gore. The bullets that had passed through both Ukrainians' bodies had smashed into the roof, globs of gooey matter stuck to the windscreen.

Thomas opened the door. The whole thing had taken just a few seconds. He dragged the unconscious Charlie across the back seat just to make the scene a bit more confused. Charlie's briefcase containing 60 bags of cocaine mixed with strychnine lay on the floor at his feet.

Thomas walked away through the darkened streets of Marylebone. He dumped his latex glove in someone's rubbish bin. It was nearly over.

It was several minutes, maybe even a quarter of an hour, before the sirens started. By this time Thomas was in a pub on the other side of Edgware Road on his second pint of Guinness. After a third he started to make his way back to Grosvenor Square. He glanced up towards Wigmore Street and saw the blue lights flashing.

At the Millennium Hotel he ordered a very large scotch and took it up to his room. He followed this up with whatever whisky he could find in his minibar.

Feeling slightly woozy, and with a sense of complete detachment, he started up his computer and logged on to the internet. He opened the message to Mel, the one giving every detail of the case apart from the attack on Jake and the deaths of the two Ukrainians that had just happened, and pressed send. Then he sent a second email and shut down the computer.

He took a long bath, washed out the bath, then he had a long shower, scrubbing his hands and face.

He went to bed but couldn't sleep.

Chapter 46

Mel woke early on Friday. Her sleep had been troubled by anxious dreams, horrible dreams in which both Thomas and Jake died violently and repeatedly. She opened her computer and saw Thomas's email. She scanned it, read it again more carefully, and printed it off. She called Jake.

"It's not even 6 yet!" Jake protested.

"The email has come through. You need to see it. I'm bringing it to you. Best get to your office as soon as you can. I'll be there in an hour."

Julia's Blackberry was buzzing too. Another shooting, this time in Marylebone. Two dead, one injured. The injured man identified as Charles Murston, junior, currently under arrest and in Queen Mary's hospital in Paddington with an armed guard. She called the SIO.

"Commander Kelso here. I'm on my way to the Yard. Can you let me have an update on the Marylebone shooting, soon as you can. Great, thanks."

She hung up. She dressed quickly and went downstairs. Her usual exit was still sealed off so she used the main entrance. The officers posted there stood to attention as she appeared. She started to walk but an officer stopped her and ushered her into a marked patrol car.

"Sorry, ma'am. We've been told not to let you wander off. I'll drive you. Where to?"

They arrived at Scotland Yard in a few minutes. Julia went to her room and put the coffee on. He phone rang. It was the SIO in charge of the Marylebone shooting.

"Morning, ma'am," he started.

"Just call me Julia."

"As you wish. The incident happened around 7pm last night. No witnesses have come forward yet, and no CCTV in the immediate area. On the face of it Charlie Murston shot the two other occupants of the car and accidentally shot himself in the knee as well. The two dead occupants are not yet identified, but they are very similar in age, dress and appearance to the two who had a go at you yesterday. We're guessing Russian or Ukrainian. Both dead men were carrying firearms, loaded, Makarov pistols. A Makarov was used to shoot them too, we've recovered that one. It was in Charlie Murston's hand. Also in the car we found a briefcase. It had a list of addresses, and 60 bags of white powder. Cocaine by the looks of it, but big ones, not single wraps. More like party bags, probably 10 grams or so in each. A lot of gear. Murston's not fit for interview yet. He's lost a lot of blood and is on major painkillers. As soon as he wakes up I'll have a preliminary chat and I'll get back to you. Also if there is anything from the lab or any witnesses."

She thanked him and hung up. The phone went again. Mel was downstairs. Jake went to get her.

Over coffee Jake read the email. She called the SIO back.

"Julia Kelso here. Tell the lab and anyone handling it to be very careful with the white powder. It's probably high-grade cocaine cut with strychnine. A

313

small dose could be lethal, and it's imperative that it remains in safe custody."

"Strychnine? Bloody hell! That's a new one!" The SIO hung up.

Jake read the email again and started making a list.

Jake called the SIO yet again.

"Sorry to be a pain. Has Murston senior been informed yet? He hasn't? Good, let's keep it that way, and as little news coverage as possible for an hour or two. I'll need to see Murston myself and I'd rather not give him notice. I'll tell his about his son when I arrest him."

"It'll be a pleasure not to see him, Julia. I never liked the arrogant sod when he was at the Home Office."

"So, there we have it, Mel. Sir Charles bloody Murston poisoning people with toxic cocaine to bring the price down, just so he could cash in on a few shipments of cheap gear. Just for money. He's killed at least 200 people. We can account for six of the seven Ukrainians he hired, five dead, one in SIS custody, one missing. We need to find him if we can.

"We need to find the rest of the coke that was stolen from the Home Office site. Thomas is pretty sure it's in Murston's mews house, which he uses as a garage. I'll arrange a search warrant. There should be strychnine there too."

"Have you seen the TV, Jake?"

The set was on in her room, with the sound off. Jake turned the volume up with the remote. The BBC business news was leading with an article in that morning's financial press about Murston Asse

Management and insider dealing in Russia. Julia called the press office and asked for copies of the FT and other financial sections to be brought to her immediately. A messenger arrived in a few moments, out of breath.

"They said it was urgent, miss," he said.

The main article was written by Luis Ortega, citing an unnamed source. The graphic was a facsimile of a contract signed by Sir Charles Murston and an anonymous person. The story outlined the double cross that had elevated and then crashed the share price of Stavroneft, a small oil and gas company. The article went on to speculate about some other deals that Murston had been involved in, and about Sir Charles's own finances. In a paragraph that must have had the lawyers up all night Luis Ortega suggested that Sir Charles Murston had been dipping into Murston Asset Management's client funds for some of his more dodgy ventures. Specifically he said that he had information that some 40 million pounds had been extracted from the company's already depleted liquid funds on no more than Sir Charles's say so that very week.

"I smell Thomas," Jake said.

Jake spent the next 30 minutes making phone calls and giving instructions, then she called for a car and driver. Her last call was to the local Borough commander covering the Murston house in Chelsea. The Borough commander agreed to have an arrest and search team around the corner when Jake arrived.

Jake and Mel went down in the lift together.

"I'll call you tonight, if I can." Jake said to Mel. "I might want to come over, if you don't mind. It might be late."

"Please do," Mel said, "I'd like that. I'll get some gin on the way home."

******

Thomas had seen the morning papers and was happy with what Luis had produced. He had sent him a version of the email just after he had sent one to Mel, just to encourage him. Clearly it had worked. The business news channels were reporting queues of Murston Asset Management clients waiting at the firm's office to withdraw their funds. There had been no sign so far of the firm's chairman, Sir Charles Murston.

At that moment Sir Charles Murston was calling Thomas Donohue for the tenth time in as many minutes. This time Thomas answered. Julia Kelso should be on Murston's doorstep any minute.

"Charles. Your day's not looking so good, is it?"

"What the fuck is happening, Thomas?" Murston had lost his usual haughty remote demeanour. He was yelling down the phone.

"You didn't think you could get away with it, did you? Really? Killing hundreds of innocent people just to make a few quid? You're crazy. You're also broke by the way. Did you know that? And your investors are lining up to skin you alive."

"Where's my money? What about Congo? What about the cocaine? What have you done?" Murston was screaming hysterically.

316

"Your money's long gone. It wasn't yours anyway. But it's gone now, and you'll have to pay for it. There's no cocaine. There was never going to be any, I just wanted to bleed you a bit more."

"You'll die for this, Donohue. No one double crosses me!"

"Really Charles? Really? We'll see. The police will be at your door any minute. You're done, matey, finished." Thomas hung up the phone, turned it off and removed the battery. It was time for Thomas Donohue to go.

He paid his bill in cash and walked out of the hotel. His work was done.

He had carefully folded all the expensive clothing he had bought, divided it into piles and as he walked through Victoria he dropped off items in various charity shops as donations. With each donation he left a twenty pound note 'towards the cleaning', knowing full well that laundered and dry-cleaned clothes would make life difficult for any subsequent investigators.

He walked to the riverside and over Chelsea Bridge. Halfway across he dropped the Thomas Donohue phone into the murky waters. In Battersea Park he went through Donohue's wallet, sifting through the contents to remove anything that might link Donohue to any specific place at any specific time. When he had finished all that was left in the wallet was some cash and a driving licence. His credit and debit cards he cut up and dropped in pieces in various bins, along with any receipts.

Thomas walked to Clapham Junction and got a bus to South Wimbledon. From there he walked to the newsagent in Lower Morden. At the newsagent he removed Declan Walsh's stuff from the deposit box, paid up for the rest of the month and left the shop. The box was empty. He kept the cash but Thomas's wallet and driving licence went into a small black plastic bag and into a dog waste bin. Thomas Donohue was gone.

He called Mel on what he called 'her' phone.

"It's done, Mel, it's over."

"I know. I've just left Jake. Can you come round tonight? Someone wants a word with you."

"I'll be there." He hung up.

Chapter 47

Commander Kelso pounded on Sir Charles Murston's smart Chelsea front door. She was in her full uniform, flanked by uniformed police officers. She pounded again, and rang the bell. No reply. She stood aside and nodded.

Two officers with a small red battering ram had the door off its hinges in seconds, she strode in. Murston was in the hallway, apoplectic with rage. His face went scarlet as he recognised Julia.

"You're supposed to be dead! What are you doing in my house, this is an outrage!" he blustered.

"Nowhere near dead. Charles Murston, I am arresting you on suspicion of murder, conspiracy to murder, attempted murder, possession of cocaine with intent to supply, attempting to administer a noxious substance, theft, fraud and money laundering, and probably some other things too. You do not have to say anything, but it may harm your defence if you fail to mention now anything you later rely on in court. Do you understand?"

He was speechless.

"Now we are going to search your house and your garage in the mews down the road."

"You can't do that!"

"I can, and I'm going to."

"I want my lawyer!"

"Not yet. He can see you at the station. By the way, Charlie's back in hospital. He's under arrest too, in possession of 60 bags of cocaine and strychnine powder. Anything to say about that?"

Silence.

"Your two remaining Ukrainian goons are dead too, like the two who attacked me yesterday. I heard on the way over here that a crowd of your investors have stormed your offices and are demanding their money or your life. It hasn't been a good week for you, has it?" Julia smiled at him.

He lunged at her, evading the clutches of a burly constable. Julia floored him easily and stood over him as he lay there, dazed and broken.

"You've ruined everything, you fucking bitch!" he screamed.

"Now that's just rude," Julia said, "handcuffs, please."

A uniform sergeant did the honours. Sir Charles Murston glared at her, and then stared at his manacled wrists. He started to struggle. The sergeant gripped his arms firmly.

The searches took a long time. Murston's situation got worse with each passing hour. The cocaine was recovered along with the strychnine. There were firearms, a few souvenirs from the Home Office raid, lists of phone numbers that would relate to the missing drug dealers up and down the country. There were stacks of files recording illicit transactions that had been run off the books, these the taxman would find very interesting. In Sir Charles's room there were piles of cash, a few bank books, and curiously his contract with Artur Kuznetsov, which clearly stated what Murston wanted him and his team to do. Get out of that, she thought.

Murston was eventually taken to Westminster police station. Julia handed the case over to a Superintendent and left Murston to enjoy his first night in a cell, the first of many. Very many.

She had calls to make, loose ends to tie up. By 8pm she was exhausted but everything was neat and tidy, handed over where needed. She was back in her office and in her civilian clothes again. She started to make her way home but changed her mind. She hailed a taxi and asked to be taken to Raynes Park.

Chapter 48

Declan Walsh, as he would now be known, waited in Mel's flat. Both he and Mel were quiet, exhausted by the recent events, anticipating Julia Kelso's anger. She arrived. In her usual fashion she left a trail of shoes, coat and jacket in her wake. She was grim faced and furious.

"Explain, Thomas, exactly why it is that you withheld crucial evidence and vital information from me? At a time when lives were at risk, including mine and yours? Why you think it's OK to fuck with a major police investigation? My investigation!" Jake's quiet tone did nothing to disguise her cold rage. She stood facing him, arms folded.

"I wasn't withholding, Jake. I was getting everything lined up. If I'd told you everything as I got to know it you would have had to jump in with all guns blazing. You know that. You might have won some battles but you would have lost the war. Murston would have been able to walk away. For him what matters is the disgrace. He's a 'death before dishonour' type, even though he's no more honourable than a sewer rat. I had to break him, publicly. Expose him to scandal, ridicule, bankruptcy. He can't walk away from any of that. You would have got Kuznetsov and the last of the Ukrainians, if you could take them alive, but you wouldn't have got near Murston or his idiot son. Not near enough to arrest and charge him, let alone convict him. Even now there's no guarantee that he'll be convicted for the killings. He's establishment, and even if he's brok he'll get a good lawyer. He can't walk away from the fraud, the theft, the financial ruin. That's why, Jake."

Kelso stood in front of him. After a moment she sighed. "You may be right. But you still could have got me killed!"

"I was there looking out for you!"

"What if they had killed you first? Then what?"

"You would have been fine as soon as the first shot was fired, whether it was by me or at me. They could have taken you if they had surprised you. Once you knew they were there they weren't a match for you, they would've had no chance. I saw what you did!"

"I never shot anyone before! I've never killed anyone before! You made me do it!"

"No I didn't, Julia."

Her eyes were welling up. She stepped towards him. For a moment he thought she was going to hit him. Instead she fell into his arms and buried her face in his chest, sobbing.

"Don't you ever do that again!" she said, "we could have been killed. Both of us!"

He held her as she calmed, then he raised her chin and kissed her gently on the lips. She kissed him back.

"I'll get the drinks then, shall I?" Mel coughed, breaking the tension.

"Sorry, Mel," Jake said, "it's just that decent blokes are so hard to find. I don't want to lose this one just yet."

"I suppose I could always find you another," Mel offered.

"Thanks a bunch," Declan / Thomas said.

Chapter 49

Declan Walsh left the UK the same way he had arrived a few weeks, or maybe a lifetime, earlier. Everything had changed. His relationship with Jake Kelso and Mel Dunn, his outlook, even his past. He boarded the ferry at Newhaven and sipped a cold beer in the bar, watching the waves break over the bows. England grew smaller behind him, the French coast appeared ahead and grew larger.

In Dieppe he was pleasantly surprised to see the battered grey Fiat where he had left it. It had a couple of desultory parking tickets on the windscreen. The French traffic wardens knew they had no chance of enforcing parking fines on an Italian registered car so they had only made a token effort to ticket it. Declan recovered the keys from the exhaust pipe where he had left them, and the car started on the third attempt. He peeled the parking tickets off the windscreen as the engine warmed up, then he pointed the car south-west and set off. He took his time, using back roads and stopping off at small hotels in backwater towns. He liked the anonymity, the lack of curiosity. He was just another traveller.

He took almost a week to get to Bordeaux. He arrived relaxed and rested, but with no idea at all about the future - apart from the next ten days, which he would spend with Mel Dunn and Jake Kelso in the rented villa. He tried not to think about it in too much detail.

As Declan was driving slowly through France, Mrs McMorrow was sitting in her lounge facing the young lawyer, who she regarded with a great deal of suspicion. Sure enough, the lawyer was a polite young woman, and her family were from the Island too, but still what she was saying made no sense.

"Can you tell me again, please?" Mrs McMorrow asked.

"Of course. My firm was contacted by another law firm in Ireland, one that we work with from time to time. It is highly reputable, above reproach I'd say. One of their clients, who insists that he or she remains anonymous, somehow heard about the dreadful thing that happened to your two daughters, Mercy and Chantelle. Their client also heard about Etienne, and was moved by the story. Their client instructed that they arrange to ask you if you would agree to a trust fund being established to support Etienne through his childhood and education, and once he has completed his education to support him in any lawful occupation."

"How would that work?" Mrs McMorrow demanded.

"Well, a fund would be set up, we would take care of that. You would receive an initial lump sum so that you could provide a stable home for yourself and Etienne, not that your lovely home is not stable, of course, but you might want to have one that you own. It could be here or on the Island, or you could stay here and have a place back home. It would be your choice. Then there would be a payment to you every month for day to day expenses, I would imagine that young boys can get costly. If you need anything else you just ask me for it. You would be a trustee of the

326

fund, along with me or a member of my firm, so you would see everything that went on."

"And what do you want from me in return?" asked Mrs McMorrow.

"Nothing at all. Just your agreement to allow it to go ahead. You don't have to decide now, it must be a big shock. I will call you tomorrow, if you like."

"I don't want charity, from anyone."

"I know, Mrs McMorrow. The client anticipated this, and their message to you is that evil people did wrong and killed your girls. Nothing can make that right, but Etienne should not be paying for that for the rest of his life. The fund can give him a fair chance, if nothing else."

"Who is this 'client'?"

"I have no idea, Mrs McMorrow."

"He or she is a crazy person, but they're right. Etienne must have a fair chance. So yes, I will agree to it. And thank you, thank him or her too."

******

Mel and Jake left London several days after Declan. Mel drove them in her red Mini with the sunroof open. They used the tunnel and the autoroutes and ignored the speed limits, singing along loudly, if not particularly well, to the CDs Jake found in the glove box. They stopped overnight in a roadside hotel and continued on early the next day. As Declan was on the Rocade ring road that snaked around Bordeaux Mel and Jake were arriving at the villa. They travelled light. Mel said the weather was still warm, an Indian summer, and they wouldn't need much in the way of clothing. So they just had a soft bag each. Mel also had a beach bag with a few books, and also what she termed her 'travelling toy box'. Jake didn't ask.

Mel rushed to open the door with the key they had retrieved from the caretaker in the village. Jake followed on, finding a trail from the hallway into the main part of the villa. Mel's bag was on the floor, as were her sandals, shorts, pants, shirt, and bra. She heard a splash. Mel's long brown body was in the pool, she swam two lengths and lay on her back with a wide smile on her upturned face. Jake smiled back.

"Come on in! It's utterly gorgeous," Mel called.

Jake hesitated, muttered fuck it why not and peeled off her own clothing. The two women luxuriated in the cool clear water, swimming slow lengths side by side.

"I'm glad, Jake," Mel said.

"About what?"

"Glad that he didn't get you killed, or himself," Mel stood facing Jake. She took her in her arms and kissed her lips. "I would miss you both, so much."

"Are you getting soppy?"

"Maybe. Let's go upstairs. He'll be here in a while and I think we should have some time together first just us."

When Declan did arrive at the villa Mel and Jake were seated at the poolside table. Mel ran to him and kissed him. Jake waited where she was. She smiled up at Declan and held her arms out to him. He went to her and kissed her.

The following morning Declan was up first and he went down to start making breakfast. Mel came down soon afterwards, a towel draped over her shoulder bu wearing nothing else. Jake followed a few minutes later wearing a light dressing gown. Mel made coffee and they sat on the terrace under a large parasol.

Jake looked at Mel.

"Haven't you forgotten something?" she asked.

"Like what?" Mel asked, examining the table for cups, spoons or plates she may have missed.

"Just guessing, but clothes maybe?"

Mel looked down at her body.

"Oh, that! I thought I would do today mostly *au naturel*, not wearing clothes. I do that sometimes. I love to feel free, with the warm air and sun on my body. It helps me forget Yorkshire weather. Do you mind? Either of you? I'll put clothes on if you want."

They both shook their heads.

"But," Jake asked, "why is it you always put clothes on when you go to bed? Normal people, like him and me, we put clothes on when we get up and take them off when we go to bed. You're doing the opposite."

Mel put her coffee mug down.

"I do put clothes on, usually, when I get up. I've just decided to do a bit of naturism this week, while it's still warm enough. As for bedtime, you will *never* understand what the word pain really means until you've leapt out of bed in the middle of the night to go to the loo, only to find that your stud has snagged and you have a ten-tog duvet hanging from your left nipple."

"Ow!" Jake clutched her own breasts.

"That's why I always wear some clothing in bed, unless I have reason not to, such as one of you two being in there with me. I told my mum once that I was interested in naturism. She said what, like David Attenborough? I had to explain the difference between a naturist and naturalist, but I still can't look at David Attenborough on the TV and keep a straight face. No, like not wearing clothes, non-sexual nudity is marvellously liberating. If we go to the beach later you can both try it if you want."

Jake and Declan looked at each other, not convinced.

Later they did go to the beach in Declan's battered Fiat, which no one would be interested in robbing. They hired a parasol and loungers, which were already set up on the sand, and put most of their things in a locker. Mel stripped off her sun dress immediately and ran brown and naked towards the blue ocean. Jake and Declan couldn't help smiling. When she came back, dripping and happy, Mel looked at her friends.

"You're still a bit overdressed for a nudist beach," she said.

After a while they relaxed a bit, got used to the idea of being like everyone else on the beach and removed what was left of their clothing. Even Declan, who had been grumbling about it all morning.

Jake stood up and stretched. "It does feel rather good. I think I need a swim."

With that, Jake jogged off down the beach, her pale skin a startling white against the blue of the sea, her blonde mop bouncing. She ran full into the breaking waves. Mel and Declan heard a squeal and saw her being engulfed in a large breaker. Fearful for her, they both sprinted down the beach towards the spot where Jake had been dragged under. Mel streaked past Declan with her long legs powering through the sand. As they neared the water's edge the laughing and exhilarated face of Julia Kelso bobbed to the surface.

"Jeez! It's like being in a washing machine!" she said, spluttering as she surfaced.

Declan and Mel helped her from the water, and they walked back up the beach.

"I can see the appeal," said Jake, "it does feel incredibly free and natural to be naked in public. But I still feel a bit nervous. What if you see someone you know, from work or something?"

"It can happen," Mel said. "One of my first naturist experiments was at a place near Hull, which was risky enough in itself. There's a naturist club there, and I went along for the day, just on my own. I was wandering around with just a towel over my arm and I walked straight into two of my old school teachers, both starkers and very wrinkly. Mr Robinson, maths, and Miss Oldroyd, economics. It was a bit freaky at first but we all got used to it quite quickly. I think they were more embarrassed than I was. I wouldn't have been so surprised if it had been the hippy art teacher or the floaty poet lady who did English, but maths and economics? Who'd have thought it?"

Later that afternoon Jake took a call from work, an update on the Murston case. Sir Charles was wailing about someone called Thomas Donohue who, he said, had put him up to the whole thing. Investigators were trying to find Donohue and had come up with a passport application that seemed to fit, he was a

British subject, born in Northern Ireland, with no criminal record and a very patchy work record. They had come up with a few small DNA samples found on the steering wheel of the Murston Rolls Royce, which they thought might come from Donohue who, according to Murston, had driven the car on more than one occasion. Donohue was now listed as a suspect and was circulated internationally as wanted for questioning. Jake listened carefully and thanked the caller.

"Declan," she said, "sorry, but we're going to have to kill you off again. Well, Thomas anyway."

"OK," he said.

The week rolled on, but Mel was starting to feel a bit hemmed in by the developing closeness between her two friends, and sensing a slowly rising panic about the dynamics between the three of them. Her compartments were beginning to overflow into each other and Mel needed to restore her order. She saw the way that Jake and Declan were behaving with each other. It was apparent to her that they were in what Mel termed 'the sweetshop phase', being intensely occupied with each other. She didn't mind, and she certainly wasn't feeling snubbed, neglected or excluded. They were just catching up on lost time. Since their arrival at the villa she had known it was possible, probable even, that Jake and Declan might form a more conventional attachment to each other, not that it wouldn't be without its difficulties in the longer term.

One evening Mel gently explained her feelings to Jake and Declan, saying she really liked them both was very happy being with them, still liked having sex with each of them and would keep on doing it as long as everyone wanted her to, but... But she could see the way things were between the two of them and didn't want to confuse things unduly, and basically wanted to leave them to it. Jake and Declan looked thoughtful, but also a little relieved.

"So it really *is* just a physical thing for you, sex? No attachment or love or emotional anything?" Jake asked.

"Yes," Mel replied, "it always has been. I'm weird like that. I really like and trust you both, I'm genuinely fond of you and I care about you, but I don't get the pull that you two seem to have for each other. I'm happy for you, really, and I'm a bit envious I think. You've got something I can't relate to."

She was quiet, but smiling throughout. She kissed them both slowly.

"I'm off to bed, you two have fun. See you in the morning."

One day that week Mel went out on her own to see some ancient cave paintings at Rouffignac in the Dordogne. The others weren't that keen on the long drive, so she went alone, very happy with her isolation for a day. Arriving back in the early evening the villa was in semi-darkness. She went upstairs and saw Jake's bedroom door open. She was on the bed with Declan. Mel stood in the doorway and watched them. Jake's legs were wrapped around him, gripping his thighs and buttocks, her arms were tight around his shoulders. Mel watched as Jake and Declan came at the same time, a powerful mutual orgasm, and she saw Jake shower kisses on her lover. He in turn held her close, his face buried in her neck. Jake opened her eyes and looked up at Mel, her face radiant and more beautiful than Mel had ever seen it. She looked deep into Mel's eyes and smiled, and went back to kissing Declan without any embarrassment and without a word. Mel stepped back into the hall. She knew that what she had just seen was not just sex. She had just watched her two friends making love. For a fleeting moment Mel wondered what making love must feel like; it wasn't something she had ever known.

And so it went on, idyllic bliss as the three got to know each other even more, to become closer friends to enjoy enjoying each other. They found that their conversations were getting even more interesting as they explored each other's minds, now that they knew understood each other so well.

On the ninth night they were a little subdued. Tomorrow they would depart, separate. They sat on the terrace around the dinner table. The wine was finished. Mel sipped at her brandy, Jake and Declan each had a glass of malt whisky.

"What's next for you, Declan?" Jake asked.

"I've some things to do in Ireland. After that I don' know. Probably maintaining a cover story, get another identity, it takes work, time. I'll need a new base for a few months. I'm going to miss you both, I know that until something new turns up to keep us busy."

"We could just stay here and go on like this together," Mel mused, knowing full well they couldn't.

"Let's just enjoy tonight," Jake said, "while everything is still calm and peaceful."

As she spoke a zephyr of cool wind rippled across the surface of the pool, and away to the west, far out to sea, a distant flash of lightning lit the sky for a brief moment. It was a reminder that somewhere, maybe far away, more storms were building.

Printed in Great Britain
by Amazon